MARKED DRAGON

THE MARKED DRAGON PRINCE TRILOGY

JEN L. GREY

FEAR STRANGLED me as my sister, Eva, sobbed while a gigantic six-and-a-half-foot burly guard hovered over her.

Her steel blue eyes glistened from the tears that streamed down her cheeks and dripped onto her heather-gray pajama top, which asked *OMG aRe YoU a GIRL GaMeR?* in purple lettering with a purple remote underneath it and matching purple plaid bottoms. Her long, dark brown hair was messy, and strands stuck to her wet face.

"Move your ass, *now*," Falkor threatened. His cobalt eyes narrowed, and every muscle in his arm bulged as he pointed toward our new prison, the royal dragon chateau. He was bulkier than anyone here, and his every word dripped with malice. He and Ladon were Drake's favored guards.

Drake's onyx eyes were locked on me. More than seven feet tall, he towered over my five-foot-two-inch body. His white button-down shirt hugged his muscles, and his black trousers showed not one wrinkle, despite the time being nearly five in the morning. His brownish black hair remained perfectly styled in short, upward spikes, making him look every inch the regal prince he was. At one point, I'd found him handsome, but now, all I saw was the face of a monster.

Five guards I'd never seen before surrounded Saphira, my loyal friend, and Thorn's parents, Vlad and Cassidy. Drake had instructed the guards to take them back to their *hiding spot*, giving no indication of where that was.

He must have known I would tell Thorn—my fated mate.

Everly, what's going on? Thorn connected, using our bond. *I'm halfway there. I won't be much longer.*

I tried to swallow around the lump in my throat, but my mouth was so dry that it was impossible. I'd messed up by coming here. Okay, *messed up* was an understatement. *Fucked up* was way more accurate but still didn't quite capture the awfulness of my decision. Drake had promised that, if I came within two hours of my phone call with Eva, he would let Eva, Saphira, and Thorn's parents go. According to dragon law, a spoken agreement was binding, but apparently, since Drake was the dragon prince, his position superseded that. *They're taking Saphira and your parents back to their hiding spot, and Eva and me to the chateau. But that wasn't the worst of it. Thorn...I'm so sorry. I should never have come here. I should've told you everything.*

Yes, you should have, he replied. *But I understand why you didn't. I just need you to hold on until I get there.*

You can't come. My heart clenched. *You'll walk right into the trap, and there won't be a way for any of us to escape.* I wanted him here. I wanted to be in his arms again, but it wouldn't happen if he didn't think logically.

Ev, he connected, his turmoil building through our bond.

I'd never liked nicknames. Well, not since Mom died. Mom had called me her little da Vinci because I shared her love of painting, and because I'd sold more paintings during my high school years than many artists did in their entire life. After her death, I'd wanted to be called by my full name...until *him. Thorn, I need you, so we need to figure out a way to save us and for you not to die.*

Saphira's mocha eyes homed in on mine. "So you want us to head back—"

A low growl sounded, and a thick hand punched her in the face.

My friend's head snapped back, and Ladon fisted her long, curly, dark brown hair at the base of her skull. Her bronze skin blanched, but otherwise, you wouldn't have known she'd been affected since her face remained a mask of indifference.

"Don't even *think* about hinting at where you're located," Ladon seethed, his ice-green irises colder. He was huge, only slightly smaller than Falkor in height. Both could easily be MMA fighters.

Vlad hissed and stepped forward. "Why don't you pick on someone your own size?" His cornflower-blue irises darkened in disgust, and his jaw twitched. Even though he was overly pale from being held captive for so long, his greasy hair plastered to his face, he wasn't cowering.

No wonder Thorn was such a strong man. His role model, the man who'd saved him from death, was fearless.

The female guard, Jessie, grabbed the chain that connected Vlad's Wolfram Dwinn collar to his handcuffs and yanked him back. She sneered as her short bleach-blonde bangs fell over her cinnamon-brown eyes and brushed the shaved section of her dark brown hair. "If you're looking for a fight, I can handle you."

"Why don't you focus on getting us back to the *hiding spot*," Cassidy said. "Then there won't be an issue." She rolled her shoulders as if trying to get comfortable. She looked worse off than the other two. Her dark golden-brown hair hung limply, her hazel-green eyes were sunken, and her splotchy tan skin made her appear sickly.

"She's right. Take the three of them away. We need to focus on the abomination's arrival." Drake flicked his wrists.

Abomination. No wonder Thorn couldn't stand the royal family. Between the king trying to have Thorn—his own son—killed, and his brother's actions, I would hate their guts, too.

The guards took Saphira and Thorn's parents away, and I took a step after them.

Clenching my hands, I tried to keep my breathing steady. "Saphira's dad is your father's advisor. Shouldn't she come with us?" I wanted Saphira by my side. She was my friend and our best chance at strategizing a way out of this.

Four guards surrounded me, cutting me off, blocking my view of Saphira and Thorn's parents as the other five guards led them away.

"Now, Everly..." Drake snickered. "She betrayed me. She was going to help my brother, the very person who desires to take my kingdom from me. That's unacceptable and punishable by death."

Death.

He planned to kill all three of them.

Eva gasped and wrapped her arms around herself, her gaze begging me to get her out of this.

Ironically, I'd tried to save her and made a worse mess of things. Acid roiled in my stomach.

The guard in front of me with yellow eyes removed a collar from his back pocket. He lifted his arms to place it around my neck.

They were going to cage my dragon. That was probably why Vlad and Cassidy didn't look well—there was no telling how long it had been since they'd shifted.

My dragon roared so loudly that my ears rang. I whimpered, "Please. No."

"Aw, see," Drake cooed, strolling toward me. His dark irises twinkled, and it wasn't from the moonlight. "She's going to behave, so that's not needed."

My skin crawled as he stroked my cheek, and I yearned for the jolt of the fated-mate connection with Thorn.

What's wrong? Thorn asked, sensing my distress.

I had to learn to lock down my emotions, or Thorn would do something irrational. I could feel his urgent desire to come get me, and I didn't need to fuel it. *Eva's upset, and Drake is disgusting.*

Eva whimpered, and my vision spotted. I had to get us moving to the chateau. Maybe there, she'd settle down.

Drake tilted his head, watching me, and sneered, "You're talking to *him*, aren't you?"

Refusing to cower in fear, I straightened my shoulders.

He chuckled, and a sinister smile spread across his face. "Perfect. Keep doing that."

I gritted my teeth. I was giving him what he wanted—fear and disgust, two emotions that would make Thorn more desperate to reach me. I'd cowered and given in to my stepdad my entire life to stay close to my twin half siblings and fulfill my promise to my mother to protect them. But this unhealthy cycle ended now...starting with Drake.

Thorn, he's toying with me to get you to come here without a solid plan. I had to keep Thorn from rushing in. *You have to fight him strategically, not with anger and fear clouding your judgment.*

Sort of like what you did, he bit back.

I flinched, a pang of regret shooting through my chest. My eyes burned, but I managed to swallow and hold my tears at bay. *I thought I was doing the right thing. Saphira told me I could trust his word. If it had worked, I would've saved four people.*

His regret wafted through. *I'm sorry, babe. That wasn't fair. Saphira still has her blinders on when it comes to the royal family. You can't listen to her. Just knowing you're there with him is driving me insane.*

No, I deserve your anger. I was foolish, but I truly thought this was the best solution. The only good thing is that I'm with Eva. I always strove to be smart. That was why I had a perfect GPA despite the challenges of completing a premed degree. But my intelligence hadn't stopped me from making a stupid decision. I'd trusted Drake's word when I knew he was a bad person.

I had to focus on the two most important things I had influence over: getting Eva and me to the chateau and getting Thorn to stop and think. "Are we going to stand out here all night?"

Drake nodded. "Good point. It'll be harder for him to reach you in the chateau with all our security measures."

That hadn't been my point, but whatever.

"Go," Drake commanded again and shoved my sister in the back.

She stumbled and fell, barely able to hold out her hands in time to catch herself. Though she was eighteen and technically an adult, she was still very young.

I started toward her, but Drake clutched my shoulder. "Where do you think you're going?"

My dragon roared, and my right hand fisted. I wanted to punch the prick in the face, but that would only make this situation more volatile and worse for Eva. "To help my sister."

Drake rolled his eyes. "She can get up on her own. She may not be a dragon, but dammit, she will learn her place." He turned to her and snarled, "Get on your feet and move."

Eva's shoulders shook with quiet sobs as she slowly climbed to her feet. Her eyes were bloodshot from tears, and I held out my hand to her. I said soothingly, as if she were a child, "Come on. We can walk together."

Nodding, she hurried toward me.

Falkor arched a brow. He glanced at Drake and asked, "Sir?"

I growled, unable to hide my disdain as my dragon surged forward.

Eva stopped and stared at me, her eyes full of fear. I wrestled myself under control. I didn't want my sister to be afraid of me.

"It's fine," Drake said and winked at me. "It's great that my future *wife* and my *mistress* get along. Hell, if I'm lucky, they'll both be pregnant at the same time at least once."

Bile inched up my throat, but it didn't burn thanks to my new dragon shifter form. He could say *wife* all he wanted, but there was no way in hell I'd ever say, "I do." There was only one person I was willing to marry, and it was most definitely not Drake.

I kept my expression neutral as I extended my hand to Eva. She hesitated before hurrying over to clutch my arm.

Ladon flanked my other side while Yellow Eyes moved

to my sister's other side. Drake followed us, and the other three guards took up the rear.

Of course, he'd put himself in the middle. He wouldn't risk not being completely protected.

We headed to the chateau, and I held tight to Eva. I didn't know how to protect her, but I hoped holding her to my side would bring her some comfort. I'd meant to save her from this hellish future, but instead, I'd gotten us trapped in it.

Thorn, please tell me you won't do anything rash, I connected with him. I needed to hear his promise, but I was also desperate to just hear him.

I won't, he answered. *But I won't stay back, and hope Drake and the king develop a conscience. I'll determine a way to get you and my parents out of there today.*

I nearly sobbed. He and I had agreed to figure out the plan together. Then I'd seen Eva's text, and I'd called her and run off alone, getting us into this mess.

Falkor had promised Thorn that his parents would be freed tomorrow morning if he turned himself in.

I didn't believe him. If Thorn came, Drake would kill him along with his parents. Thorn was in a time crunch, and though I didn't want him to risk his life, how could I ask him not to? I had done the same, though my life wasn't at stake—just my freedom.

The gigantic sunflower-yellow chateau with gray trim came into view as we exited the woods. The sizable terrace was immaculate with the greenest grass I'd ever seen. The beige, slanted roof gave the chateau a regal appearance.

Ladon and Yellow Eyes herded us to the right, away from the terrace and back entrance. When I'd flown over the estate on my way here, I'd noted that the house looked like two separate homes that were connected. He'd told the guards to take us to the guest home, so my observation appeared to be accurate.

When the other portion of the chateau came into view, I noticed the houses were connected by an enclosed walkway. The back of what I assumed was the guest side had a smaller terrace that was just as nice with a wooden door leading into the home.

As we stepped onto the gray-painted wood terrace, the back door opened, and an older man in a suit stepped outside. He was bald with gray hair at the base of his skull. Shadowy hazel eyes glanced at Eva and me before locking on Drake. "Your Highness, I've had both bedrooms prepared. I'll have maids assigned to the suites as requested."

"Make sure it gets done, Sinclair," Drake snarled, not bothering to thank the older man.

My feet stilled. Going into this house would make it all official, and everything within me screamed not to enter.

"Move," Drake muttered. "*Now.*"

My chest constricted as I entered with Eva and looked at the place that could very well be my home for the foreseeable future.

The interior was gorgeous with dark cherry wood floors and off-white walls. There was a white painted fireplace with a roaring fire. A breathtaking painting hung over it. Mesmerized, I walked past an obnoxious white couch that was clearly never used and a glass coffee table to stare at Mom's most favorite painting in the world.

It was a replica of one of *Water Lilies*, a series of oil paintings Claude Monet had created over one hundred years ago. Mom had said that the way he painted the faint ripples in the water, washing over the leaves, made her hear the faint rush of the breeze. My chest constricted at the flood of memories.

"I said *move!*" Drake bellowed.

I turned my head to find Eva stumbling over her feet again.

My dragon roared. Oh, *hell* no. This wasn't happening.

I PIVOTED past the coffee table, hot rage boiling within me. Eva wobbled and fell backward.

I managed to reach her and wrap my arms under her armpits before her ass could smack onto the wooden floor.

Drake hadn't even tried to help her.

She gripped my arms, and I helped her back onto her feet. When she was steady, I spun toward Drake and snarled, "What the *hell* was that?"

He stepped toward me, moving into my bubble. His scent of leather and brimstone hit my nose, causing my head to twinge.

Great. I hadn't gotten a migraine in forever, but his presence was making one rear its ugly head.

"Let me make this crystal clear," he breathed, a hard glint in his eyes. "You may become my *wife*, but that doesn't give you any power in our relationship. I will do what *I* want. If your sister moves too slowly, she'll get stomped on. I don't give a *shit* if you have a problem with it."

I laughed bitterly. "You're delusional if you think I'll be your *wife*."

He held my gaze, challenging me. He said cruelly, "Oh, you will be." He brushed his fingers across my cheek.

I forced myself to remain still, hiding the disgusted chill coursing through my body. I swallowed the vomit and lifted my chin. "I will *never* say, 'I do.' There's nothing in this world that could coerce me now that I know you can't be trusted."

He gripped my jaw, digging his fingers into my skin. His pupils slitted as he murmured softly, "Who said anything about *you* needing to say, 'I do?'"

My heart dropped into my stomach as Eva whimpered beside me.

Laughing, he dropped his hand and studied me. Whatever he saw made him giddy, but I couldn't stop the horror from sawing through my lungs. I'd thought I knew what being powerless felt like. Now I understood how devastating having your power stripped away was. At least, my stepdad hadn't physically hurt me. He was just indifferent and lashed out when I came around to see my siblings. Yes, I'd bitten my tongue and been submissive, but I'd made decisions for myself: my major, which college I went to, and whether I dated. I had a nagging suspicion that if I breathed too loudly, Drake would get on me. Hell, he likely would if I breathed at all.

How am I supposed to remain rational when I feel the terror swirling from you? Thorn connected, his concern slamming into me and warming my cold heart.

I didn't know how to answer that. I barely knew anything about being a dragon, and this fated-mate bond was newer than that. *I need you to. Several lives depend on it.* I wanted to tell him what Drake had said, but I feared that would tip him over the edge.

I had to get my shit together and be strong. Otherwise,

Thorn would come here and save me before they had a good plan.

Inhaling slowly, I schooled my expression and shoved the cold tendrils of fear deep down inside me. I had experience with this, or I'd fake it until I made it. "Marriage vows require *both* parties to make the promise."

"Human marriage." He tapped his chin. "By dragon law, only the man is required to say it. After all, we are the *stronger* gender. Women are needed to birth children."

"Then why have a human mistress?" If dragons relegated women to their roles as child bearers, then he shouldn't need Eva. If I could get her out of here, the situation would be slightly more bearable, and I'd have kept my promise to Mom.

Falkor growled from behind Drake and said, "The *prince* doesn't answer to *you*."

If I'd been hoping to find an ally, Falkor was a sure pass on that front. He was shoved so far up Drake's ass that I wondered if he could breathe up there.

Snarling, Drake glanced over his shoulder at the guard. "Even though what you say is *true*, she will be your *queen*, and you will not talk to her like that. Do you understand?"

"Uh...yes, sire." Falkor averted his gaze, but his neck corded as he glanced at me.

Lovely. Now the guard resented me. Who would've thought that Drake would care if the warrior talked to me that way? *He* sure didn't mind doing it.

Drake turned back to me and grabbed the ends of my hair. "I will have children with *both* of you. The son, if not sons, I have with you will be the future heir, and the sons I have with your *sister* will help keep our race alive."

Sons. He seemed pretty certain. "How do you know

you'll have boys?" I couldn't bring myself to say *we*. That was inconceivable.

He frowned and yanked on the ends of my hair. "Because I'm *strong*. You should know better than to ask such an idiotic question."

My dragon roared at the way he talked to me and the sharp pain in my skull, but I didn't flinch. I'd already let him feel too much in control as it was. "You know that has nothing

to do—"

He bared his teeth. "When I want your opinion, I'll ask for it. Until then, keep your mouth *shut*."

I wanted to tell him that science wasn't an opinion, it was facts, but I lodged the words in my throat. He wouldn't listen to me, even if I pulled out a science book and showed him that strength didn't influence which sex was born. Many kings in history had had this mentality, but in their defense, they hadn't had the knowledge at their fingertips that we did now. Drake was either too stubborn or too stupid to believe it.

Silence descended, and after a long moment, he smiled. "Good girl."

My hands clenched. He was a condescending, arrogant jerk, and someone needed to teach him a lesson.

Footsteps outside the terrace headed our way, causing my vision to blur. *Thorn, please tell me you aren't here.*

No, he answered, but his displeasure weighed on me. *But I wish I were. I'm several miles south of the dragon territory. Fifty warriors are patrolling the area. If you hadn't asked me to be careful, I wouldn't have noticed them. It's hard knowing he has you.*

The world righted itself. Thorn wasn't being reckless. I pushed the warmth of my love and approval toward him.

That's why I told you I needed you to stay focused. Drake is hoping you will do something reckless so he can capture you. Then there'd be no way you could help us.

His dragon hissed, and he replied, *I know. I have to get you out of there. I'm flying around to see what sections are less guarded and how often the warriors change shifts.*

Static filled the air, startling me. Footsteps hurried past our door as if they were heading toward the other wing of the chateau.

My gaze landed on a walkie-talkie on Falkor's hip. Something was going on.

The walkie-talkie came to life, and Ladon slurred, "Falk...or. We've...got...a lil...

prob—"

Slipping the walkie-talkie from its holder, Falkor pressed the button. "Spit it out already."

"Don't waste time." Drake gestured to the door. "Everyone but Falkor, go! Ladon's with our prisoners. The abomination could be *here.*"

My heart raced. Maybe they'd found a way out? Then my blood turned to ice. I linked, *Thorn, you'd tell me if you were here, right?* I hated to ask him, especially since I'd snuck out on him while he'd slept, but I hadn't *lied* to him, and I was certain he wouldn't do that to me. Still, I had to ask. Maybe he would if he thought it would keep me calm.

Of course, I'm not. I wouldn't tell you that and then show up a moment later. Hurt wafted from him.

In less than three hours, I'd hidden something from him and snuck out on him, and now I'd accused him of lying to me. I had *a lot* to learn about being in a relationship. *I honestly believed that, but something is going on here. Ladon was with your parents and Saphira, and he just reached out to Falkor, sounding odd.*

"We need to get them into the master bedroom." Falkor pointed toward the hallway past the living room. "We'll be more secure there."

My attention flicked to the door as my body tingled. Falkor was now the only guard here and had the collar. If we were going to attempt to escape, this was our chance. I'd have to signal Eva, somehow, when the time came.

Drake rushed past me toward the hallway. He wasn't concerned about making sure Eva and I were safe; he was just desperate to save his own ass.

Figured.

"Don't try anything stupid," Falkor breathed. "Drake might have scolded me for the way I talked to you, but I swear to you, he would rather I be forceful than let you escape."

I wiggled my fingers at my side. I wasn't surprised he knew what I was contemplating. He was one of the top warriors for a reason.

Needing a plan that might catch him off guard, I dutifully turned around. I steadied my breathing, remembering the tips from all the yoga classes I'd taken. That was the only type of exercise I could tolerate, preferring to work on limbering my muscles instead of running outside or touching other people's sweat smears in a gym.

Eva scurried over to me and looped one arm through mine. She was shaking, and sweat had beaded on her upper lip.

My jaw popped from how hard I was gritting my teeth, but I had to do something to control my anger. The measured breathing wasn't cutting it. Eva shouldn't even be here. She was supposed to be safe. This was meant to be *my* future, not hers.

"It's going to be okay," I whispered loud enough for her

to hear, which meant Drake could probably hear me from wherever he was.

Falkor snorted as if I'd told her a joke.

I clenched my hands, my nails digging into my palms and stinging the tender flesh. The pain centered me.

Eva glanced over her shoulder at the guard and murmured, "I wouldn't be so sure."

Not wanting to say more, I nodded. "Watch where you're going." Giving her something to focus on would make her feel better...or it had worked when she was younger.

Her head bobbed, and she jerked forward, the area around her eyes tightening. We were approaching the hallway, and a doorway to our left led into a ginormous kitchen. The same hardwood theme continued throughout the kitchen with a dark cherry island in the center of the room. A huge door in the middle of the cabinets matched, and I suspected it was an oversized refrigerator. The rest of the cabinets were light gray, and gray marble countertops completed the space. The island contained a sink and a dishwasher, and several ovens and stoves were set around the perimeter.

At the end of the room was a dark cherry wood kitchen table that could seat twelve with a gigantic chandelier hung overhead.

The space was beautiful and regal, everything a chateau should be. Even though I'd grown up without hurting for money, I didn't feel like I belonged here.

"You'll have the rest of your life to get familiar with the house," Falkor said. "Hurry up."

A loud roar echoed overhead, and Eva yelped, burrowing deeper against my side.

I glanced down the long off-white hallway. Gorgeous

paintings I wanted to study hung on the walls, but I forced myself not to focus on them. I needed an exit strategy.

As we approached an intersecting hallway, I turned my head and saw the front door.

My chest fluttered. It was now or never.

Drake's head popped out of the door to the right, and he snapped, "What the *hell* is taking so long? I could be attacked any minute."

"We're on our—" Falkor started, moving closer behind us.

I tapped into my dragon, and she roared. She was on board with getting out of here and back to our fated mate. I released Eva's hold on me and spun around, facing Falkor.

Falkor lifted his hands, holding the collar open. I countered by squatting and snatching the gun from the sheath on his waist.

"Everly!" Eva whimpered, but I ignored her.

I couldn't risk getting distracted.

Falkor dropped his elbows, one hitting the top of my head. The sharp throb caused my eyes to burn, and nausea rolled through me. I spun, kicking out my leg, and nearly toppled over.

Ev, Thorn connected. *What's wrong?*

Grunting, Falkor wrapped an arm around my waist. He lifted me over his shoulder upside down, my face to his stomach. The blood rushed to my head. My vision hazed, and I dropped the gun.

"Get this contained," Drake snarled, and I heard him run down the hall toward us.

A roar thundered in my mind, and Thorn connected again, *I can feel your pain.*

Unsure of what to do, I went with my gut. I grabbed Falkor's belt buckle and unfastened it. *I'm trying to escape.*

Falkor recoiled, which meant my asinine plan was working. He readjusted his weight, getting ready to flip me over, but I wasn't done yet. I yanked at the button and then the zipper of his pants, unfastening them, then shoved the pants down as far as I could reach.

"What is *wrong* with you?" Falkor growled as I got a full view of his dangly bits.

One thing became clear, unfortunately. All dragons weren't large, and my fated mate was exceptional...or maybe Falkor was one sad, lonely dragon. I wasn't sure if I meant the dragon alone because, with a penis this size, it had to be lonely, too.

Drake growled loudly. "Why did you pull your pants down in front of my future bride's face?"

I wasn't sure what made me sicker: my face full of Falkor's privates or Drake calling me his bride.

"*She* did it," Falkor rasped as he dropped me.

I caught my weight on my arms and rolled forward onto my feet. Out of the corner of my eye, I saw Falkor hurry to me, but his slacks prevented him from moving well. He squatted down. Time was running out.

I stood and reached for my sister. Then the world tilted, and it wasn't from the elbow drop.

Drake had one hand wrapped around Eva's throat; the other hand held a gun to my sister's temple.

CHAPTER THREE

MY BREATHING QUICKENED, and I grew dizzier.

Thorn's voice popped into my head. *Everly, you're in pain and terrified. If you don't tell me what's going on, I'm coming. Damn the consequences.*

I sank to my knees, pain and fear making the walls close in. I understood that my mind was playing tricks on me, but that didn't make it any better. If I lost Eva and Thorn, it would destroy me. *Drake has a gun to Eva's head.*

Behind me, Falkor hurried to his feet, and I heard him frantically pull up his pants and zip up his fly.

There was no getting out of this.

I'm on my way, he replied.

"You better think carefully about your next steps," Drake spat as he pressed his chest against Eva's back and placed his head next to hers. "One wrong move and I *will* blow her brains out."

My stomach convulsed. It wouldn't be long before I vomited up whatever was left in there. "*Please* don't. You said you need her, so I'm begging you not to hurt her." I connected with Thorn, *Please don't come. If you do, things will only get worse. I need you to find a way to get us all out of here. It has to be planned.*

His response was just turbulent emotions. I couldn't lock onto one in particular, but an icy and hot blend of terror, anger, and distress filtered through the bond.

The jangling of Falkor fastening his belt had despair pressing in on me. He was back in position, and soon, I'd be *collared.* My dragon hissed, but she didn't force herself forward, as if she loved my sister as well and wouldn't risk her life.

Drake chuckled sinisterly. "Do you think I can't find another human to use? I brought her here to make my future wife happy and keep her family close."

That was bullshit, and we both knew it. I was tired of taking it without calling the other person out. "You *knew* I didn't want this life for her. That's why I volunteered to take her place. Besides, it's not like anyone else embezzled money from your company, so don't pretend you'll do something we both know won't happen."

His hand shook, and his eyes flashed with anger. "Are you that foolish? I can take whoever and whatever I want. There are other ways to blackmail humans into giving up something precious. And...wouldn't it be something if, after you begged to take your sister's place, she died because you wouldn't submit to me?"

Every breath I took roared in my ears. I'd thought that I severely disliked my stepdad, but boy, he was a saint compared to Drake. Anger settled heavily in my chest, my dragon fidgeting inside my brain. "Fine, you win." I forced out the words, knowing they were the ones he wanted.

Warmth approached my back. Falkor. I closed my eyes, waiting to feel cool, rough metal sliding around my neck.

"Don't," Drake commanded. "That won't be necessary."

"But, sire." Falkor cleared his throat. "She can't be trusted. Not after *this*."

I didn't have to see the warrior's face to know what I would find. He was embarrassed.

The click of the gun had my eyes popping open.

Drake had loaded a bullet, and the end of the barrel was still in place. "Everly, tell us you'll behave."

Eva's eyes were red from crying, and her bottom lip quivered.

This asshole would pay. I wasn't sure when or how, but I wanted to be the one who knocked the cocky grin off his face. I choked, "I'll behave."

"Good," he cooed and dropped the gun to his side, releasing my sister.

My entire body wanted to give out, and unshed tears blurred my vision and burned my eyes, but I blinked them back. I connected with Thorn, *He released Eva. She's not in immediate danger.*

The lightness of his relief through our bond eased some pressure off me.

"Your Highness, this isn't a good idea," Falkor insisted as he moved to stand beside me. He had the collar in his hands and a scowl on his face. "She needs to be contained."

Though I knew better, I couldn't stop the words. "Since you obviously don't know how to prevent yourself from getting pantsed."

His nostrils flared, and his head jerked in my direction. "That was a cheap move. A true fighter wouldn't do that."

"It doesn't *matter*," Drake snapped. "You are supposed to be *trained* for *every* situation. If someone wants to get free, they'll do whatever is necessary." His gaze landed on me, and there was something odd in his eyes.

I didn't want to know what it was, but the emotion would no doubt further disgust me.

The vein between Falkor's eyebrows bulged. He'd never be my ally, but I hadn't counted on that, anyway. He was drinking whatever Kool-Aid Drake was serving.

I wondered why these guards were so loyal.

Wings flapped over the house, and footsteps pounded our way. Whatever was going on outside was still underway.

"You three need to go into the bedroom," Falkor commanded as he pivoted toward the end of the hallway and the front door, positioning himself so he could still watch me. At least, he thought I was worthy enough not to disregard me.

I clutched my head and stood, the pain intensifying. I needed a dark room, Advil, and caffeine, pronto. I couldn't run right now, even if I had the opportunity, especially since the adrenaline was wearing off and the pain continued to intensify.

Drake waved the gun at me and Eva, then at the room. My pulse raced, and my head pounded in sync with my heartbeat. I moved away from the front door and farther down the hall just as the back door opened.

"Get in there, *now*," Falkor hissed as he ran down the hall.

Eva was frozen, a few tears trickling down her cheeks. She wasn't crying as hard as before, but I was certain it was because shock had taken over, something with which I was all too familiar.

When I'd asked Drake to take me instead of Eva, I'd had no clue what I'd signed up for. I'd thought it would be a loveless marriage. Little had I known I'd be thrust into a supernatural world with a sadistic asshole *dragon prince*. Not that it would've changed anything—I still would've taken her place—but I would've been more prepared for *this* future.

I looped my arm through Eva's, forcing her to move with me. Drake was already at the door, scowling.

We passed a door on the left, and I noted that it was a bathroom. I'd have to get the lay of the house later when Drake didn't have a gun.

We were a few steps shy of entering the bedroom when the person who'd come in through the back door said, "Falkor, they got away."

My heart leaped into my throat as hope surged through me. I wanted to ask who, but I swallowed the words whole. *That* question would not go over well, especially with Drake still holding that blasted gun.

Someone needed to do something about that.

Drake marched back out of the bedroom, his face damn near the same shade as a tomato. He grabbed Eva and me by the shoulders, spun us around, then shoved us back toward the living room.

"You could've just *asked*," I growled, not liking being manhandled. This could easily go in the direction of physical abuse.

He snarled, "Move or I'll make you."

Eva whimpered, and I pulled her tighter against me. The shaking of her body didn't lessen as we picked up the pace.

Back in the living room again, Falkor was staring out one of the windows, his eyes narrowed. "We need to alert the warriors at the perimeter."

The new warrior was dressed in black like the others. He was tall, coming in at around seven feet, and very muscular, with a bald head and honey-brown eyes that weren't as cold as Falkor's.

"We already did via cell phone in case the escapees got a walkie-talkie and are monitoring our actions." The new man rolled his shoulders and glanced at us.

Drake's chest heaved as he stood next to me. He snapped, "How the *fuck* did this happen, Uther?"

Using every ounce of self-restraint I had, I managed not to roll my eyes. He had some nerve talking like that to men who risked their lives daily for a pompous jerk like him.

UTHER TUGGED at the collar of his black shirt. "We're not sure, Your Highness." He averted his gaze and placed his hands behind his back. "They were locked in the cellar of Falkor's house, the same as they've been for the past month. Multiple people must have been waiting nearby because, as the guards were leaving, all five of them were shot with tranqs."

My breath caught. *Thorn, your parents and Saphira escaped.* Finally, some good news.

Warmth wafted toward me as he replied, *What? How?*

One second. Let me hear the whole story. But keep an eye out for them, I replied. I'd take this small win. And if I could get Eva out, I could deal with the hell of being left behind.

Drake growled. "How long were Ladon and the others out?"

"Not long." Uther lifted a hand. "Four nearby warriors noted three dragons flying away, frantically. Three of them shifted and flew after them, while one rushed to see what had happened. She found all five guards passed out on the ground and gave them the tranq neutralizer, which stirred them awake, and allowed Ladon to contact you."

That was why Ladon had sounded so groggy over the walkie-talkie.

Drake's body shook. "You're telling me *three* warriors went after them, and they still haven't been caught?"

Uther's Adam's apple bobbed. "The three prisoners are fast and had a decent head start. The warriors are chasing their scent, but they've split up, making it hard to track them."

I relayed the information to Thorn, ecstatic that he might very well get his parents back.

Vlad knows what to do. He also knows where the cabin is, Thorn linked, but I could feel his trepidation. *I don't know if I can go back and be that far away from you.*

My vision blurred, and I blinked back tears. I didn't need to break down, especially not in front of Drake. *You have to. Go see your parents and learn everything you can from them. Then find a way to bring me back home where I belong—in your arms.*

Damn straight you do, he replied. *I'll head back to meet up with them, but I won't wait long to come back for you. I need you here with me.*

Drake rushed to Uther and pointed at the door. He bit out, "Then why are you still here? Take every available resource and hunt those three down, *now*."

Sticking out his chest as if he were unfazed by Drake's words, Uther lifted his chin. "Yes, sir. I just wanted to apprise Falkor of the situation."

"Actually, it'd be best if Uther stayed here." Falkor held out his hand for his gun. "I'll help hunt down the others. Ladon, Jessie, and I have worked closely together for years, so it'll be quicker."

"Good idea." Drake nodded and gave the gun back. "If

you need anything, say the word. If anyone can fix these mistakes, it's you."

The corners of Falkor's mouth tipped upward, the first sign of a smile I'd ever seen on his face. Of course, it would be due to a psychopath's compliment.

"Watch her," Falkor commanded Uther and pointed at me. "She tried to escape earlier, so keep her close."

At the smug expression on Falkor's face, I wanted to take him down a notch. "If it hadn't been for Drake getting your gun, I would've gotten away. Let's not pretend otherwise."

The warrior glared at me, his pupils elongating.

Mission accomplished.

"That's enough." Drake tisked and crossed his arms. "Falkor, head out and manage the search. Everly and I need to get some rest before a long day of wedding planning. It's almost sunrise."

My mouth filled with saliva, and I wanted to spit. The last thing I wanted to do was plan anything with *him*, even though I longed for a dark room to get some relief from my pounding head. I worried about where, exactly, I'd be sleeping. Sharing a bed with *him* would send me over the edge.

Falkor exited through the back door, and I prayed that Thorn's belief in his dad held true, and that the three family members would find one another.

"If these two disappear while I'm gone, there will be hell to pay, Uther," Drake warned, leveling his gaze on the warrior. "She's smart and will be my bride. If anyone threatens her, they will answer to me. Do you understand?"

The warrior shifted his weight from one foot to the other. "Yes, sire. They won't get away."

"Make sure of it." Drake turned to me, and his cruel smirk reappeared. "In three hours, I'll be back here to take you to meet my father and begin planning. You better be ready. There are clothes your size in our closet."

My skin crawled. Between him having clothes for me and referring to the closet as ours, I wanted to claw my eyes out.

He chuckled, watching my every expression. He strolled over to me and hovered his lips inches from mine. The closer he got, the more I wanted to vomit.

The thing was, I'd never be desperate enough to ever let him kiss me.

CHAPTER FOUR

HE WAS SO close that his onion breath hit my face, making me want to gag. Any reaction would only encourage him, and I'd already done enough stupid stuff for the night.

I pressed my lips together so his breath couldn't seep into my mouth. I did *not* want to taste it. The stench in my nose was bad enough. If I made it clear I didn't want to kiss him, he'd probably force the issue.

Scanning my face, he smirked. "Don't worry. Our first kiss won't be tonight." He placed a hand under my chin, tilting my face upward so we were looking into each other's eyes. "It will happen when you're clean and don't smell like *him*."

Batting my eyes, I smiled sweetly. "Then you might have to wait a while." If not bathing would get him to leave me alone, I'd happily become the stinkiest woman alive.

"Remember, I'm the one who has the power. If you want your sister to be well taken care of, you'd better behave," he warned as he pressed the tip of his thumb into my chin, causing my entire jawline to ache and increasing the pressure in my head.

Dropping his hand, he sneered. "Goodnight, my *pet*. Sleep tight. Our first day together as an engaged couple is on the horizon, and I expect you to be polished when you meet the king."

My heart raced, and I desperately wanted to hammer a hole into my head to release the pressure.

He turned and headed toward the back door. He paused beside Uther and steepled his fingers. "Make sure you watch them. When more warriors return, I'll ensure there are several positioned around the house in case my bride tries to escape. But let me be clear—if she gets away, you know what will happen."

Eva whimpered and shuffled back, putting more distance between her and the rest of us.

Glancing over his shoulder, Drake beamed.

I would have to talk to her. If she kept showing her fear, Drake's attitude toward her would get worse. He got a high from people fearing him. She was giving him that in spades.

I moved in front of her, blocking his view. I hated what he was doing to her. Drake already knew how much I cared about my sister, so there was no point in pretending I didn't.

Realizing I had no intention of moving, he left. As soon as the door shut, my lungs worked easier, and the three of us stood in silence.

Uther placed his hands in his slacks pockets. "You two look like you've had a rough night. Why don't you head to your rooms and get some rest?"

Time alone sounded perfect. I wanted to get Eva settled and try to get rid of this headache so I could stay focused. "Which room are we staying in? I'm assuming the one to the left."

Uther winced. "Actually, your and Drake's room is on the right. Eva's is the one across the hall on the left."

Tensing, I shook my head. "I'll stay in Eva's room with her." I refused to share a room with *Drake*.

He bobbed his head and sighed. "Okay. It'll be easier to watch you two if you're in the same room."

I forced myself to exhale. His reasoning didn't matter as long as Eva and I stayed together.

I turned around and found Eva rocking, her arms wrapped around herself. Her face was sickly pale...worse than when she'd had the flu after Mom had passed.

Making my way to her, I placed a hand on her arm to comfort her, but she jerked back.

Her voice shook as she said, "Don't touch me."

My chest constricted as if she'd stabbed my heart. My eyes burned, and I dropped my hand, putting space between us. I had to remember she was going through a lot, and Elliott was the one she always turned to. Not me.

"Come on, let's go to the bedroom," I said, keeping my voice steady. I braced myself, ready for her to tell me she didn't want to share a room with me, but she turned and headed down the hallway. Some of the tension left my shoulders.

We marched past the bedroom on the right, and I purposely didn't glance inside. I didn't want to see Drake's room. I needed to get some decent sleep and not have a visual of my personal hell.

Eva and I entered the bedroom on the left, and Uther stopped at the door.

He scratched the back of his neck. "I really don't want to be in there while you get ready for bed and sleep, but I can't risk you running away, either."

In other words, he was a nice guy who was stuck working for a shitty person. I could only imagine what sort of punishment Drake would inflict upon him if we escaped.

I suspected it would involve hurting someone he loved. That seemed to be Drake's style, but Uther didn't have anything to worry about because Eva and I were trapped. "All the warriors are out at the territory line, so it would be stupid to run away now."

He bit his lip. "True, but that doesn't mean you won't. I have a little girl I can't risk."

There it was—Drake's leverage against him. What sort of sick person was willing to hurt a child, especially when the dragon shifter population was dangerously low? "I promise, if I try to escape, it won't be tonight." And it wouldn't be, not with a little girl at risk, but I decided not to say that.

"Fine." He exhaled, but his face was lined with tension. "I'll stay outside the door, but if anything sounds strange, I will bust in. Do you understand?"

I nodded. "That's fair."

"You better get some rest." He arched a brow and frowned. "Trust me. You don't want to disappoint Drake."

As he shut the door, a chill ran down my spine. Ignoring the sensation, I scanned the room, taking in the dark cherry wood accents and the light gray walls. A modern bronze chandelier lit up the entire room. A king-size bed was centered against the right wall, with white silk bedding and four huge pillows. A charcoal rug ran from underneath the bed, and a dark cherry wood bench was positioned at the foot. The headboard was the same gray as the rug. Two oversized dark cherry wood night-stands sat on either side of the bed with a large bronze lamp on each one. Across from the bed, against the left wall, rested a dresser with a gigantic mirror. To the right, I glimpsed a sizable walk-in closet full of clothes and, to the left, a bathroom.

Eva stood near the edge of the bench. She appeared tiny

in the enormous room. Tears streamed down her face, and the image reminded me of the preteen who'd lost her mother.

Devastated.

I eased toward her, needing to comfort her. "Eva, I promise everything will be okay."

"You can't promise that," she said brokenly as she countered each one of my steps, easing toward the room's double windows. "And don't come any closer."

The words were a punch in the gut, but I obliged. "I *will* figure something out. I came here to protect you."

She huffed. "Well, you did a piss-poor job."

"I got kidnapped on the way here, and things took on a life of their own." I didn't want to tell her too much and risk her becoming more of a target. "As soon as I learned Drake had you, I came here. You know that."

She rubbed her arms. "Maybe it was a ploy. I mean, how can I trust you? You're one of *them*."

I pressed my fingers to my temples to ease some of the agony from my head, especially since my heart was taking a beating. "How can you ask that? I'm your sister and will always look out for your best interests."

Eva rocked back on her feet. "I...I know that. I just need time to think. My life has completely changed in the past several hours, and I'm..."

"It's okay," I murmured. She was processing the situation, and I needed to be understanding. Eva had seen me in dragon form. That was a lot to take in. "Look, I'm going to take a shower." I didn't want to wash Thorn's scent off me, but my headache was getting worse. If I didn't do something to get my migraine to recede, I wouldn't be able to sleep or think clearly.

"You're going to leave me?" She hurried a few steps toward me.

"Of course not." I gestured to the door on my left. "The bathroom is right there. I'll leave the door unlocked. If you get too uncomfortable, you can join me in there."

She sat on the bench and nodded. "Just hurry. Please."

"Promise." I forced a smile and rushed into the bathroom.

I shut the door, wanting privacy as the acid swirled harder within. I kicked off my sneakers and set my feet on the cool, dark gray tiles. There were his-and-hers sinks to the right, with dark cherry wood cabinets and a white marble top. Next to the sinks was a huge white tub, and between the tub and the toilet was a stall lined with white subway tiles and a huge shower head.

I scurried to the shower and turned on the water. A cutout cradled a bar of soap and bottles of shampoo and conditioner. A small linen closet contained towels and two white robes. I snatched a towel and threw it over the glass of the shower stall as the water warmed.

I laid my head against the glass to get the throbbing under control. I closed my eyes, and Eva's traumatized face popped into my mind. I had to do something before Drake decided it was time she took on the role of his breeder.

The acid in my stomach lurched up my throat, and I rushed to the toilet and vomited.

The world crashed down on me, and I dry heaved, letting the agony take over. I had to be strong around Eva, so this was my chance to have a moment of weakness.

Ev, Thorn connected. *What's going on? You're in so much damn pain.*

I was, and there was no reason to lie to him. He could feel my turmoil through our bond. *Eva is petrified. She didn't want me to touch her. I'm sleeping in the room Drake assigned to her and not in the room he's classifying as ours.* The last word had me heaving again.

Thorn didn't immediately respond, and I realized what I'd said. I hadn't wanted to tell him about the wedding until tomorrow.

White-hot anger thrummed into the bond. He asked slowly, *What do you mean 'the room he's classifying as ours'? If you're his breeder...* His dragon bellowed. *Is he planning to marry you?*

Thorn, I need you to stay calm, I replied and rested my head on the toilet seat. I was beyond caring whose butt might have been on it. *This is why I need you to work with your parents and Saphira. Since I'm not human anymore, he took Eva as his breeder, and he plans to make me his wife. I need you to save Eva and me.*

Were you going to tell me? he asked as our bond constricted from his pain.

I just kept hurting him. *Of course. First thing in the morning. I wanted to make sure you had calmed down.*

Calmed down? he parroted. *I will not calm down until you're here beside me where you belong, and knowing you're keeping things from me is making this a lot more difficult.*

My dragon whimpered. He was right. I needed to be honest with him. How else could I expect him to trust me? *I'm sorry. I wasn't trying to be deceitful. I just had a lot going on, and I was petrified that you would come here, now that it's clear that Drake has no intention of letting you live.* I didn't know how to do it, but I tried to push my regret and love toward him. *I swear, from here on out, I'll tell you everything. Even if I fear you'll do something I won't like.*

His hurt ebbed and was replaced with the warmth of his love, easing some of the sickness in my stomach. He replied,

Thank you. I love you, and I promise I'll get you and Eva out of there. When is the— He broke off, unable to say the word.

He didn't have to. I understood the question. *I don't know. I meet with him and the king in a few hours.*

Okay, let me know, immediately.

Are you safe? I held my breath.

We're all at the cabin. Vlad is on the couch, and Cassidy is asleep in our bed. Saphira opted for the room you were in originally.

They'd made it. My stomach settled, and I lifted my head. *Why didn't your parents sleep together?*

They stuck me in the Wolfram Dwiin room to make sure I can't sneak past them. His annoyance flickered through our connection.

I snorted as half of the worry weighing on me disappeared. His parents and Saphira were there, and they were making sure he didn't do something reckless.

Did they tell you how they got away? I was still stunned that they'd had someone in position to rescue them.

Thorn replied, *They have no clue. It just happened.*

Now that I'd gotten some sanity back, I stood, flushed the toilet, and made my way into the shower. Steam rolled from the top, fogging up the entire room. I stood under the stream and nearly moaned when the water was hot, even to my touch. Ever since I'd become a dragon, the showers had felt lukewarm, but this shower had obviously been made for dragon shifters.

Maybe whoever helped them will help get me out. My chest expanded with hope.

Thorn didn't feel as relieved. *I wouldn't count on it, and Drake will have you heavily guarded. We'll have to operate under the assumption that we're on our own.*

I hated the sound of it, but that was the best strategy. I

turned off the water and dried my body. My head was still killing me, but it was bearable enough to sleep. As I slipped on my clothes, I replied, *You're right. I hate to do this, but I have to get some rest. I don't want to miss any detail that might help with our escape.*

Link with me as soon as you wake up. I don't care what time it is or if you think I'm asleep. I need to know what's going on.

That was the least I could do after the hell I'd put us through. *Promise. And Thorn, I love you. I'm sorry for upsetting you. I swear I wasn't trying to. I was just doing what I thought would keep you safe.*

I don't need you to save me, he replied as his dragon whimpered. *I need you back in my arms, and that means I need to know everything that's going on. I know I can't act recklessly, so I need you to trust me like I trust you.*

I do, and I'll prove it, I vowed. Actions spoke louder than words, so I needed to back mine up.

His dragon purred. *I can feel your pain, so get some sleep. I'll be here if you need anything.*

I entered the bedroom and found Eva already in bed with the lights off. She'd taken the side facing the window and away from the door, which suited me just fine. I tiptoed to the bed and crawled under the sheet, facing the door.

The sheets were cool and soft, and my body melted into the mattress. I hated that the bed was comfortable, but I felt as if I were lying on a cloud.

As I closed my eyes, Eva turned to me and scooched so close that our bodies touched. She whispered, "I'm sorry, Everly. I didn't mean the things I said earlier."

I glanced over my shoulder, not wanting to turn away from the door. If someone walked in, I wanted to see them immediately. I smiled reassuringly. "I understand, and we can talk more in the morning. I'm not upset or hurt, okay?"

She nodded. "Sleep good. Goodnight."

"Night," I murmured, and my eyes closed.

A CREAK WOKE ME. The door clicked shut quietly as someone tried to enter undetected.

Chest tightening, I opened my eyes.

CHAPTER FIVE

A LUMP FORMED in my throat as my gaze settled on Uther. He removed his black hat, confirming that his entire head was bald. Dark circles lined his eyes.

I tensed and sat up, ready to defend my sister and myself. I whispered, "What are you doing?"

His brows furrowed, and his eyes bulged as he glanced back at the door, then at me. He raised his hands and sputtered, "Nothing."

Did all dragon men think women were stupid, or was that the influence of the king and Drake? I lifted my chin, ignoring my squirming stomach. "*Nothing?* You're sneaking into the bedroom while Eva and I are asleep. That seems like more than *nothing*." I clutched the covers over my breasts, though I wasn't wearing anything revealing.

He flinched. "It's not what it looks like." He sighed and rubbed a hand down his face. "I swear. I was notified that Drake would be here soon." He gestured at his walkie-talkie. "And you weren't awake. I...I heard what he said last night and didn't want..." He winced.

He didn't have to finish. Drake wanted me ready and

presentable, yet he hadn't told me what time he planned to arrive. I inhaled deeply to calm my rattled nerves. "No, it's fine. Thank you." I threw the covers off my legs and stood but paused as I stared between him and Eva. He seemed sincere, but I didn't want to let my guard down. She was human and asleep in a bed. That was as vulnerable as one could get.

"I promise on my scales I wasn't being pervy." His nose wrinkled. "I just figured the human girl could use more rest, so I was coming to wake *you*. So, you're awake, and this is awkward, and I'll be leaving now." He spun around and blurred out of the door.

If that had been Falkor or Ladon, they wouldn't have considered Eva's needs or cared if Drake got pissed at me. I'd bet they'd enjoy it. Even though I got a nicer vibe from Uther, that didn't mean I would trust him.

Knowing I needed an outfit from the other room since "my" clothes were there, I closed my eyes to calm my pounding pulse. I didn't want to go into Drake's room, but I didn't have much choice. If I wore something he knew wasn't from in there, I suspected he wouldn't let it go.

I rushed into the hall and stopped in front of Uther, pointing at him. "Do not go in there while my sister's sleeping alone. If something seems wrong, just holler. I'll be listening."

He pinched the bridge of his nose but nodded. "Understood, but you need to hurry. Drake will be here soon. He's getting ready in the main chateau."

His heartbeat remained steady, so I forced myself to enter the bedroom.

If I'd thought Eva's room was huge, I'd been mistaken. This bedroom was twice the size.

The same wooden floor ran into the room, and every

piece of furniture was white. A king-size bed backed against the wall on the left, flanked by nightstands with dark gray lamps. The bedding looked the same as in the other room. The headboard was white, offsetting the silver walls, and the footboard had two drawers built into it. A dresser and a chest of drawers completed the set.

Across from the bed, in front of two oversize windows, sat a brown leather couch and a matching recliner. The sitting area overlooked the back terrace. Two doors were set in the wall on the far right side of the room. The one closest to where I stood was cracked open to reveal a large walk-in closet, meaning the other one was the bathroom.

This was where he expected us to stay. I was thankful I'd already emptied my stomach.

The walls crept toward me as my body tingled. If I didn't get out of here soon, I'd have a full-blown panic attack. I'd been weak enough in front of Drake last night. Today, I'd do everything I could not to let him get to me. Straightening my shoulders, I marched into the closet.

I snorted. It was as large as my attic room back at my stepdad's house. Each side of the room had two rows of clothing racks that were full. In the center, a gigantic island as long as the walls held more than a hundred pairs of shoes. It was topped by a long mirror that split the area into his and hers sections. The right side of the space held the women's clothing, and hundreds of pieces of jewelry sat on one half of the island counter.

A sour taste filled my mouth. This was obnoxious. One person didn't need this much. Peter had referenced how loaded the Hale family was, but I hadn't understood that until now.

If Thorn had been the prince living here, I doubted he would've been as obnoxious about flaunting his wealth.

Struggling to breathe, I strolled to the woman's side. I had no time to waste.

I sighed when I noticed there were no jeans or cotton tops, just various dresses, skirts, and jumpsuits. Whoever had ordered the clothes—most likely Drake—was sending a clear message: no casual wear for me.

My jaw twinged, and I realized I'd been gritting my teeth for who knew how long. I forced my jaw to relax and rubbed my chest where our bond was located. It was luke-warm, so Thorn must be sleeping, but I'd promised to let him know when I was awake. I connected, *Hey, babe.*

The bond warmed as I homed in on a long-sleeved, wide-legged jumpsuit. It looked like the sort of outfit I usually wore, so I removed it from the rod to get a better look. The material was threaded with shiny teal blue, silver, and gold lurex, and it had a surplice neckline and a sash.

Hey, you, he replied, but a chill ran through our bond. *Is he there?*

I undressed. *Not yet. But had the guard not snuck in to wake me—*

Thorn's dragon snarled. *He snuck in while you were sleeping?*

I had the same reaction, but he explained why. I filled him in on the incident. I couldn't blame Thorn for getting upset. I didn't like it either. *He seems like a good guy. He heard Drake threaten me about being ready, without including a time.* I put on the jumpsuit and tied the sash around my waist. The garment fit like a glove, which had my skin crawling.

Thorn's annoyance flashed. *Because he wanted to catch you off guard and use the fact that you're not ready as an excuse to punish you. You said you're meeting the king?*

Yes. I broke out in a sweat, so I turned to the island and searched for shoes. *I don't know what I'm supposed to do or say.* Halfway down, I found a pair of simple black heels that complemented the outfit and slipped them on my feet.

He'll tell the king that he wants to...ma— He cut himself off as his anger intensified and heated.

That was inconvenient for me, seeing as I was already having a hard time controlling my body heat on my own. I inhaled to steady my racing heart and bent down. I snatched up the shorts and T-shirt I'd been wearing. *Have you talked with Vlad, Cassidy, and Saphira?*

I'm waking them up now, he answered. *One second.*

Needing a task to focus on, I marched back out into the hallway. Uther stood a few feet away from the bedroom door, as if to ensure I wouldn't wonder if he'd gone inside. I walked past him into the room where Eva still slept and straight into the bathroom.

I searched the cabinets and found the items I needed still in packages: a hairbrush, makeup, a toothbrush, and toothpaste. Someone truly had prepared for Eva's and my arrival. My back stiffened.

As I stood in front of the mirror, my legs gave out. I clutched the counter to keep myself upright, my gaze boring into my reflection.

I didn't recognize the girl staring back at me.

I looked pretty much the same, but somehow...more. I still had long, golden hair but with more volume, and the same fair skin but with a faint golden glow. My light gray eyes glistened with unshed tears, but the hurt reflecting in my irises, as if they were a mirror image of my soul, had me doing a double take.

Even when Mom had passed, I hadn't looked dead inside.

So, I did the one thing that would make me feel better. I

closed my eyes and pulled the image of Thorn's face into my mind.

His eyes were the first thing I recalled. That sky blue shade, with flecks of what could only be described as diamonds, had captivated me. When I'd first gone to find Drake at his fancy bar to bargain for Eva's freedom, those breathtaking eyes had stopped me in my tracks, and I'd almost forgotten why I'd gone there.

Then, the day Thorn had kidnapped me, he'd shifted back into human form and reappeared shirtless. I imagined his gorgeous, smooth, tan skin and his medium-brown hair hanging in his eyes. He was perfection, and with his chiseled features and muscular body, he could easily be a model.

And he was *mine*.

A soft knock sounded on the bedroom door, followed by Uther mumbling, "Drake is heading this way."

My arms gave out, and I fell onto my knees, the broken person I'd seen in the mirror taking control. Now that the vision of Thorn was gone, it hurt to breathe. I missed Thorn so damn much, and I'd give anything for him to be here with me.

Ev, what's wrong?

I didn't want to put pressure on him, but I couldn't lie. Not to him. Not anymore. *I miss you so much that my heart feels like it's been stabbed repeatedly. And Thorn, I'm scared.* My eyes burned, and I blinked to hold the tears at bay. *Eva's here, and I don't know how to protect her, and I don't know what to do.*

Trust me, I understand, and I will get you both out of there, he replied. *We're drawing a map of the chateau and dragon lands while trying to get a solid estimate of warrior numbers based on what Cassidy, Saphira, and Vlad know. But if you need me to stay connected with you—*

I took a deep breath. *No, keep planning. That's what I need you all to do. I'll let you know what I glean here. I've seen only one side of the chateau, so far.*

That side is intended for the prince, once he marries, Thorn explained, his emotions icy. *But he shouldn't stay there until he's wed, according to a long-standing tradition that every single dragon shifter knows.*

I clung to the hope that Drake wouldn't live here with Eva and me. *Pay attention to the conversation with them. Hopefully, you can find a way to get Eva and me out.*

Panic slammed into me, then eased. He answered, *I do need to focus. So far, our options aren't promising, but I'm here, whenever you need me.*

With shaky hands, I quickly put on makeup, going for a natural look since I was low on time. As I finished with my mascara and painted my lips a rosy pink, the back door to the house opened.

Throat dry, I took one last look in the mirror. This would have to do.

I spun on my heel and rushed into the bedroom. I shook Eva and said, "You need to get up. I'm leaving." I didn't feel safe leaving her asleep with a stranger nearby.

Her eyes fluttered open, and she touched her forehead. "Everly, I had the worst nightmare." Then her face drained of color.

"I'm sorry." I brushed my fingers through her hair. "It wasn't a nightmare."

Footsteps pounded down the hallway, and Uther said, "Sire, she's not in there."

Drake snarled, "What do you mean she's not *in there?*"

"She's in this room with her sister," Uther answered uncomfortably.

I heard a huff, then Drake's heavy footfalls heading our way.

Eva's mouth opened and closed.

"Stay in here while I'm gone." I kissed her forehead. "Be safe." I stood straight and marched to the door.

As I reached it, it opened, and Drake stepped in, coming face-to-face with me.

The hard glint in his eyes vanished, and his head jerked back. "You're ready."

That broken girl in the mirror flashed through my mind. That was what he wanted, which meant that was exactly what I couldn't become. He'd hoped I wouldn't be ready, so I batted my eyelashes, oozing innocence. "You asked me to be, so I set an alarm to ensure I wouldn't disappoint you."

Uther exhaled.

He'd expected me to tell Drake that he'd alerted me. Uther didn't trust me, either, and that, somehow, made me like him more.

Jaw twitching, Drake gazed at the bed.

My dragon stirred. I didn't like him looking at my sister, especially when she was in bed. I placed a hand on his chest and managed to only push him back gently.

His nostrils flared, and he glared at me.

That had been my intent. Blood rushed in my ears, but I held back the anger. "I thought we needed to meet the king." I'd do almost anything to get him away from her. She'd already experienced too much terror.

"Don't push me again," he warned, his expression turning to stone. He gripped my arm, his fingers digging into my skin, and yanked me toward the hallway.

Eva gasped as I moved my feet, regaining my balance.

He picked up speed, and I had to run to keep up with him. No doubt he wanted to make sure I understood who was in control.

As we passed Uther, his lips mashed into a disapproving line. However, when we entered the living room where Falkor and Ladon stood, they had the opposite sort of expression—both of them smirked. After what I'd done to Falkor last night, I'd made an enemy, but I couldn't find it in me to care.

Drake made a beeline out the back door and onto the terrace lawn. With each step, my heels sank into the soft earth, making it hard to keep up. A stitch formed in my side, but I pushed through, eager to get to wherever the hell he was taking me. The two guards followed closely behind, Falkor snickering from time to time at my discomfort.

As we rounded the yard toward the main house's terrace, the scent of sausage and eggs filled the air, followed by the clanging of plates. My stomach growled.

I counted four guards stationed near the tree line. Two ladies dressed in maid outfits stood off to one side of a round glass table with four chairs around it. A muscular man, who resembled both Drake and Thorn, was seated in the spot that overlooked the backyard. I knew this was the king, and the gorgeous woman next to him had to be Drake's mother.

The king had salt-and-pepper hair and a mostly gray, short beard. He appeared to be in his fifties, and he was just as large as Thorn. His midnight black eyes focused on me, and he reached over to take the woman's hand.

Drake continued to head straight to them, his face and demeanor transforming as he changed into a person I didn't recognize. He smiled, though it didn't reach his eyes, and slowed down, wrapping an arm around my waist as if to help me over the grass.

The woman smiled back sadly. Her striking baby blue eyes were breathtaking and held a kindness I hadn't expected. A breeze lifted strands of her dark chocolate-brown hair and settled them on the shoulders of her white, sweetheart-cut dress.

Releasing me, Drake hurried a few steps ahead and pulled out the open chair next to the queen. My throat hurt as I slid onto the seat, unsure of what was to come.

As soon as I sat, the breeze picked up again, and the queen's eyes widened. She jumped to her feet and stumbled away from me.

CHAPTER SIX

THE QUEEN'S abrupt movement jarred the table, and the coffee in her full mug splashed over the rim. She clutched her chest, breathing raggedly.

The king climbed to his feet. "What's wrong?"

Falkor and Ladon fanned out on the terrace, searching for signs of danger.

I didn't hear anything other than birds chirping. Her reaction must have something to do with me. My vision blurred.

"I thought you said she was human," the queen gasped.

Blood running cold, I took a hollow breath. Out of every scenario I'd anticipated, I hadn't contemplated this.

The two guards relaxed as they moved into positions at opposite ends of the terrace.

Brow furrowing, the king settled his attention back on me, and he sniffed the air. His eyes narrowed as he looked at Drake. "She is supposed to be human. What the *hell* is this? There's only one way this is possible."

The king didn't seem to know that Thorn had captured me. Even though Drake had admitted that he was behind the kidnapping of Thorn's parents, I had assumed the king had been made aware of it.

Drake's eyes darkened until I couldn't distinguish his irises from his pupils, but his expression remained indifferent instead of his usual cruel, stony appearance. He rolled his shoulders back and took the seat next to mine. "She is Peter's stepdaughter, not his actual blood."

CROSSING HIS ARMS, the king lifted his chin. "Yes, I *know* that. I saw her, her siblings and her mother, in Peter's building several times when I met with him, and all four were human."

A long-forgotten memory flashed through my mind. I was thirteen and waiting with my mother and the twins in the lobby. A man I'd heard called Mr. Hale had come out with my stepfather, looking identical to the way he did today, as if he hadn't aged a day, but that wasn't what struck a chord with me now. It was the way I remembered him staring at me and the twins with longing.

If Drake wouldn't tell them the truth, I would. "I was human until a little over a week ago."

Drake glared at me sideways.

What were we supposed to say, other than the truth? They knew I shouldn't be a dragon shifter.

The queen's jaw dropped, and she took a few steps toward me, her gorgeous eyes brightening. "That's impossible. Unless..." She took a staggered breath. "He's alive."

Out of every reaction I might have predicted, it wasn't one I would have described as hopeful.

She took her seat again and leaned toward me. She bit her bottom lip and asked, "Where did you see this man? Was it in Asheville or another town close by?"

Drake snarled, his malice slipping through. "Mother, stop. Remember how you were supposed to meet her over a week ago? You didn't because the *abomination* kidnapped her on the way to the chateau. Falkor and Ladon nearly lost their lives."

The queen's face fell, and her eyes darkened.

I wished I could say something to contradict what Drake had said, but he hadn't lied. Thorn had done that, though not for the fun of it. I had to bite my tongue, or Eva would pay the price for my outing him. But I couldn't remain silent. "He changed me to save my life."

Hope sparked back into her gaze.

"He's a master manipulator," Drake said forcibly as he reached over and grabbed my knee. He squeezed so tightly that a whimper built inside me. He wrinkled his nose. "The real reason he changed you was that he knew you were meant to be my breeder. But that's fine. I got you back and solved that problem as well."

The king lifted a brow. "What do you mean?"

Drake's expression smoothed, and the corners of his mouth tipped upward. "Well, that's one reason I asked to meet for breakfast today. I've made a decision. Now that Everly is a dragon shifter, I want to make her my queen."

The king laughed but stopped abruptly when Drake didn't join in.

"I'm serious, Father." Drake lifted his coffee mug from the table. "I've thought about it, and there is no other person I want by my side."

Though there was a plate full of eggs and bacon in front of me, I couldn't eat without puking.

"Son, you have to be kidding." The king shook his head. "She's not dragon born."

"True." Drake shrugged. "But we ensure that information doesn't become public. We can say she didn't live in the area. She's from Asheville, and I won't have anyone else as my wife."

The king rubbed his temples. "You mentioned solving your problem. How will marrying Everly, a dragon shifter, help with our reproduction issue?"

"I'm glad you asked." He released his hold on me and took a sip of his coffee. "Since Everly will live here with me, I figured, why not make her more comfortable? So I brought her sister here to be my breeder."

"*What?*" the queen choked out. "You're telling me you chose sisters for your wife and breeder?"

He was trying to come off as considerate, but even his mom could see the error in that plan.

The king slammed his hand on the table, and the glass cracked down the center. "Have you lost your mind? You took not just one child away from Peter but *two?* All you've done is brought unwanted attention to us!"

Without flinching, Drake took a bite of his eggs. "Peter embezzled money. He knows the consequences. Besides, he was thrilled to get this one off his hands." He pointed at me.

That was like a gut punch, despite every word being true.

"Wait." The queen gripped the arms of her chair. "If Thorn took Everly, how is she here?"

"I handled the situation." Drake placed his fork on his plate and leaned back in his seat. "I located Vlad and Cassidy, used them as leverage, and voila, here she is, back with me."

She smoothed out a wrinkle in her dress across her stomach. "Is that the one—" She glanced at the king.

He nodded subtly.

I assumed she was asking if Vlad was the assassin, but I wasn't sure.

The king took a bite of bacon, chewed methodically, and swallowed. "Where are Vlad and Cassidy now?"

"Free. Getting Everly back was all that mattered," Drake said stonily as he turned and brushed a fingertip down my arm. "I want all of her, and when she returned to me as a dragon, I realized I could have her as my bride."

Needing to eat something to keep up my strength, I snatched a piece of bacon from my plate. I took a bite, and my stomach gurgled in protest. This wasn't happening.

The king swallowed and placed his hands on the table. "You did all of this without talking to me?"

"You thought he was dead. I was protecting you from making another hard decision." Drake's nostrils flared, but he kept his expression neutral beyond that. "I hoped not to bother you with anything since you both struggled with the decision you made twenty-one years ago, but with Everly now a dragon, it had to come out. If anything, this situation should reaffirm the wisdom of what you tried to do—kill him. He kidnapped her, locked her up, and changed her without her permission."

The queen flinched and hung her head. She reached over and patted my arm. "I'm so sorry you had to experience that, Everly. I... I don't know what else to say."

A scream strangled me, but I prevented the noise from escaping. This guy was more than an asshole—he was sick. I cleared my throat to ease the discomfort. "He really did change me to save me." I had to keep her hope alive. "I escaped and ran when it was dark and rainy. I fell and cracked my skull... I would've died."

Her lips quivered, but she exhaled. "He wouldn't have had to change you if he hadn't kidnapped you. There's more to this story, but it's best if the world doesn't know he's alive. He's a danger." Her eyes glistened.

Despite her remorse, I couldn't help getting angry. Blood running hot, I wanted to scream at them. *Thorn is your child too, and he's a great man.* But I'd learned from my stepdad that people wouldn't listen if they didn't want to.

Drake cut his eyes to me, giving me a clear message: *Keep your mouth shut.*

I snatched the white linen napkin from beside my plate and wiped my hands. They weren't greasy, but I needed to do something with my excess energy.

What's going on? Thorn linked, and our bond warmed.

I hated to tell him, but we'd promised we wouldn't hold back anymore, so I gave him the rundown.

Disgust charged through our bond. Thorn connected, *So, the king is acting like he didn't know about Drake's plans?*

He is. Though I'd just become a dragon and wasn't used to searching for clues that could reveal a lie, I hadn't heard any changes in the king's heartbeat or breathing. *I think he's telling the truth.*

Do not believe him, Thorn replied urgently. *The royals are skilled in covering things up, and that's what Drake is doing.*

I had no reason not to trust Thorn, but something didn't feel right about the situation.

"Enough of this conversation." The king waved a hand. "This is the first time I've formally met Everly, and Mira has never met her before. This isn't what we should be discussing when we have just learned that my son—the heir —has chosen his bride."

I'd rather talk about Thorn than *this.*

"Let's not forget his *breeder*," Queen Mira murmured. "How do you feel about that choice, Arman?"

DRAKE TENSED, and his jaw twitched. "Well, *Mother*, I get to choose my breeder like I get to choose my wife."

The tension was so thick it nearly smothered me. I refused to play along and act okay about my sister being thrown into this mess.

"I don't understand why you think trying to impregnate a human will work." Her nose wrinkled, and her mouth twisted like she'd tasted something bad. "Shouldn't you try having a child with your new wife first, before bringing a third person into your relationship?"

The couple of bites of bacon I'd swallowed made me gag. Here they were talking about Drake having sex with both his wife and a breeder. I'd puked enough in the last twenty-four hours that I didn't want another round, but the sensation persisted because... Drake.

"Get her in line, *Father*," Drake snapped and sneered. "If I wanted her opinion, I would've asked for it. I'm the future leader of the dragons, and I will do what I think is best."

Queen Mira grimaced and licked her lips. "I'm sorry, honey. I'm not trying to upset you. It's just...if Arman—"

"I am *not* my father." Drake lifted his chin and stuck out his chest. "I am my own man, so don't compare me to him."

She nodded and averted her gaze, and my blood boiled.

Not only was Drake an arrogant douche, but he also treated his mother like garbage. I'd do *anything* for my mom to be alive, and to see him acting so entitled and ungrateful made me want to hurt him. He had no regard for anyone but himself.

"Let's talk about this wedding." King Arman rubbed his hands together and smiled, but a vein bulged between his eyes. "It's May, so are we thinking of a fall wedding? That would give us ample time to organize everything and give our guests time to book travel and hotels."

Some of the weight rolled off my shoulders, and my lungs worked a bit easier. A fall wedding would give us plenty of time to determine a way out of this.

"Absolutely *not*," Drake rasped. "Everly and I will be wed in two days."

"Two *days*?" Queen Mira's mouth dropped. "But darling, why? We need to have her dress made, and—"

I nodded, ignoring the black spots that crowded my vision. Here I was, thinking we might have four months to plan, and of course, he'd taken that away.

I shouldn't have been surprised. He was all about claiming me and driving Thorn crazy, so he'd show up recklessly. "Drake, I'm here. Eva's here. What's the rush?"

As soon as his head snapped in my direction, I knew I'd said the wrong thing. He leaned toward me, the evil glint in his eyes bright.

I tried to lean back, but he reached over and squeezed my leg again, so hard a whimper damn near left me.

His intent was clear. If I kept doing things he didn't like, he'd hurt me. I had no doubt he'd target my sister next.

Clenching my jaw, I held still as his mouth hovered over mine.

Thank goodness, I hadn't eaten more than a bite. When his lips touched mine, my throat burned. His lips were warm but stiff and rough. They were nothing like Thorn's, and internally, I recoiled. Though the kiss lasted only a few seconds, it felt like a lifetime. When Drake pulled away, I wanted to gargle with alcohol to disinfect myself.

Ev, what's going on? Thorn connected, his worry exacerbating my upset stomach.

My eyes burned. *He just kissed me.*

Thorn's rage exploded through our connection, and my ears pounded as his dragon bellowed.

He touched what belongs to me, he connected. *I will kill him slowly and enjoy wringing out every ounce of his pain and making him squirm. No one takes my gem from me and tries to tarnish it.*

His words should have upset me, but my dragon roared in approval. Unlike Drake, Thorn didn't think of me as property but as someone who meant the most to him, like a treasure. *I couldn't stop him. I'm sorry. We're with your parents, and he threatened—*

You don't have anything to apologize for, Thorn replied and pushed the warmth of his love toward me. *He's forced you into this, and I will avenge you.*

Oh, I plan on being right there beside you. I didn't want to kill Drake, but I'd be down for making him utterly powerless.

Always and forever, he vowed, and my heart beat once again.

Drake smirked, the power-hungry glare back in place.

He could tell that Thorn and I were connecting, and he was getting the reaction he so desperately craved.

We were playing right into his hand.

Interlocking our fingers, he placed our joined hands on the table.

Drake smirked, but he didn't radiate happiness. He was as cold as an icicle. "I can't be without her for another moment. I want to do this right and not take her before the wedding, so I'm sure we can make that happen in two days. I don't care if all the guests can't make it. We'll figure out who is truly loyal to us this way."

The queen nodded. "Of course, son. We can make that happen, but Everly and I should start planning immediately."

My legs shook. I didn't want to plan a wedding to *him*, even though I prayed we wouldn't actually go through with it. There wasn't much I could do...except one thing. I smiled brightly. "Yes, we'd better. And I would love for Eva to join in on the planning. After all, she's my sister."

"That's a good point. She is important to you and in your relationship," Queen Mira said, her brows pulling together. "Drake, please have her brought into the living room to join us."

Drake stood and helped me to my feet. "Of course, Mother." Then he leaned toward me again, and I froze, fearing he was going to kiss me again.

Instead, he whispered in my ear, "One wrong move, and you will wish that Eva was only my breeder with what I'll do to her. Now, smile and laugh."

I obliged, but the sound got lodged in my throat.

He kissed my cheek and tucked a piece of hair behind my ear. "Don't worry, love. I'll be back soon."

He spun on his heels and marched away, his dedicated golden retrievers following. With each stride that took him farther away, my stomach unclenched a little. I turned back to the king and the queen and realized that King Arman had been studying me for who knew how long.

Queen Mira stood and gestured at the door to the main house of the chateau. "Come on, dear."

"Honey, why don't you and the servants go in and get things ready while I have a moment to talk with Everly alone?" King Arman said as he patted his wife's arm.

"Oh, of course." The queen laughed, but the smile didn't reach her eyes. "Drake won't let her out of his sight often." She waved the servants in and left, leaving me alone with the king.

I tried to breathe despite my lungs screaming while I waited for him to say something.

He surveyed the area, and his gaze settled on my face. "Are you mated to Thorn?"

The world shifted, and I placed my hands on the table to keep myself from falling over. Somehow, this man...the *king*...knew, and I was certain he wouldn't approve of me being mated to his eldest son.

What would he do to me?

CHAPTER SEVEN

SWEAT POOLED UNDER MY ARMPITS, and I tried to control my breathing, but the way I had to brace myself on the table had already answered his question. *The king knows,* I connected with Thorn.

"That's what I thought." King Arman ran a hand down his face, and his eyes narrowed, deepening his faint crow's feet. "That's why Drake is so set on marrying you."

What do you mean he knows? Thorn asked, trepidation leaking into the bond.

I straightened my spine. *That I'm your mate.*

Fuck, Thorn replied as his dragon snarled.

King Arman already knew the truth, so I said, "I know it's hard to believe coming from me, but Thorn isn't a monster or someone to be feared."

"Even though he kidnapped you?" The king crossed his arms.

That was a fair question, and I needed to use this opportunity to change the king's mind, if not for me and my situation, then for Thorn. "He needed leverage to free Cassidy and Vlad."

"Drake said—" he started.

"He lied," I interjected, not wanting to waste time. Drake could come back at any minute, and I suspected he'd be in a hurry. I hated what that meant for Eva. She probably wasn't ready. At least, that would buy me more time to talk to the king alone. "Thorn took me because he'd learned of Drake's plans for me. He wanted to use me as a bargaining chip."

"And what did Drake want?" King Arman tugged at the sleeves of his white and blue striped button-down shirt.

"Thorn." I ran a hand down my stomach to ease the nausea rolling inside. "He doesn't like that Thorn exists. I don't know how he found him—"

The king groaned. "I do, and no wonder the guards have been acting strangely. Falkor was my personal guard until recently, when he said he was worried that someone was stalking Drake. Falkor has to be in on it."

What's going on, Everly? Thorn piped in. *Are you in danger?*

No. Actually, the king seems bothered by all of this, I replied, trying to stay focused on my in-person conversation. "Wait, you know how Drake located Thorn?"

He placed his hands on the back of his chair and nodded. "It was because of me."

"And you're surprised he acted on it?" I scoffed and crossed my arms. Maybe it wasn't the smartest tactic for dealing with dragon royalty, but damn, he didn't get to ignore his role in this.

Growling, he focused his gaze on me and said, "I understand your predicament, but I am your *king*. Lucky for you, you're also now my daughter, but you need to understand your place."

The hair on the nape of my neck lifted, and pressure

built inside me. Despite the flood of warmth in my chest from him calling me family, the strength of his stare forced my attention to the ground...as if I were submitting. My dragon grumbled, not liking it, but I couldn't fight it.

Then the sensation was gone, and I could glance up again.

"I've known where Thorn was hiding for twenty years." The king's face twisted in agony and something like regret.

Twenty years. That was shortly after Thorn had settled in Atlanta. "Why act now? Why not twenty years ago?"

"Because he was hiding." King Arman scratched the back of his neck. "And staying away from other dragons. I *couldn't* kill my son, not when he wasn't causing any harm." His shoulders slumped.

If I hadn't known better, I would've said he cared about Thorn. "Why try to kill him at all? And why would you tell Drake where Thorn was, knowing he'd be threatened by him?" My body heated, and I wanted him to spit out all the answers instead of making me ask him.

"I didn't know what to do after he stole my dragon. That was what my father had done to people who opposed him, and if Thorn decided to take my dragon and keep it, the entire dragon shifter race would be tossed into chaos." He clasped his hands. "As soon as I knew that Vlad was in the woods and in position to kill my *boy*, I knew I'd made a mistake, but I didn't know how to stop it. When I learned the attempt had failed, I was relieved."

My breath caught. I remembered Thorn telling me about his grandfather's abuse of the mark. "If you were relieved, why did you have your guards track him, Vlad, and Cassidy down a few days after that?"

"Falkor said if the truth got out about what I'd tried to do, my people would turn on me." He turned and stared into the tree line. "They were supposed to bring the three of them back as prisoners. I didn't expect a fight to break out in the middle of human streets."

I wheezed. "You thought making Thorn a prisoner would be better than killing him? Maybe he'd be breathing, but you would've stripped away everything worth living for from him and his parents."

He flinched. "Is that what he calls Vlad and Cassidy?"

I swallowed my snort and forced myself to soften my response. "Do you blame him? They protected him and cared for him when his own blood didn't." Family wasn't always forged by blood. In fact, those bonds formed outside of blood were stronger because people *chose* to forge them. I was learning that now, with Thorn and Saphira.

"No, but that doesn't mean it's easy to hear." His eyes glistened. "Shortly after that, I learned they were living in Atlanta. I told Falkor to keep an eye on Thorn. As long as he didn't leave the area or start working with other dragons, we'd let him be. I didn't have it in me to kill him, and I wanted him to be happy."

His sincerity crumbled some of my defenses. Even though his logic was flawed, he'd thought he was doing what was best for the dragons he ruled and Thorn. Something tugged at me, and I almost closed the distance between us and placed a comforting hand on his shoulder. Even though he'd called me his daughter, I was certain we weren't at that point yet. I forced myself to stay in place. "I wouldn't call that happy."

"Better than dead or locked in prison." He exhaled.

We were losing focus, and Drake would be back soon. "Why did you tell Drake?"

"I didn't. He and Falkor have grown close these past couple of years, ever since Drake took over the family business so I could focus on royal affairs." He scowled. "It had to be Falkor. He knew where they lived and where they went on weekends to shift into their dragons."

Tilting my head back, I narrowed my eyes. I didn't want to be gullible and easily trust this man, especially when he'd ordered a hitman to take out his own six-year-old son. "And you didn't notice that Vlad and Cassidy were prisoners here?"

He shook his head and frowned. "When I heard that someone could be stalking Drake, I shifted Falkor and Ladon to be Drake's personal guards instead of mine. I wanted my son protected, but shortly after the transition, the two guards started avoiding me and spending time away from the chateau unless they were with Drake. I figured something was amiss, but I never imagined *this*. Drake tends to get himself into trouble, but Ladon and Falkor are more than capable of handling it."

I clenched my hands as my pulse quickened. "Kidnapping and threatening to *kill* people isn't *getting himself into trouble*. That's way over the line of acceptable."

"You're right." He pursed his lips. "I'll fix this, but I need to handle it delicately. I can't hurt Drake. Not like I did Thorn."

Something snapped in my chest, and for the first time, I believed I might be able to kill someone. "Drake and Thorn are polar opposites. Thorn is an amazing man who is willing to do whatever it takes to protect the people he loves. Drake is nowhere close to that."

King Arman focused his intense stare on me. "Do you mean that, or are you saying it because he forced the mate bond on you?"

My body tensed as my dragon exploded in a guttural growl. I didn't care if he was my king. He didn't get to talk about Thorn that way. "He didn't *force* the mate bond on me. When I was human, even while knowing he'd kidnapped me, there was something alluring about him that I couldn't shake. After he changed me, I was even more confused because that attraction became a literal tug, and electricity sparked between us, intensifying the draw I'd experienced as a human." I chuckled, remembering my confusion. "I thought it was a sire bond and tried to fight it, but every day, Thorn showed me that everything he'd done was to save the two people who had sacrificed everything for him. Even when we were his prisoners, he took care of Saphira's and my every need and made us more than comfortable."

The king's brows furrowed. "You're his *fated* mate?"

I smiled, the words causing a lightness in my body. I wanted the whole world to know that Thorn and I belonged to each other. "Yes, and Drake is now trying to use that bond to force Thorn to do something reckless to save me before the ceremony." There was no point in lying about Thorn's desperation to rescue me. Drake already knew. It wouldn't make the situation more dire.

The king chuckled grimly and rubbed his forehead. "He learned that his brother was alive and would be considered the rightful heir to the throne despite his exile. Mira and I have given that boy everything he ever desired, which has exacerbated the problem. This is on me to fix."

A tightness squeezed my chest. I could read between the lines. They had spoiled Drake, overcompensating for what they'd done to Thorn. "Isn't it strange that the son you feared is the one trying to save the people he loves, while the one you spoiled is turning into the very thing you feared Thorn would become?"

"No." King Arman's jaw set. "That's not it. Drake is just

misguided. He'll have to learn, and I'm here to teach him." He nodded toward the house. "You need to join Mira before Drake gets back with your sister."

Even though I still had so many questions, I inhaled, trying to calm my shaking hands. The king was right. Drake would be here soon, and if he found me speaking with the king alone, he wouldn't approve. "Please don't tell him about this conversation."

"I won't." He turned to me. "I will have to figure out a solution without him knowing, or he'll move the wedding up. I'll find you when I have worked something out."

I'd taken a few steps toward the door when the king said, "And, Everly."

Turning back, I looked at him, and what I saw caught me by surprise.

His hand was pressed to his chest, and a tear trickled down his cheek. "Can you tell Thorn I'm so damn sorry that I had to do what I did? That I think of him every day, and his mother and I would give anything to remove the mark and reunite our family. Isolating him was the only way to keep us and my people safe, and I want to make up for my mistake. If freeing you is the way, I'll do it without hesitation...like I did Saphira, Cassidy, and Vlad."

My throat burned and constricted as if I might choke. Even though he seemed haunted, King Arman still believed he'd made the right choice. "I'll tell him, but I want to make something clear, even if you *are* my king. You did *not* make the right choice. Thorn is loyal and knows right from wrong. He's everything Drake isn't, and the fact you still think you had to do what you did proves you don't deserve to know the man he's become in spite of you." I turned on my heels and marched into the house, desperate to get away from a man who didn't value my mate.

THIRTY-SIX HOURS LATER, it was the night before my "wedding." Thorn was beside himself, and I wasn't much better. I stood at the end of the bed that Eva and I had been sharing, with Uther standing guard outside the bedroom door. Falkor and Ladon were missing in action, likely from leading the charge to watch for Thorn's arrival.

"I thought you said you were going to get us out of here," Eva whispered as she crawled to the foot of the bed. She didn't realize that she no longer needed to get close to me for me to hear her whisper.

Placing a finger to my lips, I paused my pacing. I mouthed, *He can hear you,* and nodded toward the bedroom door.

Her brows furrowed, and she murmured, "What?" no doubt thinking she was being quiet.

Oh, dear goodness. I touched her arm and gestured toward the bathroom. She and I couldn't have an open conversation unless we made it difficult for Uther to hear.

She swung her legs off the bed, got tangled up in her long cashmere gown, and tumbled face-first toward the floor. I grabbed her by the waist and yanked her against my body. She landed hard against my chest, but I didn't stumble back. I still wasn't used to my dragon strength.

"I told you that gown was a horrible idea." I snickered as I helped her to her feet.

"Hey, it feels like a feather brushing all over my body." She untangled her feet and stood. "The clothes are the one nice thing about being here."

There was no way anyone would catch me in a night-gown. My skin crawled, even in the one pair of flannel pajamas I'd found in the far corner of the closet. Every inch of me, from my neck down, was covered, and I was certain someone had left them there by accident. Every other set of pajamas was some sort of cashmere gown or fancy silk set. I'd even found a piece of unnecessary lingerie. It was sheer, and *everything* showed.

A shiver racked my body over why it might be in there. If Drake ever tried something physical with me, I'd vomit all over him, and if he touched my sister, I would kill him...or die trying.

Now that Eva was steady, I hurried into the bathroom and turned on the shower. When she followed me in, I shut the door.

"They're still coming up with a plan," I whispered louder so she could hear me. "It might be best if you don't know what it is." I wanted to protect her as best I could and keeping her in the dark seemed ideal.

She shook her head. "Don't do that. We're sisters. Equals. You've taken care of me for so long—I want to be part of the plan so I can protect you as well."

My chest expanded. "Let me connect with Thorn to see if there's an update."

Leaning against the glass shower, she crossed her arms and raised a brow.

She wasn't leaving. There was no point in fighting her. I didn't want to risk her acting out and alerting the guards that we were up to something.

I connected with Thorn, *Any update?*

We're going through our options. We think one of the hidden tunnels leading into the chateau could be our best move, or possibly blending in with the help. They'll have all entrances and the backyard guarded. The problem with the help is that the warriors will be paying attention to their faces.

The wedding was to take place at noon on the terrace, with the guests sitting in the backyard. That way, the chateau would block me from view on one side, and the guards would be on the other. Broad daylight would make it easy to see everywhere for miles.

My limbs quivered. There was no good option. Drake had everything planned with no wiggle room. The king had said he'd help us, but I hadn't heard a word from him...not that Thorn trusted him anyway.

A loud knock pounded on the bedroom door, and I stiffened. We couldn't turn the water off, or it'd look suspicious. I said, "Eva, stay in here. I'll pretend you're in the shower."

She opened her mouth, but I went to the door. As I opened it, I turned back and murmured, "Please. I need you to do this."

Rolling her eyes, she nodded. I closed the door quietly and hurried to the bedroom door. I inhaled, fearing I'd find Drake's leather scent, but it was missing.

All I smelled was Uther.

When I opened the door, the guard stood there, wearing an urgent expression. He whispered, "I need you to tell me everything. It's time."

CHAPTER EIGHT

GUT TIGHTENING, I stepped away from him. "I have no clue what you're talking about. The wedding isn't for another twelve hours." *Please, if there is a higher being, don't let Drake want to have sex tonight,* I chanted internally. He'd made it clear that he wanted to wait until after the wedding, so, I assumed, Thorn would be even more desperate to reach me before the deadline.

Uther growled and glanced down the hallway toward the living room. "Now isn't the time for games. The king needs information so he can communicate with *them.*"

"This isn't a *game.*" I suspected he was trying to pull one over on me, not the other way around. "I have no idea who the king wants to communicate with." King Arman had told me he'd find me when he had a plan. This was *not* him finding me. If anything, this could be a test from Drake. After all, he seemed to trust Uther, especially when he could hold the safety of his daughter over his head.

He sighed and licked his lips. "Look, this is *risky* for me, but Drake isn't the king yet, and my loyalty lies with King Arman."

I studied him, gauging whether I should trust him. "This wasn't what the king and I agreed to." I watched his reaction to see if it would hint at his dishonesty.

"I know, but we tried to get him here." Uther shuffled his feet.

Heavy footsteps walked from the back door toward the hallway. Ladon stepped into view and arched an eyebrow. "Is there a problem?"

Uther tensed. "I was—"

"Heading into the bathroom with me," I interjected then flinched. That could get him in hot water with Drake if I didn't tread carefully, so I had to improvise. I clutched my stomach and hunched over. "My stomach has been upset this evening, and I kinda stopped up the toilet."

Ladon's nose wrinkled. "Whoa. Stop." He lifted a hand.

I groaned. "If you don't want Uther to help me, you could. I just need someone to plunge because I sorta made a mess trying to do it myself."

The corners of Uther's mouth tipped upward, but he mashed his lips into a hard line, hiding it.

"No!" Ladon slashed the air with his arm. "Uther is fine. I just heard you whispering and—"

Stomping my foot, I tried to play the part of the future, spoiled queen. "Well, I'm *sorry*. Next time I have stomach issues, I'll announce it to everyone in the house. I apologize for my discretion." My body burned, but I took a deep breath to prevent the flush from reaching my face. I didn't want to act embarrassed, but maybe it would make the whole exchange appear more real.

Uther winced and cleared his throat. "She must be nervous about the wedding tomorrow. Why don't we just go into the bathroom and fix the issue? Let's go...see what we're up against."

"That's one way of putting it." Ladon cringed. "Dude, you may want to grab some Poo-Pourri, a mask, or *something* to protect you from the smell."

I hunched over. "My poop doesn't stink," I said through clenched teeth. Would he just leave us the hell alone, or was this some sick karma attacking me because I'd lied?

Ladon dry heaved and stumbled down the hallway, and I swore he was holding his breath.

Good to know that he couldn't stand talking about bowel movements. Who would've thought a trained warrior who'd killed and had blood splattered on him would be squeamish about poo?

"Let's get you taken care of." Uther grinned as he entered the bedroom.

I shut the door behind me and dropped the act. Luckily, Eva was in the bathroom and wouldn't hear anything. I murmured, "I'm glad he fell for it."

"You're something else." His irises twinkled before his face became stern again. "But *he* couldn't get here himself to get Thorn's number. Drake has been watching everyone who tries to get close to you, including his father."

That wasn't surprising, especially since his mom had expressed displeasure with him choosing a breeder, as well as a wife. "Why should I trust you?"

Uther lifted a brow. "Do you have any other options? You won't make it out of here, and Thorn will be captured if you don't accept our help."

My body turned to ice. I hated that he was right, and I'd been trying to deny the inevitable, but that was hard to do when someone smacked you in the face with it. "What exactly are you asking me for?" My chest tingled as I stopped trying to sense whether he was on my side. He already knew enough to take us down if he wanted to.

"Thorn's number." He pulled a cell phone from his back pocket.

I laughed. I had no clue what it was. Thorn had kidnapped me, and then we'd mated. I'd never needed his number, which I hadn't realized until now.

Uther tilted his head and observed me. He asked, "What's so funny?"

"Let me connect with him to get it." I opened myself up to Thorn and said, *The king sent a guard here to ask for your number.*

Our connection warmed immediately. *Be careful. It could be a trick,* Thorn replied.

My heart ached, the pain damn near debilitating. What I wouldn't do to be with him. If it hadn't been for Eva, I would've tried to break out of here again, to hell with the consequences, but I couldn't leave her behind. I couldn't break that promise to Mom.

Rubbing my chest where it hurt, I tried to focus on the conversation and not on how much I needed him. *I know. He knew I was expecting to hear from King Arman, and he's seemed trustworthy so far. What do we have to lose?*

Thorn's frustration increased, and my limbs shook harder. He replied, *Not much, but I hate the idea of talking to the king. I still don't believe he was behind saving my parents and Saphira.*

Has Saphira tried calling her dad? The last I'd heard, she hadn't wanted to. She didn't want to make her father more of a target than he already was just by being her blood.

We decided it was too risky, he replied, and I sensed no malice through our bond. His parents had been kidnapped, and he knew getting family more involved was a lot to ask of anyone. They were probably monitoring Saphira's parents in the hopes she would reach out to them.

Though I didn't want to push him, we didn't have a ton of time. The shower turned off in the bathroom. Eva would be joining us soon. *If we're going to give him your number, we need to do it. Uther can't stay in the bedroom with me much longer without making Ladon more suspicious.*

Thorn's dragon snarled as he asked, *A guard is with you in a bedroom?*

Maybe that hadn't been the best detail to include. *Ladon was watching us, so I pretended that my stomach hurt and said I'd stopped up the toilet. It chased him off so I could talk to Uther alone.*

My stomach tickled from the humor swirling through the bond. He replied, *Gods, I needed that. I miss you and your crazy stories so damn much.*

"You're mated to him?" Uther whispered as the bathroom door opened, and Eva stalked out.

When her gaze landed on Uther, she froze, and her mouth opened. "What is *he* doing in here?"

Uther stiffened. "I'm just about to leave." He held out his phone to me.

Babe, I connected. *Do you mind giving me a number in case the king calls? This might be our best bet. What is there to lose? They already know you're coming.* Last night, I'd even begged him to stay at the cabin and rescue me later, but he wouldn't budge. He didn't want Drake forcing me to do anything.

Fine. He huffed. *It's not like Falkor doesn't have it already.*

That was true. When his parents were being held captive, Falkor had called Thorn to inform him and give him timelines.

He rattled off the number, and I quickly typed it into the phone as footsteps headed toward us. I handed the phone back to Uther, and the warrior placed it back in his pocket just as the bedroom door opened.

I hunched over again and shuffled toward Eva. Her eyes widened as I placed a hand on her shoulder and whimpered, "It's not any better."

She blinked in confusion. As Ladon stepped inside.

"Are you going to be all right?" Eva asked, her face lined with concern.

"I... I don't know." My face burned, and I wanted to bury it in Eva's chest, so I didn't have to look at all their faces. "I'm just glad Uther unclogged the toilet."

Coughing, Uther rubbed his nose. "Uh...yeah. I'm glad I could help." He pivoted toward Ladon and strolled past the older warrior into the hallway.

"Just...try not to do it again." Ladon inched backward, too, and searched the area around me, like he expected a huge gas cloud to emerge. "And get a handle on your issues before the wedding. You can't be doing *that*," he said and gestured to my butt, "during the ceremony. Drake won't allow it."

My dragon hissed, but laughter bubbled in my throat. I was a mixture of emotions and wasn't sure which one I'd settle on when all was said and done, but laughter was *way* better than crying.

When the bedroom door shut, Ladon muttered, "What the *hell* is Drake thinking?"

That sent me over the edge. I clapped my hands over my mouth to keep my chuckles silent. If I'd truly been in this much agony, I wouldn't have been giggling uncontrollably.

"Everly, what is *wrong* with you?" Eva asked as she placed her hands on my shoulders. "You're acting like we aren't trapped, constantly watched, and being forced to have some demented relationship with an egotistical asshole who also happens to be a dragon prince."

The shaking in my chest changed to uncontrollable sobs. My smile vanished as tears poured down my face. We were screwed, and if the king couldn't find a way to save us, I'd be married off to Drake tomorrow and forced to spend my nights beside him.

Lifting her hands, Eva stepped back. "Okay, forget I said anything. I prefer laughter over this."

But there was no going back. A shiver ran through me, and I wrapped my arms around myself to get warm.

"Hey, I'm sorry," Eva whispered as she touched my arm. She crawled into the center of the bed and opened her arms.

That was exactly what Mom used to do when we were hurting. The pain of losing her weakened my legs. I clambered onto the bed and scooted over to Eva. I faced the door and pressed my back to her chest as she wrapped her arms around me.

"Cry it out." Eva squeezed me gently.

She left out the other part of what Mom would say —*Things will look better in the morning.*

My connection with Thorn warmed, and his voice popped into my mind, *Did that guard do something?* Cold tendrils of fear wafted into me, tightening my chest.

No, it's just... I'm not going to get out of here, I answered, not bothering to pretend I wasn't broken. *I'm going to be married to that prick tomorrow, and not you. I don't know if I can handle that. I want to be your wife and have children with you.*

A lump choked me when I realized what I'd said. We'd been mated less than a week, and I'd spent most of that time stuck with Drake. It would be a miracle if I didn't scare Thorn away.

We're going to have that, Thorn vowed. *You're more than my wife already because we've completed the fated-mate connection. A wedding would be a formality and a way to celebrate the merging of our souls with everyone since I'm pretty sure you wouldn't have wanted them in the bedroom when we forged the bond.*

Some of the pain in my chest ebbed, but not enough to allow me to laugh. *No, and I'm glad that telling you I wanted to marry you and have babies didn't scare you away.*

Fuck no, he snarled. *That made me ecstatic. I feel the same way. You were human for so long that I didn't want to make you feel trapped or uncomfortable. But you are never getting rid of me, and I will get you out of that wedding tomorrow. Vlad is talking to Arman now.*

Do you have a plan?

Not yet, but we're working on it. He paused and pushed warmth into me. *What I need you to do is get some rest and trust me when I say I will find my way to you. Always and forever.*

I didn't doubt his words, but sometimes, promises couldn't be kept, even those made with the best of intentions. *You can't know that. And Thorn, what's my freedom worth if you get caught?*

Fate didn't put us together to have some Romeo and Juliet ending. His determination made my worries vanish. *I will do whatever it takes to get you back here with me. Please, trust me.*

Okay. I'd walk through fire with him as long as I was at his side.

I closed my eyes and pictured Thorn's face, tracing my

finger along the sheets, imagining they were a paintbrush. The small, calming motion was enough to ease my soul.

As my eyelids drooped and closed, Eva continued to hold me.

Before I drifted off to sleep, Thorn connected with me again. *Ev, we've got a plan. You'll see me soon. We'll sneak you out before the wedding preparations begin. I love you. Get your rest because, once you get home, you won't be going back to sleep until I get my fill of you.*

My chest lightened, and I smiled. *I love you. I can't wait.* Then I drifted off to sleep.

SOMETHING SHOOK MY BODY, stirring me awake. My heart leaped.

Thorn was here. Eva and I were finally getting out of this hellhole.

I opened my eyes, and harsh reality crashed over me.

CHAPTER NINE

I'D BEEN HOPING to find Thorn standing at the foot of the bed, but instead, it was Queen Mira. She wore emerald satin pajamas, and her hair was pulled into a low ponytail.

My heart clenched, and my blood turned to ice. Thorn hadn't come. *Please tell me you're okay.*

I glanced out the window across the room and noted that the sky held the pinks and oranges of the rising sun. It had to be around seven thirty, but I felt as if I'd had only a few hours of sleep.

I'm not okay, Thorn replied, his dragon snarling. *We ran into an issue. The king said he'd open an entrance for us that only he knows about, and the damn door isn't open.*

Maybe the king hadn't meant to help free us after all. Could his real plan have been to ensure his oldest son's safety but also allow Drake to get what he wanted—Eva and me? *What are you going to do?*

I'm not sure. Thorn paused. *We're brainstorming the next best strategy.*

The queen smiled sadly. "It's okay to be nervous. I

thought you might be and hoped the three of us could get ready together."

Though I wanted to tell her no, that wasn't an option. If Drake found out I'd turned his mother away, there would be hell to pay, but more than that, I didn't want to hurt her feelings. Planning the wedding with her had been horrible, but she was the only reason I'd made it through. Mira was kind and considerate...everything that Thorn was, and Drake wasn't. Eva had been quiet, I guessed because of the way Drake had treated her that morning, and Mira had noted our discomfort and planned most everything. I probably shouldn't have let her, but I didn't have the ability to plan this wedding.

"Yeah, of course." I threw off the covers and sat up. I stilled for a second to get my bearings. Everything inside me screamed to cut loose and get the hell out of here, but I knew, without a doubt, that every warrior was working today.

She pressed her lips into a hard line and placed her hands on my shoulders. "I know the circumstances are less than ideal and Drake makes it challenging to love him."

I choked. There was no question—I *didn't* love him. My stepdad was an *angel* compared to Drake, and that was saying something. My stepdad was indifferent and cruel when I got in his way; Drake was a power-hungry egomaniac. If there was a person I hated in this world, it was *him*. But I couldn't tell her that, so I posed a safer question. "What makes you say that?"

"What woman doesn't want to plan their wedding?" Queen Mira arched a brow. "And I see the way you look at him. He chose your sister as his breeder, which—having a breeder is a tradition I'm not fond of. But that's how Drake is. He pushes people brutally far to find out if they love him."

I forced my mouth to remain closed. This was clearly how the king and queen justified Drake's actions, saying he did horrible things to test how much others loved him. But that wasn't right. Drake thought he owned the world, that he could do whatever he wanted, without consequences, not to prove their love.

Not only had the king's decision changed Thorn's life but their own, too, and for the worse.

I chose my next words carefully. "And when does he stop pushing?"

Her face turned stony, any trace of warmth gone. "Never."

This proved that some parents refused to see their children for what they were.

She scoffed and rolled her eyes. "But...there are times when I see hints of the young boy underneath. Like early this morning when Drake showed up, needing his father." Her eyes glistened as she blinked. "But that's enough of that sort of talk. Today is a happy day. My son is getting married, one step closer to taking over the throne, and I get a *daughter*."

I wanted to tell her that I was already her daughter but informing her that I was mated to her other son wouldn't be the smartest move. I wondered why she didn't know I was mated to Thorn because King Arman had realized it quickly. But she *had* given me an important clue. *I think the king still plans to help us.*

What makes you say that? Thorn connected.

Because Queen Mira informed me that Drake showed up early this morning, needing his father. I wanted to ask the queen more questions, but I didn't want to make her suspicious or risk a nearby warrior overhearing us. So, I bit my tongue, hoping to ask questions sporadically and not alert her. "Well, he's probably nervous about the wedding, too. It's a huge commitment that no one should take lightly."

"Exactly." Queen Mira's attention flicked to Eva, who was still sound asleep.

That action alone was telling.

"Anyway." She quietly clapped her hands and took a few steps back. "Why don't you wake your sister while I get a maid to bring us some coffee and breakfast? My servants will bring the dresses and makeup to you. We can get ready here to ensure Drake doesn't see you before you march down the aisle."

Nausea churned within. There was no way in hell I could eat, but a cup of coffee would be amazing. "Okay." I should have said more—she was trying to be kind—but I couldn't. I did *not* want to get dressed and dolled up for... I couldn't even finish that thought.

Of course. He's watching the king because he probably hasn't determined how Vlad, Cassidy, and Saphira escaped. Thorn growled. *We're trying to figure out another way in in case the king doesn't show up soon. The back terraces are crawling with guards, so we need to wait until some guests arrive so we can blend in.*

The queen hurried away to get things rolling...which meant my ass would be getting dressed. Last night, I'd banked on not having to deal with the whole preparation part of the wedding, but that had been wishful thinking.

Everly, you will not marry him, Thorn vowed. *I don't care what it takes. I won't allow it to happen. You won't be forced to be with someone you can't stand.*

My hands clenched. *It's you or no one.* No one could

ever replace Thorn, and I wanted to ensure he was clear about my feelings.

Warmth wafted through our bond as he replied, *I love you.*

Damn straight you do. I lifted my chin as if he could see me. *And I love you, too. You're stuck with me forever. I'm like a fungus you can't get rid of. I've set up camp in a part of you, a part you can't remove me from, and I'll keep coming back.*

I never liked fungus...until now, he teased.

My cheeks hurt, and I realized I was smiling.

Eva groaned. "Have you lost your mind? You're grinning like a fool. We aren't safe, and you're about to marry Drake!"

That was like a splash of ice-cold water. My skin itched, and I leaned toward her and murmured, "I was talking to Thorn."

"That telepathic thing?" Eva rolled toward me and propped her head on her hand. "That's still wild, but I guess it's helpful, given our situation."

Being able to talk with Thorn and having Eva here were the only reasons I hadn't completely lost it. "Yeah, but they ran into a snag this morning and are sorting it out."

Eva's eyes brightened. "But they're still coming, right?"

I nodded and rubbed the spot where the bond connection warmed. "We have to play along so we don't raise suspicions."

She saluted me. "I can do that."

The bedroom door opened, and Queen Mira rushed in with three servants behind her. It was time to get ready.

DRINKING COFFEE HAD BEEN A MISTAKE—SOMETHING I *never* imagined I'd say. But as I stood in the bathroom, taking in my appearance, the acid churned, adding to my upset stomach. I wanted to puke, but I couldn't risk getting the gown dirty.

Thorn, Saphira, and his parents were trying to find a way in, but every time they peeked out of the entrance hidden in the woods, a warrior flew over. If they stepped out, the warrior's dragon would sense them immediately. There were more guards than expected, which meant Drake must have pulled some in from nearby thunders. If Thorn and the others hadn't gotten there several hours before dawn, they wouldn't have made it into the tunnel. As it was, they were stuck and planning to move at the last possible second, when everyone's guard would be at its lowest.

My long blonde hair cascaded over my shoulders in loose curls, and my makeup was done in earth tones with brown eyeshadow, blush with a golden sheen, and a warm brown lipstick that I wouldn't have been able to pull off before becoming a dragon.

The dress had been unexpected—all gold, no white. It was a sleeveless one-shoulder sheath with ruffled beading throughout. The sweeping train gave it an elegant flare but didn't go on for miles like those in the royal weddings. The sweetheart neckline emphasized my cleavage, and the slit on the left side of the skirt ended just shy of my hip, offering glimpses of my leg. The dress was gorgeous... royal and my style.

The look was completed by glittery silver high heels that clasped around the ankle. Queen Mira had given me an elegant diamond necklace to wear and large silver diamond earrings in the shape of a dragon. I reached for the bracelet

Mom had given me, but all I touched was skin. My heart dropped, and I wished I had a token to remember her by, but I'd left it behind for Thorn.

The queen had picked out everything perfectly, just for the wrong son. My insides tore to shreds as I stared at my reflection.

High heels clacked toward me over the wood floor, and Eva entered the bathroom and stood beside me. She looked beautiful with her straight, dark brown hair and smoky eye makeup that made her steel-blue eyes pop, her lips a nude shade that appeared completely natural. Her dress was simple and elegant compared to mine. It was a matte silver with cap sleeves and a similar sweetheart neckline. The top was lace, and the long skirt was made of soft tulle with detailed ruching. She wore gold shoes but no jewelry.

"You look beautiful, Everly," she said softly and frowned.

She didn't have to explain. I knew what she was thinking—*you look great, but I wish you didn't since it's almost time for your farce of a wedding.*

I swallowed to keep down the vomit and turned toward her. "You look gorgeous, too." Not only was my life changing, but hers was, too. I suspected this was the beginning of the end for us if Thorn didn't get us out of here.

"Thanks." She averted her gaze and crossed her arms.

Any updates? I hated harassing him, but our time was almost up. If he was going to rescue me, I kinda needed him to do it now.

We're at the tunnel's opening, waiting for the guard hovering over us to leave. Then, I'll make my way out and blend in with the guests, he replied.

I choked and placed my hands on the counter, trying to

breathe slowly. *They're looking out for you. You're going to get caught.*

They're expecting me to blaze in like a crazed fated-mate monster, he replied, determination flowing through, *not someone who tries to blend in with the crowd. No one besides Falkor, Ladon, and Brenton knows what I look like, so I'll stay away from them and keep my head down. It's my best chance at getting to you. I just have to keep my cool. I'm coming for you, Ev.*

"Everly," the queen called from the bedroom. "It's almost time."

I looked back at my reflection in the mirror. I'd always been the girl who tried to make peace and not cause problems and look at where that had gotten me. I'd been hoping that Thorn would save me, but maybe I needed to save myself.

First things first. I needed something I could use to defend myself.

Eva's brows furrowed. "What's wrong?"

"Everything," I scoffed as I scanned the bathroom for something, anything, I could use as a weapon.

She followed my gaze and tilted her head. "Did you lose something?"

"No, I think I finally found something." I was done being a pushover.

Queen Mira joined us, looking every bit the royal she was. Her dark hair was styled in an elegant French twist, and her makeup was perfect. A huge diamond necklace hung between her breasts, and her strapless tulle dress featured a diamond-beaded belt that contrasted with the royal purple color of the garment.

Her smile was breathtaking. "It's time to head to the

back door. Some warriors are waiting to escort us. It's eleven forty-five."

The time had arrived.

Panic clawed my insides, and my heart raced. *Are you heading to the terrace?* I hoped he'd forgotten to inform me and was already moving into place.

The damn guard isn't leaving, he replied, his anger slamming through me.

I flinched at the internal assault, but I was more perplexed as to why I hadn't felt his turmoil before now, as if he'd hidden his emotions from me.

We're about to begin, I informed him.

I'm on my way. Nobody will stop me, he replied.

A stabbing pain assaulted my heart. *Thorn, no. The guard will alert everyone, and they'll catch you.*

He didn't respond, and the anger tamped down once more.

Dear goodness. What had he done?

More determined than ever, I forced a smile and lifted my chin, despite my knees weakening. "Okay, give me a second. I'll meet you and Eva in the living room. I need a moment to myself."

Queen Mira placed a hand on my arm. "Of course, my dear. Just don't be too long." She looped her arm through Eva's and led her out the bedroom door.

Eva glanced back at me, her face twisted with worry.

I waited until their footsteps had reached the living room, then took the hairbrush from the counter and butted the end against one corner of the mirror. It took a few solid hits, but a large section splintered off, and a crack zagged across the entire mirror. I didn't have it in me to care.

The largest chunk of glass was about three inches long

and two inches wide—big enough to use as a weapon but small enough to fit in my bra. I snatched the hand towel hanging to my left, ripped the material in half, then grabbed the piece of glass, careful not to cut my hands. I wrapped it in the cloth and delicately placed it in my cleavage, low enough that neither the white cloth nor the glass could be seen.

A strangled sensation wafted through the fated-mate bond. Breathing rapidly, I linked, *Are you hurt?*

It felt like forever before he responded.

TIME STOOD STILL as I waited for Thorn to respond. My pulse pounded in my ears, and I prepared myself to go find him.

Damn Drake and everyone else.

I wouldn't allow my mate to be harmed.

I'm fine, he replied, but his dragon hissed. *The warrior swooped down and attacked me. My magic responded...and I took his dragon.*

He was outside, and anyone who passed through could recognize him. *Thorn, don't risk yourself for me. I'll find a way out of here.* I placed my hands on the counter and lifted my head, staring at myself. My fierce determination made me look like a different person.

There's no way in hell I will wait here while you take on the royals and the warriors on your own, he replied. *I'm coming for you, Everly.*

My heart swelled. A nagging part had lost hope that there was a way out of this, but his words made my determination more desperate to prove it wrong.

"Everly," the queen called as the bedroom door opened. "It's time. We really do have to leave."

I jerked upright and tensed. She couldn't come in here and see what I'd done to the mirror. I had to go.

Taking a deep breath, I strolled into the bedroom and met her. I couldn't walk too quickly or let my panic show; otherwise, the warriors might think I was up to something. I needed to act like the broken girl they expected.

"Sorry. I just—" I forced my bottom lip to quiver, and my dragon snarled at how pathetic I looked.

"Oh, darling." Queen Mira mashed her lips together and hurried to me, placing her hands on my shoulders. "I promise, this isn't as bad as it seems. As part of the royal family, you will never want for anything."

I snorted then coughed to hide my laugh. My shoulders shook, so I hunched over, pretending to sob. Her statement was so ironic. I might have all the luxuries of living in a fancy house with servants, but I didn't want that. I wanted Thorn, my freedom, and a life with him where we didn't have to hide. None of that would happen if this marriage with Drake took place.

She kissed my forehead and murmured, "You'll be happy. You'll see. We can spend time together, figuring out ways we can help our people."

Help.

That was the one thing I'd aspired to do in my life and the whole reason I'd finished a premed degree at UHC. Mom had died of cancer, and I didn't want another child to have to experience the loss of a parent to that monstrous disease.

Though that dream might have been squashed, a new one emerged.

I could help the dragons by eliminating the biggest threat to them.

Drake.

"You're right." I lifted my head and smiled sadly. "I *can* help the dragons."

Her irises sparkled as she lowered her arms. "I knew you would be the perfect daughter-in-law."

My throat ached. She was so happy, and I planned on eliminating her child. I liked her, and I hated to do that to her, but Drake should never be in power.

Footsteps pounded down the hallway. Based on the stride, they belonged to Ladon.

"If you don't come out of there now, I'll *force* you out," Ladon threatened as he appeared in the doorway.

Queen Mira arched a brow. "You dare speak to the future queen in such a manner?"

"I serve the king and the prince." Ladon straightened. "If you want kindness, Everly needs to get moving. *Now*."

"We were heading out just as you got here." Queen Mira lifted her chin and stared down her nose. "I'm sure Arman will be intrigued by the way you're talking to us."

Ladon smirked but didn't respond.

Huffing, the queen looped her arm through mine and led me down the hallway. In the living room, I found Eva flanked by Uther and Jessie. She glanced up and exhaled loudly.

I wanted to kick myself. I'd spent too long back there, planning my vengeance.

"It's about damn time," Jessie said as she wrinkled her nose. "Drake was about to come in here."

Oh, I'd bet he was. That would've made the situation more complicated.

Hurt and trepidation coursed through my connection with Thorn.

My heart stopped, and my knees shook. *Thorn, are you hurt?*

"Whoa," Queen Mira murmured and wrapped an arm around my waist, pulling me against her. "Don't lock your knees—you'll pass out."

If only that was my problem.

Thorn replied, *I'm fine. I'm back in the tunnel. Arman finally appeared, and he's guiding us.*

Able to stand again, I smiled and steadied myself. "Thank you, and I'll try to remember that." I then asked him, *Where is he taking you?*

I don't know, Thorn replied, a turmoil of emotions rising like a tsunami. *I'm hoping it's not a trap.*

Ladon marched to the back door and opened it. To the right of the terrace, the servants had built a temporary white wall to prevent the guests and wedding party from seeing me. It was about eight feet high, so not even my guards could be seen, which might help me when I escaped.

I looked to my left...and my heart sank. Twenty warriors were posted at the tree line, but I couldn't bank on that number. Drake knew I was mated to Thorn, which meant I could be relaying numbers and people's positions. There was no telling how many were hiding in the trees, and I couldn't see them since I was in human form and not dragon.

The sun shone as it inched higher over the treetops, and the temperature had to be in the high sixties. The day was gorgeous with fluffy white clouds in the sky.

Queen Mira stood on my right as Eva appeared on my left. The three of us carefully walked forward, and our high heels sank into the grassy ground. I kept my balance, but Eva clutched my arm, nearly falling over.

"Watch it," Jessie snarled at my sister from beside the queen. "If you mess up her dress, Drake won't be happy."

I wanted to punch the warrior in the face. For a human, Eva was handling this well. I would've already fallen on my ass if I hadn't been a shifter.

With her free arm, she lifted her long skirt and focused on her feet. "Sorry. I didn't mean to grab you like that."

"It's fine." I cut my eyes to Jessie, daring her to say something else. "You can hold on to me. I can take it."

"I don't see how you two aren't falling..." Then she huffed. "That's right. You're dragons."

Queen Mira chuckled, the sound like music. "I may be a dragon, but I've had my share of falls. Being a dragon shifter doesn't make you graceful."

My arms itched to hug her. She was down-to-earth and easy to get along with. She looked every inch a queen.

My insides hardened. This had to be an act. She and the king had tried to kill Thorn. How could a kind and generous person do that? Maybe Drake was just like her. Maybe her charismatic personality hid the evil underneath.

But that didn't make sense, either. Why hide it when she was the queen?

The one motivation that explained their actions was that she and the king believed Thorn was dangerous to their people. Yet Drake was out of control and power-hungry, and they accepted him without issue.

There was no point in focusing on that. I could try to rationalize the actions of others all day, like I'd done with my stepdad for the past six years, and never understand their reasons for treating others badly.

As we reached the end of the yard, the white wall

curved, ending at the edge of a royal purple carpet where a maid stood, holding a lavish bouquet of dark purple and lavender irises and baby's breath.

My nose wrinkled, but I forced myself to smooth my expression. I'd expected this wedding to be over the top but come *on*. A *carpet* outside?

With each step we took, my heart raced harder. The faint grape-soda-like scent of the flowers filled my nose, and my throat constricted. If Thorn had been waiting for me down the aisle, I'd have raced to the finish line...but he wasn't. Losing everything was all that waited for me.

Please tell me you guys are in position. I hated to pressure him, but I was almost to the aisle. I needed him to get me the hell out of here, pronto.

We're still in the damn tunnel, Thorn answered with a growl. *Arman promised that Drake won't start the wedding without him.*

I snorted, and both the queen and Eva glanced at me.

"Sorry," I whispered. "Just nerves." That wasn't a lie, unfortunately.

I'm about to walk down the aisle. I became lightheaded and had to concentrate on moving my legs forward. I had to remember I had a weapon between my boobs if it came down to that.

Thorn's dragon snarled. *Arman says we're almost there.*

The maid was close to my age, her ash-brown hair pulled into a messy bun. She held out the flowers to me and smiled sweetly. "You look beautiful, my lady."

My head tilted back. I'd never been called that before, and I was certain I never wanted to hear it again. But that wasn't her fault—she was doing what she'd been trained to do.

I took the flowers and said, "Thank you."

She curtsied to the queen and me, then headed back the way we'd come.

"This is where we part ways," Queen Mira murmured and stopped. "Eva and I will walk down the aisle, and when the piano and violin play the bridal march, that'll be your cue."

I didn't want to wish misfortune on anyone, but if the entire symphony got a sudden stomach bug, I'd be a fan. Anything that would get me out of *this*.

"You go first, dear." The queen gestured for Eva to precede her, then smiled as a man my age, who I'd never seen before, appeared.

He wore a black tux with a white shirt and a black tie. When he held out his arm for Eva to take, his lips curled, and his cedar-brown eyes darkened with disgust.

Eva inhaled sharply, and Queen Mira *tsked*. She patted the man's arm. "Come now, Daniel. If you didn't look so threatening, she wouldn't be as uncomfortable."

"Yes, my queen." He bowed his head slightly, and his gelled, mousy-brown hair didn't move an inch. "I'm just disappointed that Drake didn't want a best man."

"You know how Drake is. He doesn't like to share the stage with anyone." The queen's chuckled held an edge. "Now, go on, Eva. He won't bite."

Releasing my arm, Eva inched toward Daniel, trying not to fall on the grass. Once she'd woven her arm through his, the two of them headed down the aisle. Before she disappeared from sight, she glanced back at me, her bottom lip trembling.

She was scared, and I couldn't do a damn thing about it.

"That is Drake's best friend," Queen Mira murmured as they vanished around the corner. "I'm sure you'll be seeing a lot of him, once things calm. He lives on the property to the left of the chateau."

No wonder the guy seemed like a jackass. He was friends with Drake.

All too quickly, Daniel came back and retrieved the queen, leaving me with Jessie, Uther, and Ladon.

Chills ran through me, and they had nothing to do with the slightly cool weather. I had to hang on to the fact that King Arman wasn't there, which meant Drake would have to wait.

Then a piano began to play the beginning of the "Here Comes the Bride" song, and a violin's soothing strokes intertwined with the notes.

My breath caught. This was not supposed to be happening. *Are you here?* I glanced at the sky, expecting to see a dragon. When I didn't, I glanced around the yard for Thorn. But he was nowhere.

We're hurrying, he replied.

"You need to go," Ladon growled from behind me and pushed my shoulder forward.

I had no choice. If I didn't go willingly, they would force me, and I didn't want to risk something terrible happening if Drake saw them dragging me down the aisle.

I gripped the bottom of my bouquet hard and took a step onto the rug. *I need you to move faster. I'm walking down the aisle.*

White-hot rage slammed into me. *That bastard.*

As I pivoted toward the terrace, I saw a hundred guests on their feet, facing me. I almost choked. With such short notice, I'd hoped no one would come.

Each chair was covered in a white cloth with a sizable royal purple ribbon tied around it. At the other end of the carpet stood a man I'd never seen before. Drake was at his side. Irises covered the terrace, and a white sheet hung behind the man and Drake, blocking the house from view.

Drake gestured for me to come to him, and I forced myself to move forward and not away. Every cell in my body screamed at me to run, but that wouldn't solve anything. When I struck, the timing had to be perfect.

As I walked past the seated guests, the hairs on my neck lifted. I'd never given much thought about the attention a bride received on her wedding day, but I felt as if the stares might crush me.

An empty chair sat in the front row next to the aisle, with Queen Mira sitting in the next seat. Eva sat beside the queen, and her eyes glistened as they locked on mine.

The empty chair had to be King Arman's.

I took the last few steps onto the terrace's wood floor and didn't look at Drake. Instead, I focused on the man standing before me.

His bronze skin was the same shade as Saphira's, and his chocolate-brown eyes examined me. Unlike Daniel, his short, dark brown hair ruffled in the wind, giving him a more natural look. He seemed familiar, and after a second, I realized why. This was Saphira's dad.

Drake straightened his shoulders. "Let's begin, Errol."

The older man's brows furrowed. "But the king—"

"Is late," Drake said forcefully. "Let's *begin*."

My breathing quickened, and I tried to control it so Drake wouldn't notice. *He's pushing to begin now.*

We're almost at another door, Thorn said.

Almost didn't cut it. Hell, there was even a song written about it.

Errol spoke, but I couldn't make out the words. It was as if I were underwater, similar to the shock I'd felt the day Thorn had kidnapped me and I'd learned about dragons.

My knees nearly gave out, and I realized fear was controlling me. I lifted my chin and focused on the piece of glass between my breasts.

I'd have to use it.

Drake turned toward me, and I realized I'd lost track of time. I'd been up here way too long—the vows or claiming would be happening soon.

"Everly?" Errol said, and I jerked my gaze to him.

I swallowed hard and cleared my throat, not wanting to sound broken. That would only make Drake feel more powerful. "Yes?"

"It's time to exchange vows. I need you to look at Prince Drake," he said with a sad smile.

He knew something was wrong.

It's time, I connected with Thorn. *Where are you?*

I'm in the chateau, he replied. *Almost there. Delay them however you can.*

Drake gripped my arms and forced me to turn to him. He smiled, but his eyes were devoid of warmth. He was playing the part he wanted the attendees to see. "Hey, I'm right here with you. No need to be nervous."

Then Errol said the words I'd been dreading. The very words I hoped he'd never get to. "Do you, my prince..." He trailed off, giving me the chance to act *now*. If I didn't, everything would be over.

CHAPTER ELEVEN

THE NEXT WORDS came too fast from Errol's mouth. "Do you, my prince, take Everly to be your wedded wife?"

My heart raced as Drake's mouth opened. I dropped the bouquet, ready to attack, just as he said, "I—"

Glass shattered behind the white curtain, and I kneed Drake in the crotch. Eyes bulging, he inhaled sharply and grabbed his junk.

Drake dropped to his knees, and the guests broke out into startled murmurs. Just as Drake opened his mouth again, the white sheet behind Errol ripped away, revealing the chateau and Thorn.

I froze, unable to look away, afraid he was a mirage.

Thorn was gorgeous, determined, and worthy of being painted. He wore his typical jeans, Timberlands, and a black shirt that hugged his body. I could see every curve of muscle, and my mouth puddled. His shaggy dark hair was a little longer, hanging in his sky-blue eyes, and his teeth were clenched, emphasizing his strong jaw.

He was here, as promised, to save me.

He raced to Drake and punched him. Then he declared,

loudly, "As the first-born prince, I do take Everly to be *my wife*." He turned to me and pulled me into his arms.

My skin jolted, electrified by our fated-mate connection, and I inhaled his scent, minty amber with a faint hint of brimstone, which indicated he was a dragon shifter. I was home, but if we didn't get moving, I wouldn't be for much longer.

I pulled back and searched those around us. Four guards stood on the terrace, their tranq guns aimed at Thorn, and two dragons were flying toward us.

"Uh..." Errol's mouth hung open as more warriors barreled down the aisle.

A broken gasp from Queen Mira had me glancing behind me.

"Thorn?" Her face twisted in agony. "Is that really you?"

He tensed but didn't take his eyes off me.

Drake got back onto his feet, though he stayed hunched over. He snarled, "Kill him *now*. Then I'll take Everly as my wife."

Thorn's roar rattled the ground and the terrace. His pupils elongated. "You will *not* have what is *mine*. She is my *fated mate*."

"What?" the queen whispered, sounding shocked, but now wasn't the time to contend with her emotions.

The tallest warrior in the back aimed his tranq rifle at Thorn just as an arrow shot across the clearing and pierced the warrior's neck. The arrows kept coming as someone launched an attack from above. The four warriors with tranqs were taken down in seconds, and whoever was on our side turned their attention to the rest.

It had to be Vlad. He had trained Thorn.

Leaning toward me, Thorn connected, *Get your sister,*

and take her inside the chateau. Top floor, the bedroom all the way to the left as you're facing the house now. When you get there, let me know, and I'll come after you.

My heart thumped. I didn't want to leave him, but he wouldn't budge until I was safe.

Gunfire came from the bedroom as bullets pelted the area below. Guests jumped to their feet, screaming, and raced toward the guest home, moving away from the shots.

Chaos was a good thing.

I pivoted and jumped onto the grass. Eva and Queen Mira were standing by their seats, immobile.

I hurried to Eva, twisting my ankle mid-stride in the damn high heels. What sort of dumbass wore heels on a lawn? Me. I was that dumbass. I bent down and removed them. "Eva, take your shoes off. We have to run."

Thorn snarled, and I glanced over as two airborne dragons swooped down at him. He bared his teeth as the earth-brown dragon extended its claws and the charcoal dragon opened its mouth. My heart lurched into my throat. But as I took one step toward him, the earth-brown dragon swiped at Thorn. Thorn's hands glowed as he dodged the talons and ran to touch its tail just as the dragon lifted back into the sky.

His hand brightened, and the dragon roared louder. Then, with each second, the dragon's roar weakened, and its body shrank. It was as if the dragon were stuck and couldn't fly away. Soon, its scales faded.

My breathing quickened as I watched Thorn's magic at work. I'd never seen anything like this before, but the pure rage on his face told me he wasn't fully in control. The magic was controlling him.

Gunfire blasted from the bedroom upstairs, but not soon enough. The charcoal dragon's talons dug into Thorn's shoulders, and it flapped its wings, lifting him off the ground.

"Thorn!" I tried to scream but choked on the sound.

Thorn released the former earth-brown dragon, and a naked man landed on the terrace. The man, perhaps in his fifties, sobbed, not bothering to get up.

A hand clutched my arm, and I turned to see Daniel.

His jaw dropped as he took in what had happened. "The monster took the warrior's dragon!" he yelled, ensuring everyone could hear him with their supernatural ears, despite the chaos.

I yanked my arm out of his grip and rushed toward Eva, but Daniel grabbed my arm again.

I'm coming, I connected with Thorn. I didn't want him to think I'd abandoned him.

Don't, he replied, the bond between us sizzling. *Get out of here.*

A strangled cry rang over the grass, and I turned to see Thorn's glowing hands on the dragon's legs. The dragon was already shrinking, but blood dripped from my mate's shoulders.

"You're coming with me," Daniel snarled, and he jerked me toward the guest wing.

I wasn't going anywhere with this douche canoe. With my free hand, I clutched the side of my dress to prevent myself from tripping. Then I spun around and kicked Daniel in the stomach with as much force as possible.

He sailed backward and smashed into an aisle chair in the third row. His head hit the back of the chair and smacked onto the ground.

Babe, I need you to go, Thorn connected, his anger and worry flooding me, squeezing my chest like a vise. *More warriors will come, and we need to get out of here. They'll run out of bullets soon. I'm sure Vlad already ran out of arrows.*

We. He was right. *We* needed to leave. I had to focus on that.

"Eva, come on," I commanded and found her with her high heels off. Good girl. She'd listened to me without arguing, for once in her life.

She nodded, ready to move.

I took her hand and glanced at Queen Mira. She stood unmoving, watching Thorn with one hand over her heart and fear etched onto her face, her expression both relieved and scared.

She was a good woman but misguided, and that had unfortunately destroyed my mate's childhood. I paused in front of her and said, "Drake made him do the very thing you and your husband feared. Thorn was in hiding until the son who could do no wrong kidnapped people, including a human he forced here to be his breeder, and tried to force a woman who is mated to another to marry him. Think on *that* next time you think there's any good in Drake."

Having said my piece, I turned to the house. The warriors were closing in now that the panicked guests were mostly out of the way, but the gunfire was still holding them off.

Eva and I hurried to the side of the terrace and up the steps just as a swirling noise swooshed toward us. A sickening impact had me jerking my head around.

First, I saw my mate. He was back down on his feet, hurrying toward me. Then a familiar scream lodged in my ears.

Saphira.

"Everly, please help my father!" she cried.

My chest tightened as my gaze landed on Errol. He was

standing where Thorn had been a moment before, a tranq dart lodged in his abdomen. He must have shielded Thorn.

I clenched my hands. I wasn't sure I could carry a dragon a foot taller than me and a hundred and fifty pounds heavier, but Saphira had sacrificed herself for me, so I had to try.

Just go. I'll get him and be right behind you, Thorn connected as he rushed to the older man.

I gritted my teeth until my jaw ached. *Your shoulders.*

I'm fine. I promise, he connected as he bent and threw Errol over one shoulder.

"Errol!" the queen yelped, springing into action.

Things were escalating. As I turned back toward the house, an arm wrapped around my waist and yanked me against a chest.

The leather smell that hurt my head invaded my senses. Of *course,* it'd be Drake.

"Let her go," Eva snapped and stepped toward me.

Drake's chest shook with laughter, and I twisted my head back and saw a sinister smile on his face. He said, "Never. She's mine."

He's going to die, Thorn bellowed from ten feet away and moved toward me despite carrying Errol.

The time had come. I reached inside my bra and removed the glass. The sharp edges cut my hand, but I didn't give a damn. I was going to kill this sick asshole.

I stabbed him in the chest, and vomit rose in my throat. I'd never wanted to kill someone, but Drake's death would solve the majority of our problems.

A metallic stench swirled around me as something warm trickled down my hand.

Blood.

Drake jerked back, and his nostrils flared. "You *bitch*! You're going to pay—"

I punched him in the nose. "I will *never* be yours. I'd rather die than see your face ever again."

Blood gushed from his nose, and his black suit had a wet stain from where I'd stabbed him. Unfortunately, I'd missed his heart, but the wound should slow him down.

Everly, Thorn said.

Right. We had to go. Kicking Drake's ass felt good, but I'd rather get out of here.

"Stop her!" Drake shouted as he pinched his nose.

I grabbed Eva's hand and was dragging her to the door when a tranq came flying at me. Trusting my gut, I stopped in my tracks, yanking Eva behind me just as the dart whizzed past.

They'd expected me to keep moving and had aimed with that in mind.

Thorn opened the back glass door, and Eva and I ran toward it. More tranqs shot at us, and when I was half a foot from running inside, one of them hit Eva in the arm.

She yelped, and I spun, lifted her up like she was a baby, and raced inside the doors. She felt as light as a child. *Heck yeah.*

I was surprised to find no guards inside. How was this possible?

"Leave me here," Eva said slowly, the drugs taking hold.

"Shh." That would never happen.

Gunfire continued to burst out back as we ran through the large living room. The light gray walls reflected the sunlight with slightly darker, luxurious couches centering a large tiled chimney. The same dark cherry wood floors ran throughout this side of the house, including the gigantic curved stairway. With each hurried step we took, the bronze chandelier swung as if it sensed impending doom.

Taking the stairs two steps at a time, we reached the top floor. Thorn turned left, heading to the bedroom he'd indicated earlier. The hallway was long and had the same light gray paint, but large crystal chandeliers hung every ten feet. We passed by a few mammoth, black cherry wood doors, but I didn't have to question where we were heading.

It had to be the door at the end of the hallway, the very one King Arman stood in front of with a lit candle.

His gaze landed on Errol, and he frowned.

Great. He wouldn't allow us to leave with his advisor. What else could go wrong?

He opened the door and waved us in. As soon as Thorn and I entered the room, he shut and locked the door behind us. The candle held a strong scent—French vanilla—and it diluted the smell around us.

This had to be the king and queen's bedroom. It was massive, taking up the entire side of the house. Windows overlooked the back, facing the terrace where Vlad and Saphira stood, shooting guns, and the front of the house, where Cassidy was firing.

Saphira's long, curly, dark brown hair was swept back in a low ponytail, and her mocha-brown eyes squinted as she fired the weapon. Her skin was back to its normal gorgeous bronze color. Vlad stood beside her with a rifle. His wavy, caramel hair was no longer greasy, and his cornflower-blue eyes were locked on the fighters below. His ivory skin looked almost ghostly next to Saphira but was alluring in its own right.

Cassidy's dark gold-brown hair hung in her face, but her hazel-green eyes were focused outside. Her light tan complexion was closest to Thorn's.

They each wore a black shirt and jeans.

None of the guards had been stationed inside the chateau. They hadn't expected a threat to come from inside.

Like the rest of the house, the same wood accents were present, but that was where the similarities ended. A gigantic bed with a gold frame sat against the far wall. A royal purple blanket sat folded on the end of the bed, on top of a white comforter. Above the bed, a circular section of the ceiling was cut out, platter style, and painted a royal purple in the center where a bronze chandelier hung. To the right, a spectacular gold-framed painting took up the entire wall, with two purple chairs that had been pushed against the bed in front of it. On the other side were an enormous black cherry wood desk, a sectional, and a table where a huge sunset puzzle that had only been partially put together.

My heart hammered, and despite my new dragon strength, my sister was getting heavier...enough to make me winded. I'd hoped that my days of forcing myself to exercise were behind me, but even as a dragon shifter, I would have to work out.

King Arman hung his head, then glanced at Thorn, Errol, Eva, me, and back to Thorn. Gesturing to everyone in the room, he said, "I hope you realize how much I'm giving up and betraying by helping you."

My eyes widened. He had to be kidding. *That* was what he'd wanted to say when Thorn would be leaving again and never returning?

"That's worse than trying to have your own son killed and then guilting him when you're trying to set something right for him?" I lifted my chin despite the sweat beading on my face from how damn heavy my sister was. "Please, spare us the theatrics. You wouldn't be in this situation if it wasn't for Drake."

Saphira snorted.

I was so sick and tired of the royals' attitude. They'd tried to kill Thorn, then had given him up, while Drake—the epitome of a douchebag—could do no wrong. Something was messed up in their heads, and I was done tolerating their stupidity.

"Now listen here—" King Arman started, but then a loud groan echoed through the room.

CHAPTER TWELVE

MY HEAD WHIPPED toward Vlad and Saphira, and my ears thundered. Vlad stumbled back with a tranq dart in his arm. He gripped the tranq and tossed it to the floor, swaying on his feet.

He was going to black out at any second.

"You have to *leave* now, before you can't." King Arman rushed to the huge painting and slipped his hand behind the bottom right corner of the gold frame.

Saphira wrapped an arm around Vlad, tossed him over her shoulder, and ran from the window. Tranqs pelted the area where the two of them had been standing seconds ago, and I realized that another round of warriors was in place.

Feet pounded below as the painting and frame slid sideways.

"Go." Arman pointed at the passage he'd revealed. "I've arranged for someone to pick you up at the other end, but it'll be several hours from now, so stay in the tunnel until I can divert the warriors and you can get out unseen. Do *not* fly. They'll be searching for your scents. Go south. My contact will meet you on the main road a few miles beyond the dragon lands."

Cassidy was the first to move. She rushed to the king and lifted a brow. "They won't believe we didn't harm you."

"Fine," he snarled as he placed the candle on the nightstand and broke the window next to the bed so it would appear as if we'd escaped. He came back to stand in front of her. "I deserve it, so do it."

A deep growl emanated from Thorn, and he handed Errol off to Cassidy. "Let me."

Hurt and anger swirled inside me from him, and I wanted to tell him not to strike the king. But if I ever got a chance to knock out my stepdad, I'd do it without hesitation. He'd been awful to me, but not nearly as bad as King Arman had been to his son.

Nodding, Cassidy adjusted Errol in her arms and took off into the hidden passage with Saphira right behind her, carrying Vlad.

More warriors clambered up the stairs.

Air sawed through my lungs, and I moved to the opening and waited for Thorn. I wouldn't leave without him. I'd lay Eva down and close the door before I allowed it to come to that.

"You saw the button I used earlier to open the passage. It'll close it as well." The king lifted his chin. "Do it and *run.*"

Something hard slammed into the bedroom door. The guards were almost upon us.

Thorn punched the king in the back of the head, and the king's eyes rolled back as his body lurched to the left... landing right on the bed.

My heart warmed as I entered the passage with Thorn right behind me. He spun around and pressed the button just as the bedroom door cracked, and the secret door slid shut, cutting off the noise.

A stale scent replaced the sweet smell from the bedroom.

Thank goodness the king locked the bedroom door, I connected as some weight fell from my shoulders.

We still need to be quiet in case the guards can hear us, Thorn replied. He turned carefully toward Cassidy and Saphira, who stood a few feet away, and held out his arms to take Errol back from his mother. Saphira then handed Vlad over to Cassidy.

The tunnel was about ten feet wide and twelve feet tall with cobwebs hanging throughout the area. Thorn appeared more massive in the small space.

There was no light, but that wasn't a problem with my dragon eyes. If Eva woke up, she'd be spooked. *Is there a place with more light?* I cradled my sister close to me. My brow creased. She'd been tranqed with the same drugs as Errol and Vlad, and she was a small human.

Yeah, there's light at the other end of this tunnel where we need to wait, he replied and held out his free arm. *Let me take your sister. I can tell how uncomfortable you are.*

Could I hide anything from him anymore? Even when I'd left to give myself up, thinking his parents, Saphira, and Eva would be released, I hadn't managed to hide that I'd sneaked out for long. He'd sensed me and awoken before I'd reached Drake.

I shook my head. *I've got her. You're already carrying Errol. If you're going to take a second person, get Vlad. He's significantly heavier.* If anyone needed a reprieve, it was Cassidy.

I want to help my mate. He frowned, and his disappointment swirled through me.

My cheeks hurt from the huge smile that spread across my lips. *If my sister wakes up, she'll be more comfortable if I'm holding her. Let me be there for her. Please? After all, she was captured because of me. This is the least I can do.* My shoulders slumped. Her life was forever changed because I hadn't done enough to protect her.

His irises darkened. *You do realize she would've been his breeder anyway if you hadn't interfered, and you wouldn't have gotten caught up in this if you hadn't been so selfless. If it's anyone's fault that you two got dragged into this, it's mine. I kidnapped and changed you.*

I exhaled and tried to be logical. He and my siblings were the only three things that hindered my pragmatic side. When I faced any other problem, I could separate my feelings from my actions...but not when it came to them. Never them. *It's the king, queen, and Drake's fault. Your biological parents for being closed-minded assholes, and Drake for being a narcissist who believes he owns the world.*

He brushed his fingers along my cheek, the jolt sizzling between us. I closed my eyes and damn near moaned from his touch. I'd missed him so much that it physically hurt.

Saphira quietly cleared her throat.

My gaze flicked to hers. She arched a brow and nodded in the direction of the tunnel we needed to be heading down.

We better move, I connected, staring into his gorgeous eyes, which reminded me of my favorite shade to use for painting the sky.

The lines around his eyes tightened. *You're right. I can't risk them finding you.* He stepped around me, and I wished that Eva hadn't been a barrier, so I could've felt his muscles brush my breasts as he passed. But we'd have time to reconnect later.

"Let me take Vlad, too," he murmured and reached out his hands.

Cassidy smiled but shook her head.

She wanted to take care of her mate. I could respect that. She was taller than me, so his huge frame didn't overpower her like Thorn's would've done mine.

Saphira took the lead and headed toward the exit. Her pace was slow and methodical, instead of relieved and carefree. We weren't out of the woods yet, literally, or figuratively. Cassidy was between Thorn and Saphira, and I took up the rear.

Being in the back was so worth it. I got to watch Thorn's ass the entire way and admire how his back muscles rippled from carrying Errol. I normally stuck to painting landscapes and faces, but there was a time and a place for exceptions, and the next time I got my hands on brushes, paints, and a canvas, his entire body would be one of them. Although...I would leave out certain delectable places. I didn't want anyone else to ever see them. Those parts were all *mine*.

My body warmed just remembering him naked.

Warmth flooded through our connection as Thorn connected, *Do you like what you see? I can smell your arousal.*

My face flamed. Not because he could smell it but because that meant Cassidy and Saphira could, too. I hadn't even officially met Cassidy, and *this* would be the way I was introduced to her. If we hadn't been in such a dangerous situation, I'd have run away and hidden. *Your mom is going to hate me.*

What? He slowed and glanced over his shoulder.

Shock pulsed through our bond, and my breath caught.

His brows furrowed. *Why would you say that?*

Because I'm ogling her son, and she can smell what he does to me. I closed my eyes for a second. *Why else?*

He grinned and winked. *Oh, she understands. I've smelled many things I'd rather not have been privy to while growing up with those two, and they're fated mates, too.* His nose wrinkled at what I assumed were those memories.

Maybe we could all pretend that no one had smelled anything. I was downwind from them.

"Oh, gods," Saphira groaned. "They're not together ten minutes, and it smells like a brothel."

Then again, maybe not. Though I loved Saphira, I would have no problem killing her at this moment. Too bad I hadn't dislodged the glass from Drake's chest so I could stab *her* with it.

Thorn chuckled, his happiness wafting through the bond. "What I'm more intrigued by is why you know what a brothel smells like. Did you visit, or did you work there?"

"Thorn Wight," Cassidy exclaimed and turned around, careful not to bump Vlad into the wall.

There was no doubt about it—she was his mother. The mom tone was unmistakable, and my heart ached from remembering my own mom.

His shoulders shook. "I'm twenty-seven years old. I can give Saphira hell when she's making my mate feel uncomfortable."

I wanted to bury my face in Thorn's back for many reasons, but mainly so Cassidy couldn't see me. Instead, I lifted my chin, faking that the banter and attention didn't bother me. "I don't know what you're talking about. I'm in the very back. You can't smell anything."

Saphira twisted to look at me. She placed a hand on her hip and arched a brow. "You wanna bet? I wouldn't be surprised if the warriors tracked us down. That's how strong it is."

I narrowed my eyes just as a deep moan echoed in the tunnel.

"Please, for the love of the gods, stop talking about my son and his mate," Vlad grumbled as he rubbed a hand over his forehead. "My head hurts, and there are things better left unsaid."

I could get behind that sentiment. We should drop it and not address the elephant in the secret passageway...or the dragon that ate the elephant...or whatever.

We all paused, and Cassidy squatted as Vlad stood and leaned against the side of the tunnel, blocking Saphira from view. I had to wonder if he'd done that on purpose, but some tension left my shoulders.

"At least, the king came through for us." He yawned and stretched his shoulders.

I glanced at Eva, then at Errol hanging over Thorn's shoulder. I bit my lip. "How come you woke up before Errol?" I understood why Eva remained unconscious. She was human and had a slower metabolism, but Errol had been shot first.

"I removed the dart before all the liquid leaked out." He pointed at Errol and my sister. "If those two still have the dart lodged in them, we need to remove them. The darts have a slow-release mechanism to keep people asleep longer."

That would've been nice to know a while ago. I kneeled and dropped Eva's legs to pull the dart from her arm. I was already worried about the dose she'd gotten, but to know more had been trickling in made me panic. I hadn't thought about pulling it out while we'd been running for our lives.

"How did I not know that?" Thorn grumbled. Using his free arm, he felt Errol's side and yanked out the dart.

Vlad shook his head. "I learned about the upgrade when we were kidnapped."

My heart sank. All of us had suffered so much.

"Do you think she'll be okay?" I couldn't hide the worry in my voice. "She's human."

"Yeah, it'll knock her out longer." Vlad stood, though his legs wobbled under him. He glanced up and down the tunnel. "How much longer until we reach the exit?"

Saphira was back in view, and she pushed a stray curl from her face. "We're halfway."

"Let's keep pushing." Vlad smacked his cheeks to wake himself up. "We need to listen so we know when we can risk leaving."

The king had said he would handle the warriors, but if Drake had his way, he would go behind his dad's back and force them to keep watch in large numbers. We could hope, but there was no guarantee we would make it out of here tonight. I only hoped that whoever was coming for us wouldn't give up.

I kept hold of the dart, careful not to stab myself with it. I wanted to get an idea of how the contraption worked and what sort of anesthetic they'd used to subdue us.

The time for lightheartedness was gone, and even though our moment of levity had been at my expense, it had given us a reprieve from the tension. Vlad was right. We needed to get into position so we could meet our next contact.

The five of us walked, though a little slower since Vlad was still impacted by the drugs. I focused on Eva's breathing and heartbeat, ensuring it didn't slow enough to cause alarm.

Something skittered past my feet, startling me. *Rats*. My skin crawled. They were gross disease carriers, especially the ones that lived underground.

Light shone at the end of the tunnel, but there was no obvious exit, just a dead end.

A lump formed in my throat until I noticed the light was coming from above.

How odd.

The closer we got, the clearer the exit became. It was over the tunnel. When we reached the end, I looked up and saw tiny holes that allowed us to see outside.

Something caused the light to vanish, and a scream lodged in my throat.

Thorn turned and placed a hand on my arm. He connected, *It's a guard walking past the rocky edge. They blocked the sun. No one has found us.*

Forcing myself to breathe steadily, I tried to focus. His touch grounded me, and I turned and rested my head on his arm. I needed his touch after being separated for so long.

He wrapped his free arm around me, and the jolt thrummed between us as the five of us who were awake stood in silence.

When there was no noise from outside, Vlad's jaw twitched. He exhaled and glanced at the two people still passed out in our arms. "I know this isn't ideal, but we need to get out of here after the next round of warriors passes."

My brows furrowed. "But the king said we should wait." We couldn't risk getting caught again. Darkness would give us more coverage.

Concern wafted from Thorn as he and his dad locked gazes.

He was keeping something from me.

I swallowed hard and narrowed my eyes. "What aren't you telling me?"

Thorn hung his head while Vlad crossed his arms. Vlad said, "If you don't tell her, I will. Waiting will only cause us to have to fight the warriors again."

"Just tell me," I gritted out.

Saphira rolled her eyes. "I'll do it."

She turned her attention to me...and winced.

CHAPTER THIRTEEN

THE ONLY THINGS that kept me grounded were Thorn's arm around me and holding Eva to my chest. I was about to scream at them to tell me, but if I was too loud, a warrior might overhear me.

"Drake will take matters into his own hands and use every possible resource against us." Saphira bit her bottom lip.

Nausea churned within. "Elliott and Peter." Drake would target my brother—Eva's twin—and my stepdad. Though I didn't truly care about Peter, my siblings did. He was their last remaining parent, and I would do anything to ensure they didn't lose him.

I sagged against Thorn, wanting to punch something. I hadn't thought of that, which infuriated me, but I knew Drake would never stop looking for someone to use against us. People like Drake couldn't let anything go. He would always hunt us.

Babe, I'm so sorry, Thorn connected, and his face twisted. *I wish—*

It's not your fault. We wouldn't have this conversation again. *We'll find a way out of this.* I should've killed Drake when I'd had the chance, but I'd missed his heart. Part of me was relieved that I had—I didn't want to kill *anybody*—but if I'd succeeded, we might not be in such a dire situation.

My blood cooled, and I arched a brow at Saphira. "You do realize that also goes for Brenton and Tyson, right? You're officially lumped in with us if they realize you helped attack the warriors back there."

Saphira hung her head as if she hadn't thought of that.

Cassidy growled softly. "I wish our thunder link worked the same as a wolf pack. Saphira could find out what's going on with the search and what their plans are."

I blinked, trying to understand. "How would she know that?"

"Wolves can communicate with everyone in their pack." Vlad tapped his forehead. "Just like you can with Thorn but with everyone. If our bonds worked the same as a wolf bond, and since you're part of our thunder now, the four of us could mindspeak to one another."

That would have been handy, especially with the whole wedding debacle.

"Ugh," Errol moaned, and his foot jerked.

Saphira exhaled, and her shoulders relaxed. "Dad?" she whispered and squeezed between Cassidy and Vlad.

Releasing me, Thorn kneeled and gently set Errol on the ground, propping him against the wall.

Be careful. There are cats, I connected with him. *Do you think that's smart?*

They're more afraid of us than we are of them. Thorn looked at me with a smile, then studied my face. *Or...maybe not?*

I hugged Eva closer and squinted. *Do you know how*

many diseases they carry? Hundreds. And several of them are deadly.

Remember, we're dragon shifters, not humans. We don't get sick, but don't put Eva on the ground, he replied and stood. *That's a different story.*

I grimaced. There was no way I'd risk my sister like that.

The sound of flapping wings had me holding my breath. I understood that warriors were searching for us, and I feared we would give ourselves away if we weren't careful. I exhaled slowly then inhaled deeply to calm my racing heart.

Errol's eyes fluttered open, and he glanced around the tunnel. "Where are we?"

"In a secret passageway," Saphira answered as she squatted in front of him. "We're waiting for the warriors to pass so we can get away."

He locked his attention on her and leaned his head back against the cement. He whispered, "Saphy, thank gods you're here."

"I'm sorry you got involved in this." Her eyes glistened as she touched his arm. "I had hoped it wouldn't come to this, but with what Drake has been doing, I couldn't stand back and pretend not to notice."

"None of us can any longer," he said as he patted her arm. "I was supposed to go with you all, anyway. The king pulled me aside last night and informed me of his plans."

His heartbeat remained slow, but it could have been calm due to the drug still coursing through his blood, so I couldn't tell if he was lying.

I hated to be *that* person, but we couldn't blindly trust anyone...not after Saphira's uncle, Brenton, betrayed us. "You officiated the wedding. You almost married me to that asshole."

Rubbing his forehead, he sighed. "I know. I'm sorry.

The king and I didn't expect him to start the wedding without Arman in attendance. It was unprecedented. Then again, we assumed he had a sense of honor for our traditions. Clearly, that is not the case."

Errol had pointed out that King Arman wasn't there, and Drake had pushed him to start, putting him in a dangerous position.

He frowned, his irises darkening. "At least, you married the right person."

My head jerked back, and my heart ached. "Wait. That counted?"

Hurt wafted through our bond, Thorn's feelings adding to my shock. Indigestion burned, but it wasn't from the coffee this morning; it was from the guilt over how I'd made Thorn feel.

"Yes. He is a prince—even though people thought he was dead. That was why I worded the question the way I did...so that any prince could speak up." Errol exhaled and sat upright. "I hoped Thorn would do what he did."

I'm sorry if you didn't— Thorn started.

No, I want to be married to you, I interjected. I couldn't fathom hearing the words I knew he was going to say. *I was just hoping it wouldn't be at a wedding someone else planned, and I wanted both of us to be able to say an 'I do.' Not only that but to also commit to each other among the people we wanted as guests, not random strangers watching in the hopes of getting on the good side of King Arman and Drake.*

He sighed and pushed a piece of hair behind my ear. He connected, *I didn't think of it like that. Just that I couldn't let Drake have you.*

Our buzz zinged, and I closed my eyes, treasuring the

moment. It had been far too long since we'd been together, and my dragon was growing restless. She wanted to connect with him, but here and now was *not* appropriate. *I know. You have nothing to feel bad about.*

Footsteps pounded above us, and dirt sifted through the holes and landed in Vlad's and Cassidy's hair.

Vlad placed a finger to his lips, and all of us went quiet.

I could only hope Eva stayed silent in her sleep.

Instead of focusing on the noise above, I listened to her heartbeat and breathing. Neither had slowed more, but I wished she would wake up soon. She was getting heavy.

Let me have her, Thorn connected as he gently took my sister from me and cradled her in his arms the way I had. *She's my sister, too.*

My heart warmed, and I stared into his eyes. I thought him touching my sister might bother me, but it didn't. There was no doubt he was all mine, and he was helping her to take care of me. *I love you.*

His eyes twinkled, stealing my breath, and my heart skipped a beat. *I love you, too.*

Every time warriors passed by, the light was blocked for a few seconds. Their footsteps were strong and steady, and more dragons flew overhead. There were a few minutes between the warriors, and as soon as the next group ran past, we would have to make our move.

We had to get to Elliott and Peter before Drake did, or we'd be right back in the situation I'd just escaped. And next time, Drake wouldn't wait to get what he wanted. He'd kill Thorn, marry me, and make Eva his breeder.

Eva turned her head, and I held my breath. Of course, *now* she'd stir. Hopefully, it was just from being jostled.

When we move, I need you to promise that you'll keep

going, no matter what, Thorn connected, his determination flaring through our bond.

I placed my hands on my hips as my blood heated. *What the hell does that mean? I'm staying beside you the entire time.* I was done splitting up. The past several days had been horrible, and I refused to go through that again. *Just because I did something stupid doesn't mean it's your turn.*

He pressed his lips into a line, but his shoulders shook gently. *I meant if I need to handle one of the dragons.*

With my sister in your arms? I scowled, allowing myself to get annoyed with his quiet laughter. At least, he was wise enough to attempt to hide it.

Fair point. I may have to hand her off to Vlad. Carefully, so that my sister wasn't bothered, he leaned over and kissed my forehead. *We all have to get to safety, me, included. If Drake captures me, he'll use me against you, and that is something I will never allow.*

My lungs worked a little easier. He wasn't planning to sacrifice himself.

The footsteps above quieted, and Vlad moved to the right side of the hole. He placed his feet into the small cement slots I hadn't noticed and climbed up. He touched the top of the covering and paused, looking down at us. "Is everyone ready?"

We glanced at one another.

Cassidy bit her bottom lip. "Errol, can you climb and run, or do you need more time to let the drugs wear off?"

"I'll be fine." Errol stood and placed his feet shoulder-width apart, then lifted his hands, stretching side to side.

That was one of my favorite moves in yoga.

"Wait." Saphira clenched her hands. "What about

Brenton and Tyson? I know Brenton betrayed us, but not Tyson."

"Don't worry about them," Errol said as he gestured for Vlad to open the lid. "We've handled it."

My brows furrowed, but Vlad opened the lid before we could ask more questions.

He stepped out, and Cassidy hurried up and climbed out behind him. Once Saphira and Errol were out, I scurried up the small makeshift ladder. The cement was jagged, likely from not being used much, and my bare feet ached as I climbed.

Thank goodness I hadn't worn my high heels, or there was no way I would've made it.

At the top, I placed my feet on the mulchy ground. I turned to help Thorn out, but he was already gracefully climbing up the awkward cutouts, carrying my sister.

It was a good thing he'd taken her from me. I wasn't sure I could've done that.

Vlad shut the lid, the top looking just like a rock on a slight incline. I never would've guessed it wasn't natural.

Out of the corner of my eye, I noticed movement.

Warriors.

They were heading this way. More must have joined the search. We'd wasted too much time, and now we were vulnerable.

Cassidy murmured, "Come on." Grabbing Saphira, they took off running.

Pointing at me and Thorn, Vlad indicated for us to head out.

I pivoted to run but stilled when I noticed Thorn not budging.

"Errol and I are still impacted by the tranq. We'll slow

you down if we take the lead," Vlad rasped. "Go, before we lose Saphira and Cass. You have the human girl."

Thorn growled but took off, running at a pace I could keep up with. Vlad and Errol hurried behind us, and we dodged and wove through the trees.

As I ran, my dress caught on twigs and branches, slowing me down. The warriors hadn't noticed us, but they'd pick up our scents once they reached the spot where we'd come above ground.

The constant breeze would help. I could only hope we would be far enough away before anyone caught our scents. *How far is it to the dragon territory border?*

Four miles, Thorn replied. *If we keep up this pace, we should be out of this area in thirty minutes.*

Thirty minutes. My legs were already stinging from scratches, and we'd gone maybe a quarter of a mile. With each passing minute, I hated this dress more and more.

Saphira and Cassidy slowed down, and we soon caught up with them. The six of us ran in rhythm, and I kept my eyes locked in front of me to make sure I didn't get injured more and wind up not being able to run on my own. We were already carrying one too many people, but Eva wouldn't have been able to run as fast as the rest of us.

A few squirrels and a skunk scurried away, and I tensed every time. I kept expecting someone to jump out from behind a tree and tranq one of us. *Where are all the warriors?*

Probably still close to the chateau, but they'll spread out soon since they haven't found us, Thorn answered. *They didn't expect us to get very far, or we would've already been spotted. King Arman didn't lie when he said no one knew about the secret passage.*

At least, there was that.

Errol grunted from behind. "Tell Cassidy to go slightly right, so we'll run into the road."

"Absolutely not," Vlad snapped. "That's taking us toward the houses."

"That's where Arman left a vehicle for us," he huffed, out of breath. "If we go down first and then right, it'll take more time."

Vlad sighed but didn't respond.

Cassidy veered right, pushing Saphira that way, confirming Vlad had relayed the message, after all.

We picked up the pace, and if someone had asked, I would've said we'd been running for hours. My feet were raw from the rocks and twigs I jogged over. Soon, a road appeared, and I spotted a black SUV.

Saphira stopped. "You've got to be kidding me. He'll take us straight back to Drake."

My attention landed on Brenton, and my blood froze. She was right. We couldn't trust him.

As I opened my mouth to agree, the sound of flapping wings caught my attention. I spun around to find three dragons flying toward us, their eyes locked on me.

Just when I'd hoped we might get away, we now had *two* problems.

Thorn handed me Eva and turned toward the dragons. He raised his hands, making his intentions clear, while Vlad removed a pistol from around his ankle. The two of them stood side by side, ready to fight.

I spun around to find Cassidy with a gun, rushing toward Vlad and Thorn, while Saphira marched directly to her uncle, her hands clenched at her sides.

"Saphira," Errol rasped as he rushed forward, intending to be involved in whatever was going on with his brother.

My chest constricted. I didn't know what to do: help my

mate or get into the car so I could hide my sister from the battle.

The dragons roared louder as they reached us.

There was only one thing I could do.

CHAPTER FOURTEEN

TRUSTING MY GUT, I forced my legs forward. My dragon roared as my chest clenched since I wasn't standing beside my mate, fighting, but I had to get my sister to safety first.

My lungs burned. I thought to my dragon, *I'm coming back to him. But what do you think will happen if I try to help and become an easy target because I'm holding my sister? The dragons know we're mates. They'll use me against him. I'm protecting him better this way.*

Some rage ebbed, so I continued toward the SUV. *I'm not happy about this, either.*

Just like when I'd handed myself over to Drake, my dragon begrudgingly relented. She was all about protecting Thorn too, but her instinct was more animalistic. She wanted to fight everyone that threatened him.

I connected with Thorn, *I'll be right back. I'm just going to put my sister in whatever getaway vehicle King Arman arranged for us.*

Stay safe, Thorn replied. *The three of us can handle*

them, and I can focus better if you're not in danger, espe-cially after being apart for so long.

My heart panged. He hadn't meant to hurt me, but we'd been apart because I'd been foolish enough to trust Drake. Granted, I wasn't sure what would've happened if I hadn't snuck away. For all I knew, things could have been worse, but they might have been better.

At least I'd learned we couldn't trust Drake, even when it came to dragon law. He'd confirmed that he thought himself above it, by word and deed, and he'd intended to keep or kill all five of us despite what he'd promised.

Saphira reached Brenton and shoved him in the chest.

His emerald eyes widened as he stumbled back, and the sun reflected off his dark brown complected head. He straightened, rubbing his hand through his black goatee. "Clearly, you haven't been informed who the getaway driver is."

She laughed bitterly as her irises darkened. "Like I'd ever trust *you* again."

"Saphy, he's telling the truth," Errol murmured. "The king asked him to wait for us here. In the tunnels, you even mentioned needing to protect him and Tyson, and this is why I said not to worry about it."

The sounds of dragons roaring and swooping filled the air, adding to the tension. I didn't care that Brenton had betrayed us, because Thorn could take his dragon if he led us back into danger.

"I didn't mean to betray you that night." Brenton tensed. "I was followed, and I only became aware of it a few minutes before you three showed up. You arrived just as they got into position. I had no way to tell you."

I reached the SUV, a black Nissan Pathfinder. Someone was in the passenger seat, but the windows were dark enough that I couldn't make out their face. "Who's in the car?"

"What?" Saphira gasped and rushed to the driver's side window. "You brought Tyson into this?"

"Like I said"—Brenton's nostrils flared—"we're going with you. We aren't coming back."

I'd have been more worried if Tyson hadn't been in the vehicle. That would mean Brenton did plan to come back. "If we take their phones, any electronics, and switch cars at the first opportunity, we can ensure they don't contact Drake." I nodded to the empty road. "Unless you can make another car appear out of thin air?"

Saphira fisted her hands as Errol placed a hand on his daughter's shoulder. "Brenton is telling the truth. Drake overheard my conversation with him and was suspicious. He assigned guards to watch him, and I couldn't warn him because Drake forced me to stay with him."

Her face was lined with worry, but I didn't have time to stand here while their drama unfolded. I adjusted Eva in my arms and opened the back driver's side door. I gently placed Eva in the seat and spun back around in time to see Cassidy fire the first shot.

The navy dragon that had been attacking her flew back, but I didn't see the bullet pierce its skin. There was no blood or injury, as if the bullet had bounced off its scales, making it flinch back.

Thorn's hands glowed as he held a hunter-green dragon's lower jaw, forcing its head up. The dragon's mouth was open, trying to bite Thorn, but its body was shrinking.

Our bond sizzled like before when he'd taken the dragons of the warriors at the wedding. It was different from our fated-mate jolt, and I guessed I was sensing his magic.

To my mate's left, Vlad held both a gun and a knife. He

slashed at the talons of the lemon-yellow dragon trying to lift him.

Though things appeared under control, that could change in a moment. "Saphira, please keep an eye on my sister." I took off running toward my mate and his parents.

"Yeah, sure," Saphira deadpanned. "Not that you gave me a choice."

Under normal circumstances, I'd have grinned, but not when my mate was being attacked.

I had to get to him.

Thorn's attacker's scales were vanishing, and the dragon was human size again. Blonde hair appeared, as well as a human female's face. She was naked. He wasn't doing anything wrong, but my dragon didn't care, and a deep growl rumbled in my chest.

The female warrior dropped, her head smashing into the ground. Her eyes rolled back as she passed out on impact.

The navy dragon swooped down, and Cassidy turned, aiming her gun, but when she pulled the trigger, it didn't fire.

It was jammed.

The navy dragon's gigantic mouth opened to bite her, but Thorn spun around and punched the dragon in the eye, seconds before it could lock down on Cassidy's arm.

Head jerking back, the dragon snarled, its teeth grazing Cassidy's upper arm. Blood oozed from the scratches.

Now that Thorn was helping her, I'd help Vlad.

Turning my attention back to him, I watched as the lemon dragon circled the clearing and barreled back toward Vlad. Vlad raised the knife in his hand, not the gun, and I wanted to scream at him to shoot the dragon. When Cassidy had, it had slowed the dragon down for a minute.

The lemon dragon had all four sets of talons extended. Smoke trickled out of its nose as it homed in on Vlad. He crouched, and I realized the dragon's strategy would work.

When I was less than ten feet from Vlad's back, the lemon dragon struck him as the swirl of Thorn's magic surged through our connection—Thorn was taking the navy dragon's dragon.

Vlad swiped at the lemon dragon's front talons as the back ones dug into his sides. The dragon flapped its wings, lifting Vlad off the ground.

Vlad groaned and dropped his weapons. The knife fell at my feet, missing my big toe by a foot, and the gun fell farther away from me.

I bent, swiped up the closest weapon—the knife—and jumped, barely catching Vlad's feet.

Warm liquid hit my face as Vlad grunted from carrying my weight. I hated to make his injury worse, but I didn't know what else to do. I didn't feel comfortable shooting a gun and didn't want to risk hitting Vlad accidentally. The knife had seemed like the smartest choice. Now I was having second thoughts.

"I'm sorry," I said and tried to climb Vlad's body.

My dress flapped in the breeze, tangling around my legs, and I couldn't use my hands to climb him because of the damn knife. Every second, we lifted higher, my dress tangling around me even more.

Instead of helping, I was making matters worse, and we were about ten feet off the ground.

Everly! Thorn connected below, the cold tendrils of his fear gripping me. *What are you doing?*

Trying to save Vlad, I replied as the wind hit my face, splattering Vlad's blood all over me. *But it's not going so well.*

I see that, Thorn growled. "Cassidy, get to the car."

I had no idea what was going on down there. Vlad gritted his teeth as he leaned down, face twisted in agony, and extended a hand to me. I turned the knife so the blade rested in my palm and gripped the handle so I could hand it to him without stabbing him.

The lemon dragon roared and rocked forward, heading toward the ground. My body lurched as our momentum changed, giving me enough of a boost to use my arms. I got the butt of the knife into Vlad's hand.

The sound of additional wings weighed my limbs. *Thorn!*

It's just me, Thorn replied as his plum scales came into view. His front talons gently grabbed my sides as the lemon dragon jerked and shrieked.

Thorn's talon's dug into my side a little as he connected, *Release Vlad. I've got you.*

Sides protesting, I obeyed, trusting my mate. Thorn lifted me to one shoulder, where I grabbed onto his scales and hoisted myself onto his back. My skin buzzed from our touch despite us being in two different forms.

The lemon dragon flew upward to get away.

Thorn flapped his wings, soaring toward the dragon as Vlad shoved the knife into one of the talons that held him. The dragon shrieked and threw its head back in agony. The talons retracted from Vlad's side, and blood poured from the wound. I wouldn't have known he was injured if I'd been watching him, because Vlad didn't pause as he sliced into the other talon.

The dragon dropped him just as Thorn swooped below, catching Vlad in his talons. The lemon dragon soared away. Backup would be here soon.

I didn't even think about shifting. I should've shifted at the first sign of an attack, but I'd dumbly stayed in human form.

We were all trying to stay in human form so we could use our weapons and get to the vehicle quickly, and it was going fine, until it wasn't. Are you hurt? he asked, flying toward the waiting vehicle.

I smiled tenderly, and my chest expanded so much it hurt. *I'm fine.* Just a little banged up but better off than Vlad and Thorn.

He landed softly and placed Vlad on his feet. Cassidy stood by the car and helped Vlad get into the vehicle as I climbed down Thorn's back and glanced behind.

The two warriors whose dragons Thorn had taken were out cold. The man had landed awkwardly on his knees, making him appear to be in the child's pose with his naked butt facing us. Unfortunately, I learned a very uncomfortable fact about this stranger—he had a caterpillar butt crack. It was so damn hairy.

"Everly!" Saphira shouted from the SUV.

Thankfully, that yanked my gaze away from the sight I'd never be able to unsee. *That* vision was one I would never put on a canvas.

Cloth hit my face, and I grabbed a pair of large jeans and a shirt.

"I understand he's not bad looking, but the last thing I want is him butt-naked in the car with us, rubbing all over you after being separated for so long." She jumped back in the car and climbed into the backseat.

Thank goodness for this. I didn't want anyone seeing Thorn naked for longer than necessary.

I turned to find him already back in his gorgeous muscular human form, and I drank in the sight, even as I tossed him the clothes. He grabbed them and quickly dressed, connecting, *Get into the vehicle. I'm going to grab my phone real quick.*

As I stuck my head in the door, I noticed Brenton was already behind the wheel and Errol was in the front passenger seat. Eva was propped against the passenger side window with Saphira in the middle next to her and a teenage boy, who had to be Tyson, was in the seat on the other end. Luckily, the middle row was also a three-seater, but four of us needed a spot.

I bit my lip. I could sit on the floorboards once the others got settled.

Cassidy slid in first and scooted across to the spot behind Errol. Vlad settled into the middle seat. Strong arms wrapped around me as Thorn picked me up like a princess and arranged me on his lap in the final seat. He slammed the door, and Brenton peeled away without missing a beat.

Thorn tightened his arms around me, and I breathed in his scent as the jolt surged between us. The car swerved as Brenton desperately drove away, but as usual, Thorn protected me from any discomfort.

"We've got to get to Everly's family home quickly. Drake will send people there as soon as that yellow dragon tells him we got away," Thorn said, his chest vibrating against mine.

I purred before I realized what I was doing. Being somewhat safe in his arms was the most comforting thing I'd felt in forever.

He tilted my face toward his and kissed me. The jolt between us sizzled, and my breathing caught as my body flamed. Kissing him was like a drink of water after being stuck in the desert. My dragon roared with his as his tongue brushed my lips.

"You weren't kidding, Saph," Tyson said from behind

us. "Not even a minute in the car, and they're making out, while she sounds like a cat."

And that was enough to remind me we had an audience, two of whom were Thorn's parents, so I pulled myself away.

"Do I ever exaggerate?" Saphira quipped.

Errol chuckled. "Don't answer that, anyone. It's a trap."

Face burning, I looked behind me and took in Tyson. His skin was a shade darker than Saphira's, and his eyes were a warm olive. His midnight black hair was cut short, and he was smaller than Thorn and Vlad, but still muscular. His attention was on his cousin, his face filled with adoration.

Saphira had mentioned they were close, and the way he looked at her confirmed it.

Though they were trying to lighten the mood, I couldn't joke around, not until Elliott and Peter were with us and Eva was awake.

We hit a bump, and Vlad grunted, grimacing in pain.

"Babe..." Cassidy said with concern.

"I'm fine." Vlad forced a smile. "Just a little beat up. After a good night's rest, I'll be better."

No one responded, the lighthearted atmosphere gone.

Once Brenton had the address, the vehicle descended into silence, and I laid my head against Thorn's chest, listening to the one noise that trumped the sound of a paintbrush on canvas—his heartbeat.

WE PULLED up in front of the two-story robin-egg-blue house. My skin crawled. There were no strange vehicles in sight, and Drake wouldn't risk flying here in dragon form, especially during the day. But there was no telling how far behind us he was or how Peter would react.

The only good thing was that my white Audi A4 was still in the driveway, in the cutout section to the left of the white garage.

Thorn opened the door and helped me out. "Just Everly and I will go in. That way, there will be fewer people to get situated if someone arrives."

No one questioned him; the leader he was meant to be shone through, but I paused. "What about Eva?"

"She'll recognize me. It's fine." Saphira nodded and gestured to the door. "We don't have time to wait."

I swallowed. *Why don't they go on? It's not like we can fit Elliott and Peter in the car with us. We'll take my Audi.* I hated to do that, but if Drake showed up, I didn't want all of us to get caught.

I'll tell them. Go on inside and get them ready.

I turned and rushed to the door, bending to retrieve the key under the mat. I slipped it into the lock and opened the door, then jerked back, surprised at what I found.

Peter was pacing behind the black leather sofa, and Elliott sat on the couch in his normal spot. They turned their heads toward me as Peter scowled. His chestnut-brown eyes hardened, and his light brown hair was messy on top like he'd been running his hands through it, the gray on the sides adding to the troubled look. His brown suit jacket was thrown over the back of the couch.

He took a hurried step toward me, stabbing his finger at me. "Drake just called. He told me you'd be coming here. What the hell have you done?"

"Dad," Elliott murmured. He looked identical to Eva; the only differences were that he was taller, and his hair was significantly shorter. "He's not a good dude. He took Eva in the middle of the night."

"Because *she*"—he shook his finger again—"didn't follow through."

My submissive side wanted to placate him, but my dragon roared. We didn't have time to waste. I lifted my chin. "Grab a few things, and let's go. We have to get away before Drake gets here."

Elliott jumped to his feet, but Peter lifted a hand and said, "We aren't going anywhere. We're going to hand you back to him and get Eva back."

My body jolted as Thorn entered the house and stepped up beside me. He growled, "The hell you will."

CHAPTER FIFTEEN

UNABLE TO STOP MYSELF, I leaned on my mate. For the past six years, I'd had no one on my side when it came to dealing with my stepdad and siblings, but not anymore. My throat thickened as my love for Thorn overwhelmed me.

Peter's nose wrinkled. "Who the *hell* are you?"

Slipping his arm around my waist, Thorn lifted his chin. "Her husband."

Even though the wedding hadn't been a joyous occasion, I *really* liked hearing him say that word. It wasn't as if he could throw the word *mate* around yet. Unfortunately, Elliott and Peter would be learning about the dragon world, soon enough.

"What?" Elliott gaped. His eyes were so wide I feared they might pop out of their sockets. His attention settled on me. "Is that true?"

I beamed, unable to keep a neutral expression. "It is." I leaned my head against Thorn's shoulder.

Peter took a menacing step forward. "You'll have to annul it so we can get Eva back from Drake. You said you would take her place. Then you run off and *marry* him? I knew you were a piece of—"

"You better stop right there," Thorn warned as he released me and marched over to Peter. He grabbed Peter by the collar of his button-down shirt and lifted him. "One insult thrown her way, and your life will be a lot worse than anything Drake can do to you. Do you *understand?*"

Sniffing, Peter blanched. "Yes."

"Good," Thorn snarled and dropped him. "We've got to leave *now.*"

I glanced out the door, expecting Drake to be here, but found Brenton pulling out of the driveway and heading toward downtown. At least, that group would be out of harm's way. We needed to be right behind them.

"Uh..." Elliott raced to the television and unplugged the gaming system.

Out of *all* the items he could focus on bringing, it would be that. I almost told him to forget it, but Eva could use a sense of normalcy and comfort. Playing games with her twin would give her some semblance of being back home.

"I should get stuff from my bedroom." Peter headed toward me to climb up the stairs, which were in front of the door.

We can't let either of them out of our sight, Thorn connected as he followed Peter. *And we need to go. Warriors will be here any second.*

I stepped in front of Peter, blocking the stairs. "We have spare clothes. You two will be fine." I connected, *Can you come here? He'll try to go upstairs as soon as I move to get my keys.*

Peter's hands clenched. "Get out of my way, Everly. This is *my* house, and I'll do as I want."

"Can't you trust me?" Every time we got near each

other, he treated me as if he resented my presence. It wasn't enough to prevent me from coming around, though, since the twins were my half-siblings. He did seem to care about them, but ever since Mom had gotten sick, he'd channeled his malice toward me. Whenever I'd visit to keep my promise to Mom about taking care of my siblings, I'd avoid my stepdad as much as possible. Inevitably, he'd treat me like I was scum he merely tolerated. "We're trying to keep Eva safe."

He snorted. "You're trying to keep her safe? Then where the hell were you when Drake came for her? You left to protect her, yet she was taken anyway. You're selfish, even if you pretend you aren't."

His words stung because they were true. I had failed my mom and Eva, but not on purpose. But I sure as hell wouldn't fail them again.

Our connection grew uncomfortably hot from Thorn's rage. Hands fisted, he marched over to Peter and growled, "Clearly, you didn't understand, and I will not tolerate your disrespect."

"You listen—" Peter started and spun back toward the living room in time for Thorn to punch him in the side of the head.

Peter hit the back of his head on the stair rail and dropped, crumpling onto his side. Elliott yelped.

I blinked, trying to comprehend what had happened. Then a deep, hearty laugh shook my shoulders. "That's one way to shut him up."

No one talks to my wife and mate that way. Thorn's eyes softened. *You deserve the world, and I intend to give it to you and beat anyone who hurts you or stands in your way. That asshole was doing both. He's lucky that's the worst he got.*

Though Thorn and I had met under less-than-ideal

circumstances, I wouldn't change it for the world. It had gotten us *here*, and if I died today, it would be while knowing what it felt like to be truly loved and accepted and what loving someone unconditionally felt like. Many people didn't get to experience that in an entire lifetime. *I love you.* Even those words didn't seem momentous enough for how strong my emotions for him were.

And I love you. He smiled. *We'll have to continue this discussion when we get back to the cabin.*

I winced. Here I was, standing around like a lovesick schoolgirl, when our enemy would be beating down the door at any second.

Enemy.

Wow.

If someone told me a month ago that I'd be in the middle of a supernatural drama, I would've taken them to seek help.

"I'm ready." Elliott lifted the gaming system and controllers. "As long as I've got these, I'll survive. Just don't punch me like dad."

The sad thing was, he meant it. "Don't run your mouth like him, and we won't have a problem. Besides, we'll ensure you have deodorant, soap, shampoo, and a toothbrush. Basic hygiene is a must."

He tilted his head and held out the gaming system to me. "Says the sister who's standing in the house with blood in her hair and running down her face and splashed all over some gaudy gold dress while barefoot."

I jerked back. He had me there. I touched my face, and sure enough, I felt dried blood. Vomit inched up my throat, but my dragon hissed at my human theatrics.

Where are your keys? Thorn asked as he lifted Peter and

tossed him over his shoulder. His muscles rippled, and my body warmed.

Right. Keys.

I shook my head, refocusing on the threat and not my mate's tantalizing body, and hurried past the sofa into the kitchen and grabbed my keys from the basket on the counter.

My chest ached. This might be the last time I saw the kitchen that Mom and I had decorated shortly after she'd been diagnosed with cancer, but I pushed the memories away. I dangled the keys from my finger. "Let's roll."

Opening the door, Thorn rushed outside. I waved Elliott on, wanting to take up the rear. I pressed the unlock button, so Thorn could get Peter situated in the vehicle, while the two of us were slower coming out.

With each step Elliott took, parts of his gaming system jostled, causing him to slow even more. I bit the inside of my cheek to prevent myself from snapping at him. Maybe allowing him to bring the system hadn't been smart. If we got caught because he was too slow, my good intentions would lead to disaster.

When we stepped onto the long porch, Thorn was shutting the back passenger side door of the Audi. Elliott shuffled down the stairs, and I locked the door and replaced the key under the mat. Though I doubted it would make much difference, I didn't want whoever came by to think we were frantically on the run, even though we were.

Thorn slid into the driver's seat, which somehow didn't annoy me. I liked to be in control, but with him, being a passenger didn't bother me.

Ten years later, we finally reached the car. Yes, I was being dramatic, but damn, it sure felt as if it had taken that long. I opened the back driver's side door, trying to get Elliott to hurry, and as soon as he swung his feet into the car, I slammed the door shut and ran around to the front passenger seat.

Thorn pressed the button to start the car, and as soon as the engine turned, he backed out of the driveway.

I buckled my seatbelt and took deep breaths like I learned in yoga. It wasn't as effective, since I couldn't do the stretch that went along with them inside a moving car.

Elliot sighed and fidgeted behind me, trying to get situated. "You said you were trying to keep Eva safe? What did you mean by that? Isn't she with Drake?" Though he was trying to control his voice, it grew thick with emotion.

As Thorn drove down the street, I turned in my seat and smiled sadly. "Actually, I was with her. She and I escaped, but she was tranqed, and some of our friends and Thorn's parents are taking her to the same place we're heading. You'll see her soon."

Eyes glistening, Elliott let out a shaky breath. "She's not with him, either." He leaned his head back against the headrest and stiffened. "Wait. She was *tranqed?*"

Tires squealed, and I jerked my head forward. Several large black Suburbans turned the upcoming corner and barreled toward us.

There was no doubt who they were.

Warriors.

A lump formed in my throat. At least, we weren't at the house. I could only hope they were so focused on getting there that they didn't notice us, especially with my tinted windows.

When the third and final SUV passed us, the vehicle slammed on its brakes.

No. This couldn't be happening. *Thorn,* I connected.

"I know," he rasped as he pressed the gas pedal, taking a

turn at a much faster speed than I was comfortable with. He expertly maneuvered the car as tires screeched and the SUVs cut hard, spinning in our direction.

Thorn glanced in the rearview mirror as we approached the main road leading to downtown. "Elliott, it's going to get rough, so hold on."

"Is that them?" Elliott breathed, watching them out the back window.

I gripped the black leather center console and the door handle, my gut heaving as Thorn turned onto the main road. A car blared its horn behind us as we cut them off, but Thorn didn't ease off the gas.

My mid-size sedan was significantly smaller than the Suburbans, so we were able to swerve through vehicles efficiently.

The Suburbans raced behind us, honking their horns, and weaving through the traffic after us, but we were gaining distance.

My heart hammered, and I grimaced as Thorn cut another person off. The car slammed on its brakes, honking, and the lead Suburban slammed into the back of the car.

The car flipped around from the impact and wrapped around a telephone pole.

My hands shook. *Thorn, I need your cell phone.*

His brows furrowed, but he fidgeted in his pocket and handed it to me.

I expected him to take the next left that would lead us away from downtown, but he remained on the main road.

Dialing 911, I connected with Thorn, *Why are we going downtown?*

If we take the main road, we won't be able to lose them, he replied as his hands gripped the steering wheel.

The 911 operator came on the line, and I informed

them of the accident and that the person who'd run into the smaller car was chasing us. I then mentioned two more Suburbans were still pursuing us. After telling her where we were heading, she told us that police officers would intercept us.

As soon as I hung up, Thorn connected, *That's actually a smart plan.*

Just make sure they don't catch up to us before the police arrive. I rolled down my window and chucked the phone.

Ev, what the hell? Thorn connected, surprise flickering through him. *Dad or Mom may try to call us.*

I winced. I hadn't considered that. *Sorry, but I had to toss it, so the cops don't follow us.*

He nodded. *Right. We'll just need to tell them when we can.*

The traffic light turned yellow, and Thorn punched the gas. My car lurched forward, and Elliott grunted as his knees hit the back of my seat. My kidneys complained.

We sailed underneath the light just as it turned red, and I glanced in the side mirror.

I'd hoped that the Suburbans would stop, but they swung into the opposite lane and swerved past the handful of vehicles between us.

Luckily, traffic wasn't heavy, and another wreck didn't unfold.

Thorn's knuckles turned white, and soon, sirens sounded. Two cop cars rushed past us toward the Suburbans and blocked the lane, preventing them from following us.

My head fell against the headrest.

Now, we have to get to the cabin before another car finds us, Thorn said as he took the next left and headed out of the city.

As soon as the long, winding roads with less traffic surrounded us, I relaxed. We were heading in the opposite direction from the dragon lands, which meant we shouldn't pass any guards.

Thorn took my hand, the jolt thrumming between us. He connected, *Lay your head back, and get some rest. We're safe now.*

After the torturous week, a nap sounded fabulous. I placed my head on his shoulder and breathed in his scent. I needed to touch him, and even in the slightly uncomfortable position, I was out fast.

Everly, Thorn's voice popped into my head, and my eyes fluttered. *We're at the cabin. Do you need me to carry you in?*

The offer was tempting, but with Elliott and Eva around, I needed to be strong. I lifted my head, my neck aching from the position I'd slept in. *No, I'm fine. You deal with Peter.*

He nodded, his gorgeous eyes locked on me. *That's what I thought you'd say. Let's get you inside. I've been waiting for this moment for far too long.*

"What is this place?" Elliott asked from behind.

I opened my door and climbed out. "Your home for the foreseeable future."

He followed my lead. Standing outside the car, he leaned back inside to gather his gaming system. "And Eva is in there?"

Glancing to the right, I noticed the black SUV parked there. "She should be inside."

Thorn tossed Peter over his shoulder, and as we walked

up to the one-story log cabin, the front door opened, revealing Eva in a pair of brown sweatpants and a white T-shirt. She rushed into my arms.

I stiffened, having expected her to run to Elliott.

"Thank goodness, you're okay. They told me you were, but I needed to see it with my own eyes." She leaned back, touching her chest.

My eyes burned, but I forced a smile. "We made it, and we brought Elliott and your dad here."

Her attention flicked to Elliott, and a huge smile lit her face. She took a step toward him, her arms outstretched.

Elliott shook his head. "Dude, you just hugged her, and she's all bloody. I know I love my game character like that, but that's pretend. So, like—"

Eva didn't hesitate and threw her arms around him. She whispered, "You brought our game."

He scoffed, "Of course, I did."

Thorn walked into the hallway, and I followed him. We found Saphira, Errol, and Brenton in the den, sitting on one of the black futon couches, and Vlad, Cassidy, and Tyson on the other. The charcoal walls didn't seem so dark this time around, likely because I'd spent time in actual Hell. My gaze landed on the white back door and continued out the square window to the woods.

"Thank gods, you two made it back." Cassidy sighed. "I was just about to call you to see if everything was okay."

Saphira snorted. "I take it Peter wasn't the most agreeable."

"He was an ass," Thorn growled as Eva and Elliott entered the cabin and shut the door. Then the two of them joined us in the den.

"I'll take him into the Wolfram Dwinn room and lock him up." Thorn nodded back toward the hallway. "Then I need a minute alone with Everly so we can talk and clean up."

That was the room he'd put Saphira in when he'd first brought us here. The tungsten had been forged with Thorn's own royal dragon fire, and not even dragon shifters could break through the metal or shift when surrounded by it. Peter would be very securely locked in.

I inhaled swiftly. There was no telling what Thorn wanted to say, but I deserved to hear whatever he needed to get off his chest.

"Sounds like a plan." Cassidy went into the kitchen as she continued, "Vlad needs to clean up too, and I'll cook us something to eat. Everly has to be starving."

Food sounded amazing, but *after* I cleaned up. I wanted the blood off me.

I turned to the twins. "Will you two be okay for a bit?"

Eva pointed at the gaming system. "Hell yeah. I've been jonesing to play."

The two of them hurried to the television and started setting everything up.

As Thorn and I turned down the hallway toward the bedrooms, Saphira muttered, "Just keep it down. We all have good ears."

We reached the first door on the right, and Thorn nodded at it. "Go ahead and get in the shower. I'll be right there."

He probably wanted me to get clean before we talked, and I couldn't blame him.

I entered the bedroom and breathed in his minty-amber scent. The stark off-white walls and the queen bed with the same purple sheets we'd made love in for the first time now felt like home.

I walked past the bed and the dresser to the bathroom

and turned on the shower. As the water warmed, I bent to grab a towel from under the sink. I tossed the white towel over the shower rod and heard the bedroom door shut. When I glanced up, Thorn was leaning against the bathroom door frame.

Turning to him, I rubbed my arms.

Then he gestured for me to come to him, an unreadable expression on his face.

My heart nearly stopped. What did he want?

CHAPTER SIXTEEN

I STRAIGHTENED, trying to find some sort of calm. This was the first time we'd been alone since I'd snuck out in a poor-ass attempt to save Thorn's parents, Saphira, and Eva. If he wanted to yell at me, I deserved it.

My feet moved toward him without me giving it much thought. We'd been apart for too long, and at least, I'd get to be near him when he told me whatever he had to say.

Inhaling, I had to get something off my chest. "Before you say anything, I just want to say again how sorry I am. I know I fu—"

He kissed me, cutting off my words, and connected, *None of that matters. I just need you.* His tongue brushed my lips, begging for entrance.

My body thrummed as our dragons purred together inside our minds. I hadn't expected this, but it was a more than welcome surprise. We were mates and had been apart too long. We needed to connect again.

To be one...even for a few moments. One soul, one body, one everything. The way we were meant to be.

His minty scent engulfed me, making me dizzy. I

opened my mouth to him...and my skin cracked as something that had dried on my face stretched.

Blood.

Ew. He was kissing me while I was covered in blood—though it was mostly Vlad's. I took a step back.

Thorn's forehead lined, and he tilted his head. "Did I do something wrong?" His concern wafted through me.

"*No*," I said forcefully. I glanced down at my chest and the splotches of blood. "I *want* to kiss you and—" My face burned as I cut off and waved at his body. "You know." I cleared my throat.

He grinned wickedly. "Nope. Not a clue. You'll have to spell it out for me."

I stuck out my tongue, well aware this was the happiest I'd been since the last time I'd seen him. "Well, some would say that leaving you guessing works in my favor." I scrunched my nose and sighed. "But can we hold off until *after* my shower? I'm covered in blood and want to wash off the stench of the chateau."

Pursing his lips, he closed the distance between us and slid his hands around my waist. He connected, *Actually, I've got an idea I think we and our dragons will approve of.* He unzipped my dress and tugged it, so it fell to the laminate floor, leaving me in nothing but my white strapless bra and black panties.

His gorgeous blue eyes glowed, and his pupils slitted as he ogled me. My breath caught, and my body flamed with desire.

Even covered in blood, you're the most gorgeous woman I've ever known. He growled as he unhooked my bra and tossed it aside. His fingers slid underneath the line of my panties and pushed them to the floor. *Pure perfection.*

Sliding the curtain to the side, he nodded toward the tub. *You should get clean.*

I nodded, my body humming. I damn near tumbled into the tub, and he laughed, deep and sexy. "Don't get hurt. I need you in top form."

My body blazed hotter than ever as he shut the curtain.

I stepped underneath the hot water, enjoying the way it splashed over me. Pink water puddled around my feet as the blood rinsed off.

Thorn moved around outside the curtain as I scrubbed my fingers through my hair and down my face, removing the dried blood that tried to stay behind.

The curtain opened again, and Thorn stepped into the tub.

Need bloomed heavily within me as I ogled him from head to toe. Every inch of him was more chiseled, muscular, and huge than I remembered, perfection compared to the statues of gods that people had sculpted so many centuries ago.

He leaned toward me and moved to my right, snatching the shampoo bottle from the side of the tub. I huffed in frustration, and he smiled.

"Turn around," he murmured, and I didn't hesitate.

The warm water hit my front as he worked up a lather in my hair. His fingers dug into my scalp as the berry smell of the shampoo swirled around us. My stomach clenched with need, even as he relaxed me.

His hand touched my waist, turning me around. I leaned back into the spray, rinsing the shampoo from my hair and body.

Leaning over again, he squirted conditioner in one hand and took a bar of soap in the other. When I turned around, he worked the conditioner into the ends of my hair while his other hand rubbed the bar of soap over my body.

After a minute, he used both hands to clean my body and placed the soap back on its shelf. I turned to rinse off, but he shook his head and connected, *I'm not done yet.*

His left hand cupped my breast, rubbing suds across my nipple, while the other one slipped between my legs. Unable to stand, I leaned against the back wall of the tub, allowing the water to wash over my body, but he didn't relent. His thumb rolled over my nipple as his fingers circled within my folds. Tension built, and my breathing turned erratic. As ecstasy coursed through me, I moaned, and Thorn kissed me, swallowing the noise.

After my body stopped quivering, I pushed him off and smiled wickedly. I arched a brow. "My turn."

Just like he'd taken care of me, I washed his hair, and my fingers grazed the mark that haunted him at the base of his neck. I hadn't gotten a chance to study it because of all the drama. It looked more like a tattoo than a birthmark, showing a detailed image of a dragon. I was lingering, my hand itching to trace the outline, when he stiffened and turned around to rinse the shampoo from his head. A twinge of discomfort swirled between us.

I didn't want to make him feel awkward, so I moved on to do what I'd been looking forward to most—cleaning his body. I followed every curve of muscle and slid my hand downward to find him hard.

His body shuddered as I stroked him, trying to make him feel like he'd made me feel. His hips swiveled, increasing the rhythm, and he leaned toward me, capturing my lips.

Safety and happiness meant being with the one person who was made for you in a way that couldn't be replicated.

He pulled away from my lips and kissed down my neck. When he reached the base, he nipped like he had the night we'd claimed one another. He grabbed my hand, removing it from his body.

I moaned, wanting to keep going, but he lifted me, placing my back against the wall as he slid inside me. Our dragons roared as he slowly slid in and out, and I wrapped my arms around his body.

I wanted to pleasure you, like you did me, I connected, but I was already matching his pace, spreading my legs to feel him deeper.

Oh, you will. Don't worry. He snarled as he nipped at my throat and quickened the tempo. *This is the only way I want my ending—with me deep inside you.*

His words urged my dragon on, and I dug my fingers into his back, needing to mark him in the way he was marking me. He groaned as his fingers dug deeper into my skin.

Our love for each other mixed with our growing euphoria. Releasing his hold, he took my hands and pinned them against the wall as he kissed me again.

We orgasmed at the same time, our pleasure blending. I wasn't sure how long our bodies thrummed from the high, but when we finally came down, the water was cooling.

Guiding me back under the stream, he rinsed us off. A loud knock sounded on the bedroom door.

"I hate to, uh...interrupt," Cassidy called out, "but dinner is ready, and it's going to get cold."

My stomach growled, and Thorn laughed. The sound was carefree and warmed my heart so much it could burst.

"We're getting out," he called back as he turned off the water. "But you guys don't have to wait on us. Eat."

Part of me didn't want to get out of the shower despite

the chill. That meant my mate would get dressed—a true tragedy. I'd been more worried than I'd let on about not seeing him again, and I hated for any part of him to be covered. But it was better than everyone seeing him naked.

He wrapped the towel around me and kissed the top of my head. He connected, *We need to get you fed.*

I pouted. "But we could stay here and have sex again."

"There's no question about that." He winked as he snatched another towel from underneath the sink and dried himself. "As soon as you eat and we handle Peter, I'm bringing your sexy ass right back in here to make love all over again."

Batting my eyes, I dropped the towel lower, exposing the top of my breasts. "Or we could go for round two now."

Behave. Though I want to ravish you, one thing is more important—making sure you're taken care of, which means eating. He strolled out the door, dropping the towel so I could see his tight ass walking away. *Besides, it's selfish. If you don't eat, you won't have the energy to have sex all night. So, a small break is winning.*

All night.

I liked the sound of that. I hurried and got dressed, not wanting to be left behind.

Dinner went better than I'd imagined. I'd thought it would be awkward, but Cassidy, Vlad, Thorn, and I sat around the dinner table, while Tyson, Eva, and Elliott played a shooting game. Saphira, Brenton, and Errol sat on one of the futons, watching them play, while poking fun at Tyson whenever he died.

It was almost as if we'd known one another a lot longer than we had.

Cassidy had cooked steaks and potatoes and made a salad. I hadn't had a good home-cooked meal since Mom had died, so the moment was bittersweet but delicious. The only thing nagging at me was my stepdad, who must have still been passed out since he wasn't making noise from the back room.

I lifted a bite of steak to my mouth just as Saphira strolled into the kitchen.

"So..." She leaned against the window in front of me, grinning wickedly as she crossed her arms. "Eva told me you were in over your head with Falkor."

Inhaling, I dropped my fork, and it hit the plate with a loud clank. A sour taste filled my mouth as I glanced from her to my sister.

Eva paused the game.

Elliott jumped from the floor and spun toward her, scowling. He rasped, "What the *hell*? Cheater! I was winning."

"You still will be. Chill." She turned around to watch the exchange between Saphira and me.

My jaw dropped. "You *didn't*." She'd *told* Saphira. The little traitor.

"I hope your mouth didn't do that when you were hanging around there." Saphira smiled devilishly. "Unless you're a biter." Her attention homed in on Thorn. "Is she a biter?"

I wanted to die. That was a moment I didn't want to relive *ever* again.

Thorn placed his arms against the table and frowned. "What does Everly being a biter have to do with Falkor?" His irises darkened as he glanced at me.

"We're missing something." Cassidy wiped her mouth with a napkin and set it down. "Does anyone want to enlighten us?"

"No!" I yelled at the same time Saphira replied, "Yes."

Everly, what's going on? The concern wafting from Thorn had my nerves jumping.

"It was something that happened the first night Eva and I were *there*," I replied, wishing Saphira hadn't brought the story up.

Vlad's jaw clenched. "Did Falkor do something to you?"

Smoke trickled from Thorn's nose, and I realized Elliott didn't know about dragons yet. I glared at Saphira and said, "She's making it sound worse..." I paused. The whole situation had been horrible. It couldn't have gotten much worse. "More..." I didn't know what to say to diffuse the situation.

Thorn slammed his hand on the table, cracking it. I was reminded of King Arman.

"Dude!" Elliott's eyes bulged. "You broke that huge-ass table. I need to work out with you. The ladies would be flocking to me like moths to a flame."

Thorn wasn't calming down.

"I tried to escape the first night we got there, and Falkor grabbed me and threw me over his shoulder, my face to his chest. I had what I thought was a bright idea." I closed my eyes and rubbed my forehead, not wanting to see anyone's reaction. "If I pantsed him, he wouldn't be able to walk without stumbling, and Eva and I would have time to run away."

Relaxing, Thorn rolled his shoulders. "So why is she insinuating—"

I had to get it out before I couldn't. "Because I didn't consider where my head was in relation to his..." I twisted my face as the food inched back up.

"Junk." Saphira snorted. "His junk was in her face. She went balls deep."

My eyes flew back open to see Saphira beaming as she

studied Thorn and me. She was enjoying watching me squirm and Thorn's fated-mate reaction.

Brat.

"Whoa." Elliott lifted a hand. "You gave a dude a blow job to escape?"

"*What?*" I glared at him. "Of course not. Why would you think that?"

He gestured at Saphira. "She said 'balls deep.'"

This was getting worse. My face heated. I did not want to be discussing *this* at all, but especially not with my twin siblings. "She thinks she's being cute and clever."

"Oh, she's *not*," Thorn growled, his pupils slitting.

Cassidy clapped her hands. "Well, this has been fun." She mashed her lips together, but the corners of her mouth tipped upward.

"Though the execution didn't go as planned, her strategy makes sense." Vlad nodded. "When you're in a bad situation, you might have to try unusual methods to get out of it." He patted Thorn's arm. "You have a very smart mate."

"Mate?" Elliott's face was lined with confusion. "You mean wife, right?"

"Yes, wife." Thorn placed an arm on the back of my chair. "And Saphira, if you bring that up again, I won't hesitate to lock you in the back with Peter." He grinned so wide he showed his bottom teeth.

Her face fell, and she crossed her arms. "Fine. I've been locked in a horrible room for far too long and unable to shi—"

I glared at her, cutting her off.

Her mouth dropped, and she cleared her throat a little too loudly. "Shit. Unable to shit." Her cheeks turned red as she realized what she'd said.

I laughed wholeheartedly. That was what she got for

giving *me* shit. The thought made me laugh even harder because the saying had the word *shit* in it. I was losing my shi—mind.

Elliott flinched and stepped back. He whispered to Eva, "These people are weird and make me uncomfortable. When Dad wakes up, I hope he'll push for some answers."

I tensed. I wished there was a way I could shield him from this world, but it was impossible. Drake was making sure of that.

Everly, he'll be fine. Look at Eva. She's already adjusting to everything, even though she's human, Thorn connected and leaned over to kiss my cheek. *They're your family and love you far more than you know.*

I wasn't sure that was the case. Both Elliott and Eva had always seemed indifferent to me.

A loud bang came on the door as Peter shouted, "Help! Someone help me!"

Lovely, the asshole was awake. Elliott was about to get his wish because Peter had to understand what we were up against. If he didn't cooperate, he could make our lives a whole lot harder.

Thorn and I stood and marched down the hall with Elliott, Eva, Cassidy, and Vlad right behind us.

It was time to face the devil that had haunted me for so long.

CHAPTER SEVENTEEN

AS I APPROACHED the bedroom to confront Peter, my body coiled tighter. This man had been indifferent to me for the fourteen years I'd lived with him, and after Mom had passed, if I'd stayed in his presence too long, he'd become cruel. To keep my promise to Mom to protect my siblings, I'd had to lie low and not push him so he would allow me back into *his* home.

Avoiding him was ingrained in me.

But to keep that promise to Mom, I had to face him. If I let him push me around, Eva's life would become worse than death, and Elliott would likely die.

I turned left to continue down the hallway, passing the door to Thorn's room and the second bedroom, which Thorn had originally placed me in when he'd kidnapped me on my way to the chateau.

Outside the door to the bedroom that held Peter, I stood still and tried to gather my wits. My racing heart wasn't helping matters; instead of slowing to help my calm settle in, it was going faster.

You don't have to do this, Thorn connected and placed

a hand on my shoulder. *You can go back to the living room, and I'll handle him. It would be my pleasure and honor.*

His anger thrummed through our connection, and I came close to smiling. Who would've thought that having a man who was willing to protect me at all costs would be this damn thrilling? Before Thorn, the thought of anyone taking care of me had sat uneasily with me. I didn't want to wind up like Mom, whose husband had essentially turned his back on her in the months before her death. I wanted to be independent and self-reliant, but now I realized I could be those things with a strong man beside me, which meant I had to be part of this conversation. "It's something I have to do."

Elliott fidgeted and asked, "Uh...who are you talking to? No one said anything."

I flinched. I'd been so focused on Peter that I'd answered Thorn out loud. My carelessness would make Elliott more uneasy, so the truth had to come out.

I glanced at Eva, who nodded as if she already knew what I was thinking.

Peter banged on the door again, yelling, "Somebody, please help me!"

Let's just do this, I connected with Thorn. I'd learned a long time ago that dragging out something you didn't want to do only made the anxiety worse. Elliott's uneasy glances were already making my skin crawl.

Okay. Thorn removed the key from his pocket and unlocked the door. As soon as it clicked, Peter gasped and stumbled back from the door.

I snorted. I couldn't help it. He'd begged for help, but when someone came, he clearly regretted it.

The door swung open, and Peter came into view. He

rubbed his head where Thorn had punched him, and his irises were dark, like he was in pain.

"Headache?" I asked, strolling into the metal-lined room.

The dark metal reminded me of aluminum foil, and it covered the entire space from floor to ceiling. The room was set up similarly to the other two bedrooms with a bed against the outside wall, a barred window to the left, and a small dresser in the far-right corner. A door on the left led to a tiny bathroom, which was covered in metal, as well.

He scowled. "Yes! Your *husband* knocked me out and locked me in a room. Wait until I get out of here."

Thorn entered and stood next to me, and Peter cowered.

"Dad?" Elliott rushed inside the room and stopped a foot away, his worried eyes scanning his father. "Are you okay?"

"No, I'm not *okay*." Peter dropped his hands and glared at Thorn and me as Eva, Cassidy, and Vlad tensed. My stepdad continued, "They forced us to leave against our will, and now they've dragged Eva into this. Drake will have my head."

Eva shook her head. "They didn't *drag* me into this. They got me out of it. You have no idea what Drake is like."

"Please." Peter wrinkled his nose. "If Everly hadn't run off with this walking steroid-induced muscle freak, she'd be with Drake, taking your spot as she promised, and *you* wouldn't be involved."

Head tilting back, Elliott looked at me, brows furrowed.

"Do *not* talk about my son that way," Cassidy hissed between her teeth, stalking forward, her pupils slitting. "He's a better man than you by leaps and bounds."

Vlad caught her wrist and tugged her back into him.

This was what Peter did. He tried to control the situation with harsh words and manipulation. I was so over the entire thing. "Maybe if you hadn't embezzled money from the Hales, neither I nor Eva would be involved."

"What?" Eva gasped. "You embezzled money from them?"

Not wanting him to change the subject, I told her, "That's why you were initially promised...as payment. I found out and took your place, but things went awry. If Peter hadn't stolen money, this would be a non-issue." Although, I couldn't get too upset about it. It had led me to Thorn.

Nostrils flaring, Peter stepped around Elliott to get closer to me. "If it weren't for Kelly, I wouldn't have had to embezzle money. Her sickness damn near ruined our family."

A cold realization washed over me. "Is that why you were so cruel to her in the end? Because treating her cancer was putting a strain on you financially?" I'd always wondered what had changed him from a caring husband and father to someone who ignored us to the best of his ability.

"Yes, she was going to die. Why stay in the hospital and rack up all those bills?"

My vision turned cloudy, and my eyes burned. "Because she was in intense pain and didn't want to die in our house, where Eva and Elliott would have had to watch her dead body be carried out. She didn't want those memories to haunt them."

"So, she wanted to be a burden?" Peter snorted darkly. "*My* burden, which forced me to deal with *you.*"

Though I'd always known he felt that way, hearing it was worse than I'd anticipated. At least, it was out there—

the elephant that had been shadowing our relationship if you could call it that.

Thorn snarled and stepped in front of me.

But Cassie was the one who spoke in a deep rasp. "Listen here. The day you chose to marry Kelly was the day you took on the responsibility of not only being a father to the twins but to Everly, too. If you didn't want that responsibility, why marry her?"

"Because she got pregnant." Peter ran his hands through his hair. "I wanted an heir for the family company, so I asked her to marry me. When she was healthy, it was tolerable. She handled all the children, but when she got sick—" He took a step back toward the wall.

Hurt was etched onto Elliott's and Eva's faces. Eva whimpered, "I always told myself it was because you were dealing with losing her, but that wasn't it." She stomped her foot and clenched her hands. "Then you were willingly going to hand me over to a dragon shifter prince to be his *breeder?*"

Peter huffed and rolled his eyes. "Don't be dramatic. The Hales may be strong and powerful, but dragons and being a breeder? Come on!"

"She's not being dramatic." It was time for Peter to understand what he'd done, though I doubted he'd care. "They are dragon shifters, and he had no intention of making Eva his wife."

"Wait." Elliott stumbled back a few steps. "Is that why your eyes do weird things, and you were talking about shifting to get away?" He bit his bottom lip and glanced at me. "But you...you're not one. How could you be with him?" He gestured to Thorn.

I licked my lips and stepped around Thorn to see my brother better. Thorn placed a hand on my arm, the jolt thrumming through my body. His action, and the way his feelings swirled through our bond, told me everything I needed to know without him saying a word—he was right here with me.

"That's the thing." I inhaled, trying to keep my voice level. "I am one. Now."

His jaw dropped, and his attention flicked between Thorn and me. Finally, he asked, "Did he bite you?"

Saphira laughed from the living room, confirming everyone in there was eavesdropping on the conversation.

Damn dragon hearing.

"He turned me, but not with a bite." We were getting off-topic, but Elliott had a right to some answers. "I fell and would've died if he hadn't used his abilities to change me so I could heal faster."

Elliott inched away, his legs hitting the footboard of the bed.

Sighing, Thorn lifted his hand slowly. "Don't worry. I won't change you."

His shoulders relaxed marginally.

"Don't be an idiot," Peter scoffed and smacked Elliott on the back of his head. "You're completely gullible if you believe that."

A low snarl emanated from my chest as I stepped toward Peter. It was one thing when he treated me that way, but I would not tolerate him treating my siblings like that. "Touch him again, and what Thorn did to you will be a walk in a park compared to what I will do."

Peter scowled.

"Dad, it *is* true." Eva moved to stand between Peter and me. "I saw people shift right in front of my eyes. Dragons are real, and Drake wants to use me as a breeder."

"Why?" Peter tilted his head back and winced as if the

movement hurt. "If they're dragon shifters, why would they need a human to have kids with? Seems like it would weaken the genetic line, especially with someone like her." He waved his hand at me.

"Clearly, you didn't learn what happens when you insult my mate." Thorn sneered and tugged me behind him again.

Vlad cut his son off. "Though tactless, Peter asked a fair question. In general, we live to be around five hundred. Because of our long-life expectancy, our women don't reproduce very often. Normally, each couple is successful with one child, two if they're lucky. Over the last two centuries, more dragons have died than have been born, so our numbers are getting dangerously low. Drake thinks the solution is to attempt to have multiple children with a human, while also having a wife to bear a true heir."

"He's operating under the assumption that dragon magic is strong enough that any child born will be a dragon." Cassidy rubbed her forehead. "Though, no one I know can prove that. For all we know, the human could die."

Elliott wrung his hands together. "Let me get this straight. Drake is a dragon prince who wants to screw both my sisters, and we're hiding from him to ensure that it doesn't happen?"

I nodded and leaned into Thorn's side, needing his support depending on how my brother reacted.

Eyes bulging, Elliott beamed. "That's *badass*. Dude. I should've played *Spyro* when it came out on the PS. I could've prepped on how to fight dragons!"

I rolled my eyes. Everything led back to video games with him.

Eva chuckled. "Really? Badass? Not what I was going for, but I was Drake's prisoner when I found out. But I'm sure our daily battles in *Demon's Souls* will suit us just as well."

Peter's attention homed in on me. Disbelief poured from him, but I didn't give a damn. He'd soon learn we weren't lying.

"I'll take my chances." Peter lifted his chin, though he moved his head slowly. "Release me, before I call the cops."

"How will you do that?" Thorn bared his teeth. "I took your phone, but you should already know that."

Peter harrumphed. "When I don't show up to work tomorrow, people will search for me. If you let me out now, I'll blame it on *her*." He pointed at me.

Lovely. He was willing to let his own stepdaughter go to jail without batting an eye.

"That's a risk every single one of us is willing to take." Vlad nodded to the door.

He wanted us to leave, and I was more than willing.

Cassidy walked out the door first and paused at the frame. "I'll bring you some dinner, but it's best if you stay in here."

"What?" Peter hissed. "You're going to lock me alone in here where I can't watch over my own kids?"

Now he was playing the doting parent?

"It's fine. Elliott and I can stay in here with him." Eva gestured to the door and flicked her gaze to me. "I'm tired anyway, after the crazy afternoon."

"But the game!" Elliott pouted. When Eva gave him a look, he exhaled and said, "Can wait 'til morning."

I hated to leave them in here with Peter, but something told me Eva had her own agenda. I followed Vlad out the door but paused and said over my shoulder, "If you need anything, just holler. I'll hear." Then I continued without looking back, not wanting to see Peter again.

Thorn shut the door behind us and locked it. "Dad, here." He reached around me to give Vlad the key. "Everly needs to rest after everything that happened today. I'm going to put her to bed."

His father smiled. "That sounds like a good plan. We won't be too far behind you. My wounds are healing, but rest will speed up the process. Cassidy and Saphira were already talking about sleeping arrangements, so we can take it from here."

After learning why Peter resented Mom and me and everything in between, the day had caught up to me. I hadn't gotten back to Thorn a moment too soon because I wasn't sure I could've gotten through this alone.

Thorn placed a hand on the middle of my back, guiding me to our bedroom. "Oh, and Everly," Vlad called out. "Welcome to the family. I look forward to spending more time with you when we're all better rested."

At his sincerity, the pain swirling through me ebbed, and I smiled in return. "I look forward to the same and to being part of a family."

As Vlad turned back to the living room, Thorn and I stepped into our bedroom. I crawled into bed as he shut the door and quickly joined me. I snuggled against his chest, listening to his breathing and heartbeat. There was no sound more beautiful.

My body thrummed from having his arms around me.

He kissed my forehead, his lips so warm and firm. *Ev, get some sleep.*

What happened to all the sex? I teased, but my eyes were shut and unable to open.

His chest shook with quiet laughter. *Oh, it'll happen, but we have tomorrow and every day after. I won't lose you again. Rest now because you'll need your stamina.*

My cheeks hurt from smiling as I drifted off to sleep.

The smell of bacon, eggs, and pancakes hit my senses, and my eyes cracked open. The comforting jolt of Thorn still buzzed across my skin, and I glanced up to find him watching me.

His sky-blue irises sparkled, and a tender smile filled his face. *You are somehow more gorgeous while you sleep. I hadn't gotten a chance to watch you sleep before now.*

I winced. Though he hadn't meant it maliciously, guilt still weighed on me. After all, I'd snuck out on him after our first night together, after we'd completed our bond.

My stomach grumbled, and my mouth watered. I wasn't sure how I could be this hungry.

Untangling from me, Thorn stood and gestured to the door. "Your food awaits, my lady."

I rolled my eyes just as Cassidy called from the kitchen, "Everyone, come and get it before it gets cold."

I crawled out of bed and ran my fingers through my hair to tame the beast on top of my head then quickly grabbed one of my outfits from the duffel bag. I put on a pair of black shorts and a flowy, olive-green top, while Thorn dressed in jeans and a navy shirt.

We held hands as we walked into the kitchen, where every seat was already taken, even one of the futon chairs with Tyson, Saphira, and Brenton.

Peter, Eva, and Elliott were sitting at the table between Vlad and Erroll. Though Peter wasn't handcuffed, I wasn't concerned with Vlad and Cassie nearby. They could handle him.

Thorn and I filled our plates and hurried to the vacant futon to eat breakfast.

I enjoyed sitting next to my mate while hearing chatter about normal topics around the kitchen. Peter was silent, but everyone else discussed the weather, hiking, and what we should do today. Of course, Elliott was hell-bent on playing video games.

Saphira and Tyson were trying to one-up each other with some sort of roasting. I caught that Saphira had a mouth bigger than the Eiffel Tower. In many ways, those two reminded me more of siblings than cousins.

You're happy, Thorn connected as he set his plate on the coffee table in front of us.

There was no point in denying it. *It just seems normal, which is amazing after going through hell. Let's go on the hike with Vlad, Cassidy, and Errol.* I used to hate hiking but getting out into nature after being trapped in the chateau for so long sounded perfect...and being away from Peter made it even more appealing.

Just no sliding down any hills, Thorn teased and kissed my cheek.

A cell phone rang, breaking the moment.

I glanced over my shoulder and saw Vlad remove his phone from his back pocket. His jaw tensed. "It's the king."

"King?" Elliott echoed. "Wait. Is that Arman?"

"Elliott, what did we talk about last night?" Peter snapped. "They're just messing with us, and for some reason, your sister has agreed to go along with it."

"I told you it's all *true.*" Eva huffed as the phone rang a third time. "And it was pure hell being there."

Neither of us wanted to go back.

Cassidy pointed to the phone. "You better answer."

Standing, Errol moved behind Peter and placed a hand over my stepdad's mouth. Peter grunted and tried to move his head, but Errol didn't budge.

With Peter contained, Vlad answered, "Hello?"

My dragon ears could hear it all. King Arman said,

"Run. Now. They've found you, and a huge group of warriors is heading your way."

Vlad hung up, and the room went silent, except for Peter's mumbles.

My blood turned cold. Just when I'd felt safe enough to want to hike, this happened.

"How did they find us?" Brenton's hands shook.

I should've realized this last night. "Didn't you say he had a phone?"

Thorn nodded. "Why?"

"His biggest client is the Hales. They gave him a phone to ensure they could reach him at all times." And it was in the house with us. We should've thrown it out last night.

Peter laughed, and as soon as Errol removed his hand, he said, "I told you last night that, if you let me go, I'd blame it on her. But no."

That was why he'd been so cocky.

"Drake tracked us with it." Vlad groaned as he jumped to his feet. "I took the phone away from him last night while you were showering, but I didn't think about them tracking it."

"We've gotta get out of here." Errol glanced at Saphira, his eyes wide with fear. "They'll be here in less than thirty minutes. Is there another place we can go?"

"No." Vlad pinched the bridge of his nose. "Since we lived in Atlanta, I sold my backup houses because the city was so expensive. I only kept this one because it was close by."

"It doesn't matter where we're heading as long as we get Everly away from *here*." Thorn climbed to his feet so fast he damn near blurred. "We can shift and get out of here."

"Shifting will help them track us. Our scents could linger in the air." Vlad licked his lips. "We'll have a better chance at getting away by vehicle." He glanced at the phone. "There is a place we can go, but we should rent two cars, so they won't be able to spot us easily when we're farther from the city."

Thorn and Eva had to get out of here. Drake would take Eva to be his breeder and kill Thorn. Neither was going to happen.

Elliott blanched but ran toward the television and began unplugging the gaming system. Instead of asking about shifting and scents, he'd decided to use the extra time to salvage his games...again. A reaction I would never understand.

"Mom and Dad, take the truck keys on the key chain by the front door. We can't risk leaving the truck behind in case they can glean information about the full name I go by now," Thorn instructed and turned to me, placing his hands on my shoulders. "Eva, Elliott, Peter, Everly, and I will take her Audi. Everyone else, get into Brenton's vehicle. We've got to go."

Everyone dispersed. Elliott strode out of the cabin, balancing the gaming system, with Eva right behind him. I snatched the keys from the hook by the door and unlocked the car, climbing into the passenger seat.

That was when I realized Thorn and Peter hadn't come out. Thorn wouldn't delay unless something had gone wrong.

Peter had to be up to something.

"Stay here," I instructed and opened the car door in time to hear a loud crash from inside the cabin.

CHAPTER EIGHTEEN

I SHOULDN'T HAVE RUN out without making sure Peter was following. I should've known he'd try something, but instead, I'd left Thorn to handle my stepdad alone. Of course, Thorn knew he couldn't be trusted.

Anger flared through our connection, and my blood boiled. Whatever Peter was doing had pissed off my mate.

The front door was still open, so I breezed into the living room in time to watch Thorn punch Peter in the head. His eyes rolled back as his body crumpled. Thorn didn't even try to catch him. He let Peter's body hit the wooden floor between the kitchen and living room.

"What did he do?" I breathed as I reached Thorn's side.

A metallic stench hit me. I looked at his upper arm, which had a deep cut. My jaw clenched.

"I'm fine." He bent and tossed Peter over his shoulder. "He snatched a knife when we were all dispersing and used it on me when I tried to force him to leave."

My chest constricted. "I'm sorry."

"For what? Your mom marrying a douchebag?" He took

my hand and tugged me to the door. "It's not your fault. Stop taking on that responsibility."

His words were like a slap to the face. I often apologized for things that weren't my fault, but in this instance, I felt like it was. *If it wasn't for me, Peter wouldn't be here cutting you.*

Having you in my life has made me the happiest I've ever been, he replied as we stepped back outside. *I'd happily let him cut me every day if that was the price of finding you.*

My chest ached from the way it expanded. I'd never felt so happy, even when Mom was alive.

Mom.

I froze. "I need my bracelet." Mom had given me the bracelet after getting diagnosed with cancer. I'd left it behind with Thorn when I'd run off to hand myself over to Drake. I'd wanted to leave a piece of myself behind for him, and it was the one item I truly valued.

He squeezed my hand and replied, "That's what I was getting when Peter grabbed the knife." He patted his jeans pocket. "It's in here. I'll give it to you once we get into the car. I know how much it means to you and didn't want to leave it behind. We might not be able to come back."

Tears burned my eyes. Of course he'd done that for me. In the short time we'd been together, he'd come to know me better than I knew myself—in some ways, anticipating my needs before I did.

Vlad backed up the white, beat-up pickup truck and rolled down the window. "Follow me. I have an idea where we can go."

Nodding, Thorn rushed to my Audi and tossed Peter in the back driver's side seat. Eva resettled in the center as I hurried to the front passenger door. I was all for Thorn driving, especially if the dragons arrived before we got away. I didn't want to try to outmaneuver them, and I suspected Thorn was more than capable of doing it.

As soon as I shut the door, Vlad pulled out, and Brenton followed right behind him.

Thorn slid behind the wheel and started the engine.

When he put on his seat belt, he winced, reminding me of the cut on his arm.

My shoulders drooped. *I can drive if it's uncomfortable for you.*

I'm fine. He put the car in reverse.

Vlad and Brenton took off, driving faster than normal, and unease settled over me. In one swoop, Thorn had put the car in drive and caught up.

The dirt road jarred us as we ran over branches and pebbles.

Eva sighed. "Did you have to knock him out?"

I glanced over my shoulder to see Peter slumped against her.

"He stabbed me, so be thankful that's the worst he got." Thorn tightened his hands on the wheel. "No promises if he's rude to Everly again. I don't care if it's just a scowl. I will do more than knock his ass out."

My dragon purred, and my heart skipped a beat.

"Uh...is that noise coming from Everly?" Elliott asked from behind me. "Because I'm certain there's no cat in here."

My face flamed. Thank goodness Saphira wasn't here, or she'd start in on the cat jokes again.

Do not be ashamed. Thorn reached over and took my hand. *A dragon purring means they are happy and feel loved. The sound is dead sexy.*

I bit my lower lip, and some of my spirits dampened— I'd never heard Thorn purr when he was with me. But now, while we were trying to get away from impending warriors, wasn't the time to discuss that.

Glancing at the sky, I exhaled when I didn't see any dragons. The woods thickened around us as the three vehicles hurried down the dirt road. We were still in danger because we hadn't passed another house, and if the dragons got close, they'd know it was us.

"Seriously." Elliott cleared his throat. "Is that a dragon thing? Purring?"

He wouldn't let it go.

"No clue." Eva groaned. "She never did it back at the prison." Something thumped in the back seat, and I assumed it was Peter hitting the door, but I didn't care enough to look.

"Wait!" Elliott squeaked. "Drake put you two in *prison*? No fucking way."

Thorn fisted his hands. *You didn't tell me that. I thought you were in the guest house.*

"She meant it metaphorically. Neither of us wanted to be there, and warriors were watching us constantly."

"Everly even had to pretend she had stomach issues to try to talk to one of the warriors alone," Eva snorted.

Every rash decision I'd made would haunt me for the rest of my life. Even if I managed to forget for a while, Eva and Saphira would constantly remind me of every ridiculous thing I'd done. I was surprised the twins hadn't brought up the time when I was sixteen and Mom had asked me to mail her and Peter's tax returns, and I'd bought a penny stamp to send it. I'd been so confused about why anyone would buy more expensive stamps when they sold some for a penny. When Mom had explained, she'd exclaimed that, for someone so smart, I did some pretty silly things. Not that I would dare bring up that story to any of them.

"Oh." Elliott leaned forward. "What kind of stomach issues? Like the explosive kind, the cramping kind, or the scent-alone-could-kill-everyone-who-came-into-contact kind?"

I sighed. My siblings had never been interested in what was going on in my life...until now.

The corners of Thorn's mouth tipped up, and he glanced at me. "That's a valid question."

Traitor. I squinched my nose at him.

"Everything with you is either poop or blood." Eva huffed.

"Yeah. The two best things in life," Elliott scoffed. "You need blood to get the oxygen to your organs, and you need to poop to get rid of the stuff your body doesn't need."

Unfortunately, he wasn't wrong.

Elliott grasped the headrest as he leaned forward. "So, which poop issue did you pretend to have?"

The best thing I could do was answer and hope we moved on. "The kind that clogs the toilet, but despite it being pretend, I'd rather not talk about it."

"Mad respect." His hands disappeared as he sat back in his seat. "A total twofer. Cramping *and* smell."

The main road came into view, and some tension left my body. If we could blend in with the traffic, we might be home free.

We turned west. *Where are we heading?*

No clue. Thorn flicked his attention to the sky. *Dad has figured something out. I'm sure we'll stop somewhere soon to rent some vehicles. The last thing we need is for Drake and the warriors to be searching for your and Brenton's vehicles. Drake could issue an alert on the Dragonnet, and dragon shifters would be watching for us.*

Dragonnet? There were so many things I still had to learn.

He nodded. *It's an intranet for dragons. They post announcements, news, and any speeches the royals desire to deliver. It's the one-stop space for all dragon happenings, activities of other thunders, and all other relevant information.*

Now I remembered that he'd mentioned it before.

Out of the corner of my eye, something moved high in the sky. I turned my head...and my breath caught. Forty warriors were flying so high that no humans would be able to make them out...but I knew they had dragon sight.

We'd barely missed them, and luckily, there were now several vehicles on the road. They didn't expect us to know they were coming.

Thank goodness King Arman had warned us.

Thorn, I connected.

I see them, he replied and took my hand. *We'll be out of here before they realize we're gone, and they won't be able to track us down by scent.*

That didn't mean they wouldn't scour the area. My pulse quickened, but I forced myself not to tense. I didn't want to alert Elliott or Eva that something was amiss.

"Oh, hey." Thorn released my hand and reached into his pocket. He removed my bracelet and placed it into my hand.

The white gold was warm, and I ran my fingers across the interlinking small hearts and diamonds that clasped in the back. With my other hand, I touched the two white gold hearts hanging down. The first heart was inscribed with *Everly* and the other with *The love between a mother and daughter is forever*. A lump formed in my throat as my heart swirled with emotions. I'd do anything to have her here with me, but at the same time, it was also best that she wasn't here now. She'd be another pawn for Drake to use against me, and he had enough of those.

I put the bracelet on and took Thorn's hand again, enjoying the jolt of our connection and the smooth metal against my skin.

Lean your head back and get some rest, he said and squeezed my hand comfortingly.

I arched a brow. *Really? We just woke up.*

He cut his eyes to me. *At least, try to relax. Or I'll get Elliott talking about poop again.*

Who are you? My mate or Saphira? I leaned my head back, pretending I was upset. *You look like Thorn but sound like her. I'm all sorts of confused over here.*

If we weren't in a hurry to get away, and if your siblings weren't in the back seat, I'd make sure to alleviate all of your confusion. He winked.

Heat swarmed through my body, and he grinned wickedly.

Tease, I connected.

His look stole my breath. He was so damn handsome in every way. I couldn't wait to paint him one day. I had to; he was a masterpiece.

Using the buttons on the steering wheel, he turned on the radio and scanned the stations. I fidgeted and got comfortable, staring out the window as "Blackhole Sun" by Soundgarden played, thankful that I had Thorn in my life.

Two hours later, we were pulling out of an Enterprise Rent-A-Car in two Suburbans. Apparently, Vlad was a man of many talents and had fake IDs for himself and Cassidy, so they'd put the cars under their aliases and opted for the company's rental insurance.

We parked the other vehicles across town in a motel lot. If the warriors found them, they wouldn't automatically realize we had rented cars.

Everyone from my Audi climbed into the Suburban that Cassidy was driving, while everyone else climbed into the one with Vlad. We put Peter in the passenger seat so we could keep an eye on him. He sat silently pouting, which I was all about. It was just as good as him being unconscious.

Thorn sat behind Cassidy, and I opted to take the seat behind Peter, since I had shorter legs, which left Elliott and Eva in the far back. Elliott had pulled out a Nintendo Switch, which he and Eva were playing. I swore the boy had a game stowed away everywhere.

As soon as we got on the interstate, heading northwest again, Thorn tapped his hands on his leg. "There's only one place I can think of in this direction, but Vlad would never take us there."

My mouth went dry. That sounded ominous. *What are you talking about?*

"His family thunder." The area around Thorn's eyes tightened. "He hasn't been back there or even spoken to anyone, including his parents, since we hid away in Atlanta."

"Desperate times call for even more desperate measures." Cassidy glanced in the rearview mirror. "We have nowhere else to go."

"What about a hotel?" The last thing I wanted to do was put more people in danger.

"We don't have unlimited funds, and Drake will have dragon shifters searching for us. They know what we all look like." Cassidy watched the road. "We can't get jobs and risk them finding us, we can't go back home to Atlanta, and the cabin has been compromised. We literally have nowhere else to go. I tried talking him out of it, but we're out of options."

My leg bounced. *Maybe I should go back. If he has me—*

Thorn's pupils slitted, and he growled so loudly that the car shook. "That is *not* an option, Everly. If you so much as think that again, I will not let you out of my sight...*ever*."

"Whoa," Elliott gasped from behind me. "That's badass, but I *never* want to get on his bad side."

"It took *this* for you to realize that?" Eva sighed. "Not him punching out Dad twice?"

"Eh. Dad's an ass." Elliott's tone held some anger.

Peter glared over his seat at his son, but surprisingly, he remained silent.

If Thorn hadn't been so angry with me, I would've pushed the topic more.

"I'm not trying to upset you but look at how many of us are on the run. Going to another thunder could add more people to that number," I said and took his hand, but he didn't squeeze back like normal.

"What Thorn is trying to say, not so eloquently, is that there is one thing Drake wants more than you." Cassidy changed lanes, following Vlad. "Thorn. Even if you handed yourself over, he won't stop looking for us. Vlad and I were captured before you were promised to Drake."

I hung my head. Regret surged through me. "You're right. I wasn't thinking." I stared at the floorboard and removed my hand from Thorn's.

At the last second, he snatched it back. *I know you're trying to help, but I just got you back, and you're already considering doing the same damn thing all over again.*

You're right. Why did I keep wanting to sacrifice

myself? I wasn't a martyr, nor did I want to be. I just wanted *him* and my siblings safe...no matter the cost. But they were right. Even if I turned myself in, that wouldn't be enough... not for Drake. *I'm sorry.*

I need to know you won't ever do something like that again. He clutched my hand tighter.

I promise. I don't know what I was thinking. I wanted to kick myself for even considering it.

Some of his worry eased. *Good, because otherwise, I might have to give you a spanking.* A twinkle returned to his eye as his playfulness swirled inside me.

The vehicle fell back into a comfortable silence.

<hr>

AN HOUR LATER, we passed through the small, quaint town of Mount Airy, North Carolina. Several miles past that, we turned onto a gravel road.

The Suburban bumped and jolted as we passed a few ranches and drove deeper into the woods. The houses were spread a few miles apart, and I was surprised the dirt road continued for so long. This had to be the thunder neighborhood.

Fifteen miles from the last paved road, Vlad pulled into a driveway. Before the vehicles were turned off, the front door of the white ranch house had opened, and an older man and woman rushed onto the wooden porch.

Vlad got out of the Suburban. "Mom. Dad. We need your help."

"You're alive," the man said, his voice quivering. He was close to seven feet tall with gray hair and a matching beard with a few hints of brown. He took a step toward Vlad but stopped when Thorn climbed out of the car.

"My baby boy." The woman's voice shook as tears trickled from her slate-gray eyes. Her hair was ashy blonde, several shades lighter than her son's. As she passed her husband, Vlad's father grabbed her arm.

The warmth vanished from his cobalt eyes. He glared at Thorn then flicked his attention to Vlad. "What have you done?"

CHAPTER NINETEEN

MY HEART STOPPED. Vlad's parents recognized Thorn...but how? He'd been in hiding since he was six, and the only reason the royals knew what he looked like was because he'd shown up to save me.

"I can explain." Vlad lifted a hand. "But it would be better if you let us into the house before others see us."

His dad's body coiled, but his mom rushed over and hugged Vlad.

A lump formed in my throat. There was no way he was going to let us in. I clenched my hands, jumped out of the Suburban, then marched around the hood, ready to aid Vlad.

"Aiden." Vlad's mother pulled back and placed a hand on his father's forearm. "He's our son, and we've both missed him dearly. We can at least hear him out."

Huffing, Aiden scanned the area behind us. Pain flashed in his eyes. "Fine." He patted his mate's arm before dropping his hand and schooling his face into a stern expression. "But all of you get in here. The last thing we need is someone from the thunder seeing you without warning."

"Agreed." Vlad swirled a finger around, indicating we needed to move.

As Thorn hurried past me, his arm brushed mine, and the jolt surged through my body. Every touch from him was like a high I never wanted to come down from.

My siblings climbed out of the car, and my attention landed on Elliott. As expected, the Nintendo Switch bulged from his pocket. No wonder he wore baggy jeans. How else could he carry around his electronics?

I snapped my fingers and gestured to the game. "Leave it in the car."

"What?" Elliott lurched back and stuck out his bottom lip. "But they'll be talking, and I'll get bored."

Sometimes, it was hard to remember he was considered an adult. I lifted my head. "Boredom helps creativity. It's healthy to be bored from time to time." Mom had often told me that whenever I'd complain. One day, when I was a toddler, I'd gotten so bored that I must have driven her to her breaking point. At the time, we'd been tight on money, so she'd decided to splurge and buy some finger paints, starting my love of painting.

Elliott and Eva never learned that love because Peter had bought them all kinds of gadgets to keep them entertained.

His irises darkened with hurt. "Now you sound like Mom."

My heart panged, and I smiled sadly. "I'll take that as a compliment."

"Hurry up," Aiden rasped as he held open the front door.

I couldn't blame him for his uneasiness. If he knew who Thorn was, he knew he was inviting trouble into his home.

Vlad held out his hand, and Cassidy hurried to him as Thorn dashed to the driver's side back door to monitor Peter. My stepfather climbed out, and they glared at each other as we headed to the house.

Head hanging, Aiden sighed. "Dammit, Alina. They also brought humans. I should've listened to my gut."

"You did." Alina brushed a hand over his shoulder before stepping into the house. "You just needed me to guide you."

Vlad and Cassidy paused in front of the door, and Aiden blew a raspberry as he stepped to the side, allowing our group to enter.

One by one, we walked into the house, Thorn and I taking up the rear.

We stepped into the living room. It was large enough to hold all thirteen of us, but only two hunter green couches faced each other in the middle of the room. A black coffee table sat in the center with an open laptop on it. The walls were off-white, and a beige carpet ran everywhere I could see. The house must have been built in the eighties because it had popcorn ceilings.

Thorn walked behind a couch, and Peter went to a corner of the room. I stopped close by, so I could keep an eye on him.

Aiden's mom smiled as she strolled to Cassidy. "You're mated to my son."

"I am." Cassidy beamed. "I'm so glad to finally meet you."

Saphira snorted and plopped onto a couch. "Someone stand in front of the door. We don't need this one getting away." She gestured to Peter.

"Man." Elliott shuddered as he strolled over and sat next to her. "Let me tell you, even if he did get out, his sense of direction's crap. Dad can't find anything in Asheville, and he's lived there his entire life."

Good to know, Thorn connected as he moved beside me and took my hand. *Your brother is a wealth of information.*

He is. I hadn't even known that about Peter. This was the most talkative Elliot had ever been. It was like meeting a new person.

"Well, maybe we should let him go, then." Tyson sat across from Saphira, his brown eyes sparkling with interest. "He's been a pain."

"Even when the cops told him to come to my friend's house, he got lost." Elliott snickered.

Peter scowled. "Let's not bring up that night. No one wants to relive the phone call from the cops informing me that they found my *son* at a party with his pants down."

Saphira's brows furrowed. "Why were your pants down?"

"Of course, someone would ask." Eva grimaced. She knew the story.

"Senior prom." Elliott pounded his chest. "Me and some of the guys drank a lot and wanted to see how fast we could extinguish the bonfire."

Eva closed her eyes as if something were haunting her. "They decided to do it in front of us girls. Let's just say Dad was pissed when he didn't get the deposit back for Elliott's tux. Pee on a bonfire is one of the worst smells I've ever experienced in my whole life."

Errol took the spot on the other end of the couch Tyson was sitting on. The older man leaned back and murmured, "Thank gods I had a daughter."

"Oh, don't worry, Uncle Errol. Saphira has done—" Tyson started.

Saphira pointed at him and snarled, "Do *not* finish that sentence."

Chuckling, Brenton took the middle spot between his son and brother. "Yes, son. Don't."

"Is this why you came?" Aiden asked as he crossed his arms and glared at Vlad, who stood next to him. "To talk about peeing on bonfires? We don't hear anything from you for twenty-one years, and then you pull up with *him*"—he pointed at Thorn—"and three humans who aren't supposed to know about our existence."

Cassidy bristled but didn't say anything...at least out loud.

"No. They just *talk*. Incessantly." Vlad rubbed his hands together. "And I didn't reach out for the past twenty-one years to protect you."

"From what?" Aiden spread his arms. "Because it sure seems like you brought a shitstorm to our door."

"We thought you were dead." Alina stepped between Vlad and Aiden and placed a shaky hand on her son's arm. "We knew if you were alive, you wouldn't just disappear without a word, but it's apparent we were wrong."

Vlad ran his hands through his hair. "Remember the last job I left to do?"

Aiden's brows furrowed. "You mean the one you refused to tell us about? Something about the king and our security?"

"Yes," Vlad answered as he took Cassidy's hand. "The king hired me to kill someone who posed a threat to the dragon nation."

"Badass." Elliott bobbed his head, his eyes wide. "That's epic."

"It wasn't." Vlad cut his gaze to my brother. "I soon learned that the mission was to kill the six-year-old prince and his nanny."

Tyson sneered. "I knew the king was no good, especially with how he caters to his jackass son." He flinched and glanced at Thorn. "No offense."

Muscles tensing, Thorn shrugged. "Doesn't offend me. Vlad's my dad in all the ways that matter."

"Wait!" Elliott jumped to his feet. "You're a prince, too." His mouth dropped. "And you married my sister. Holy shit. I'm royalty!"

"I don't think that's how it works, E." Eva shook her head.

Errol chuckled. "That's definitely not how it works."

"Aw. Man." My brother sat back down like the world had treated him cruelly.

Patting his leg, Saphira winked. "Royalty is just a state of mind. If you think it, you can become it."

"Fuck, yeah." Elliott's entire body bobbed.

"Let me get this straight." Aiden rubbed the back of his neck. "The king hired you to do a job, and not only did you not follow through, but you also hid your targets from him?"

"He was a six-year-old *boy*," Cassidy snarled and turned to Aiden. "You'd be okay doing that if it was *your* job? And might I add, Thorn is an amazing, sweet, and loyal person. He doesn't deserve any of this."

"Sweet and loyal?" Aiden parroted and motioned to Peter. "We saw the video of the wedding where he kidnapped *her*." He gestured to me. "He stole people's dragons!"

Hurt, guilt, and love swirled from Thorn as he watched the situation unfold. I hated that he had to go through this, and I wouldn't let Cassidy and Vlad defend him alone. I lifted my chin. "Yes, he came to save me from being forced to marry a man I didn't want. And he, along with Vlad and Cassidy, *saved* my sister from becoming Drake's human breeder. He took those dragons, but we were outnumbered, and they were attacking us."

Aiden deflated. "They were forcing you to marry Prince Drake?"

I nodded.

"There's a more pressing question." Alina glanced from me to Eva. "Your sister is human? How is that possible?"

"I changed her." Thorn placed his hands on my shoulders. "And by doing so, I created my fated mate, who Drake tried to take away from me, after kidnapping Vlad and Cassidy."

My skin buzzed from his touch, and I leaned back against his large chest.

"The humans are here because Drake wants the one girl as his breeder and would use the other two to get you to turn yourself in." Aiden rubbed his temples and looked at Vlad. "You sure got yourself into a difficult situation."

"One I would gladly get into all over again if given the opportunity." Vlad focused on his parents. "When I attacked Thorn and Cassidy that day, twenty-one years ago, that little boy—the one the king was so desperate to kill— was more concerned about saving his nanny than himself. Yesterday, he walked into fire, knowing he was risking his life, to save his mate and her sister. In the twenty-one years in between, no one knew Thorn was alive. Everyone thought he was dead, and did he do anything to cause problems?"

Silence was the answer.

"You know he didn't, or it would've been all over the

Dragonnet, like the wedding is now." Vlad clasped his hands together. "We have nowhere else to go."

"I hate to interrupt and ruin this moment." Errol stood and placed his hands in the pockets of his dark slacks. "But won't this be the first place Drake looks for us?"

"Not the first." Vlad rubbed his mouth. "But they will come eventually. We need to make a plan instead of rushing everywhere."

I sighed. This was only a short-term solution.

Hey, it'll be okay, Thorn connected and wrapped his arms around me. *No matter what, they won't get you or Eva again. As soon as we get settled, I'll get us fake IDs, so we can get the hell out of here.*

I turned and stared into his gorgeous eyes. *Eva and I aren't the only ones I'm worried about. I don't want anything bad to happen to any of us.*

He brushed his fingers across my cheek and rested his forehead against mine. *We'll make sure they're all set up before we go.*

Why did he keep mentioning leaving? My throat went dry, but I didn't want to get into that discussion right now.

"Over twenty years ago, they were watching this location like a hawk, and Vlad never made so much as a phone call to us." Aiden's voice thickened. "They'll probably search wherever they tracked you to before checking here again. But they *will* come, and it will be sooner, rather than later. You can't stay here."

My limbs trembled, and my pulse pounded in my ears. My attention flicked to Vlad, whose face had gone white and stony.

He'd expected his parents to help us.

"Fine." Vlad lifted his chin. "I get it. But for what it's worth, I wasn't trying to hurt you."

"No. It's *not* fine." Cassidy stepped around him and stared both his parents down. "Do you know how hard he struggled with not reaching out to you? Every holiday, every birthday, hell, even on your anniversary, Vlad fell apart, wishing we were part of your lives and part of the thunder he grew up with. He sacrificed his world to protect Thorn, me, and *all* of you. He didn't want to burden you with the knowledge that would make you a target for the king's abuse and maliciousness. But now we're here, asking for the help you're so upset he didn't ask for twenty-one years ago, and you're turning us away? Why? For vengeance? To get back at him for protecting us?"

Even if Thorn hadn't told me, I would have known they were fated mates by the way they defended each other. Cassidy wouldn't let Vlad's parents hurt him without having her say.

"Why did he decide to stop protecting us?" Aiden lifted a brow. "Are we no longer worthy?"

Cassidy laughed bitterly. "That's not it, at all. He finally found a reason to come home. He's been hoping for one every day for the past twenty-one years, but nothing could justify it. Now, there *is* a reason, and your son needs your help. This was why I tried talking him out of coming here to begin with."

"That's what people do when given a chance." Thorn released me and took my hand, tugging me to follow him as he stepped up beside Vlad. "They disappoint you. All these years, Vlad talked about what an amazing man you are, but you're no better than the king. Let's go. We've wasted too much time here."

Thorn let go of me and forced Peter toward the door. Saphira and the others stood from the couches, and our group moved to leave.

When Vlad touched the doorknob, Alina called out, "Wait. Please don't leave. Not yet."

Aiden growled. "Alina."

I turned around to see the older woman glaring at him as she said, "You had your say. Now it's *my* turn to get stuff off my chest."

CHAPTER TWENTY

I HOPED whatever she was about to say would be in our favor. So far, in the face of Vlad's sudden resurrection, she'd been the more level-headed of the two.

Vlad didn't turn. He continued to face the door, his hand on the knob. Cassidy stood close, ready to defend her mate.

"Your father has made it clear where he stands, but as soon as you walk out the door and leave, he'll regret it." Alina flexed her fingers at her sides. "And, even if he doesn't, I won't stand here and turn my back on my son, even if Aiden is the leader of our thunder."

"Alina," Aiden growled, but the older woman ignored him.

"Unfortunately, I do agree it's too risky for you to stay here. Not just for us but for our thunder. The royals could be on their way here now. I can give you cash so you can rent rooms at a hotel the next town over, and I'll make some calls to find a place for you to stay in the near future."

My lungs inflated more freely again. I'd thought we

were doomed, and his mother was helping us, although mainly for Vlad's benefit.

Grimacing, Vlad slowly turned and looked at his mother.

The rest of us shuffled to the side so we weren't blocking their view of each other.

"Thank you," he rasped, his eyes glistening.

Though I hadn't been around him long, I already knew he was a strong, smart man, yet his parents had so much influence over him. From what I'd seen, parents didn't understand the lasting impact they had on their children until random moments of clarity like this.

My heart ached, and my fingers caressed the pendants of the bracelet Mom had given me. Even six years later, her loss still gaped inside me, especially when something good or bad happened, and I reached for the phone to call her, only to remember that was impossible.

Thorn pushed warm love and comfort through our connection, knowing exactly what I needed. Though I no longer had Mom, I had him, and that meant more to me than the world.

"Of course." Her body shook harder. When she stopped in front of him, a tear trickled down her cheek. "But it comes with one stipulation."

I tensed. I'd thought this had been going so well. Had that been an illusion?

Vlad huffed. "Which is?"

"You *can't* disappear on us again," she murmured and hugged him. "I can't survive it a second time."

His face crumpled, and Cassidy glanced at Thorn, then flicked her eyes toward the door.

She wanted us to leave, so I wasn't surprised when Thorn said, "Let's give Vlad a moment with his parents.

Everyone, get in the Suburbans. We'll leave as soon as he's ready." He walked over to Peter, standing close, not willing to risk my stepdad trying to run.

Saphira nodded. Gently nudging Alina and Vlad out of the way, she opened the door. We walked to the vehicles and climbed into the ones we'd ridden in here. Thorn put Peter back in the front passenger seat and got into the seat behind him to keep watch. He didn't trust Peter to sit behind us since he seemed to be trying to find a way to escape. At least, this way, he couldn't try to talk Elliott into doing something stupid like jumping out the back.

The front door opened, and Cassidy marched out with a sizable duffel bag.

Will Vlad be all right? I asked Thorn.

Removing his phone from his pocket, Thorn nodded. *I'm just glad Alina intervened. Vlad used to tell me his dad was fair, but tough, and I should be thankful Aiden wasn't the one who raised me. I thought Vlad had been exaggerating because he didn't coddle me at all. He allowed me to learn things on my own, and when something didn't work out, he was there to help me pick up the pieces, but he never fought my battles. I didn't think there could be a tougher man out there than him, but I saw how it was just now with his dad.*

Cassidy walked to the Suburban in front of ours and opened the door, then spoke to the people inside.

He's hurting, even though that doesn't make it right. I didn't want it to sound as if I was mitigating the agony Vlad had to be experiencing, but if the child I'd assumed was dead for the past twenty years suddenly reappeared, I'd be conflicted too. Half pissed that they'd let me grieve for that long and half overjoyed that they were alive. I could imagine the turmoil Vlad's parents were going through.

Cassidy turned to us, and Brenton jumped out of the back and into the driver's seat of that vehicle.

When Cassidy got into the driver's seat of our car, she exhaled a long breath and sat for a moment before stowing the duffel bag by Peter's feet. She started the engine and put the vehicle in reverse. "Vlad is staying here while we find a place. I'll let him know where we end up, so he can give his parents the address before shifting and joining us." She backed out of the driveway onto the gravel road. "Once we get away from here, we'll pull over and figure out where to stay."

"What about a hotel?" Eva asked from the back. "One that takes cash?"

"Do hotels actually take cash anymore?" Elliott scoffed. "I've never had more than five dollars in my pocket. I use Dad's credit card for everything."

In one way, I was glad my siblings were so sheltered, but that created a whole other set of problems for them in the world. "First off, we're likely talking about a motel, and second, we have to be careful where we stay, or Peter could cause problems."

"Problems?" Peter scoffed and snapped his head my way. "You mean trying to free myself and my children from a *kidnapping*?"

Thorn leaned forward, placing his hands on Peter's shoulders, and growled, "Do you need another lesson?"

My stepdad's response was a loud swallow.

"We can't risk anywhere too close to other people and that isn't soundproof." Thorn swiped his phone. "Can you give me a credit card that's under a different alias from the one you used to rent the cars? I found a house that can accommodate a group our size in Stuart, Virginia, thirty minutes from here."

"Perfect." Cassidy slowed the vehicle and took out a pink wallet with a rose engraved on the front. "Here. Tell me the address."

When he took the wallet from her, she pulled up the car's GPS and typed in *Stuart*. As soon as the directions loaded, she pressed the gas and headed back onto the main road.

I leaned my head back and closed my eyes, trying to release the knot that kept twisting in my stomach. Each time my heart pounded, I swore I could hear wings flapping, but there was nothing in the sky. I needed to get a handle on my nerves before I did something stupid and made a scene.

***

THIRTY MINUTES LATER, we pulled up to a three-story house that appeared to have been built in the eighties. The bottom half was brick, and the top half was wood panels. It resided on forty acres of property, which meant any neighbors nearby shouldn't be able to hear Peter.

There was a garage, but we parked both vehicles in the driveway, facing the road in case we needed to exit quickly. Ten steps led to a front porch with four teal Adirondack chairs angled invitingly toward each other. Behind the chairs was a large wooden door with a glass storm door in front of it.

As soon as the engine turned off, Peter sighed.

I wondered if there was anything like dragon metal that we could use to put him into a deep slumber until we got things settled. If dragons were real, then maybe Maleficent existed too, and she could spell something for him to prick his finger on and sleep for a hundred years.

One could hope, but Thorn had mentioned only wolf

and bear shifters. I hadn't asked about vampires, witches, demons, or angels.

My heart thudded, and my skin crawled. The idea of vampires wigged me out more than the others. I rubbed my neck where my pulse pounded under my skin.

Thorn glanced at me and linked, *I won't let him be rude to you. I'll knock him out in a split second if that will make you feel less uneasy.*

That's not it. My throat constricted with how much I felt for him. *I was wondering if vampires, witches, angels, and demons are real. I'm a dragon shifter, but I don't know anything about the supernatural world.*

His gaze softened. *Vampires and witches are real. Angels and demons are not. We won't run into vampires out here. They live in cities where their food source is all around. The bigger the city, the more vampires live there. Witches tend to live out in the woods and keep to themselves. Out here, we're more likely to run into witches than vampires, but even that's unlikely. Witches can sense energy, and they'd know we're here. They wouldn't come near us unless they needed something for themselves.*

Everyone got out of the vehicle, and Thorn connected as he stayed close by Peter, *The code is 4181210 to get in the house.*

I walked up the steps, opened the storm door, then punched the code into the device above the doorknob. There was a click, and I pushed the door open. We entered a large den with wood paneling and maple hardwood floors. Two black couches sat across from each other with two large black ottomans between them and centered in front of a large flat-screen television. In the back of the room was a fully equipped pool table.

Across the room from the front entrance, a double

sliding glass door overlooked a flowing river. If I'd had a canvas and paints, this would've made for a perfect land-scape to paint.

We piled into the house, and Thorn gestured to the wooden stairs on the right. "There are two bedrooms upstairs. A second master, which I thought Vlad and Cassidy could have, and another room with twin bunk beds and a full-size bed."

"Maybe I should go lie down." Peter crossed his arms. "I have a headache due to some menacing dragon hovering over me."

Thorn beamed. "Take the one upstairs with the bunk beds."

"I'll watch him," Saphira offered with a smirk. "I've wanted to have a *chat* with him since the first time I heard him speak to Everly."

"Saphy," Errol gasped and nodded toward the twins.

"Nah, it's fine." Elliott waved a hand. "Just knock Dad out, and I'll watch him. He's easier to be around when he's asleep."

My eyes widened. Peter had never been very involved with the twins, but he wasn't rude to them like he was to me. I'd thought he didn't interact with them much because I was around, but maybe I'd been wrong.

I stopped breathing. Maybe I'd broken my promise to Mom before I even realized it.

Thorn turned to Peter. "All it'll take is one hateful tone, word, or attack, and I *will* knock your ass out again." He took my hand. "If you even look at my *wife* with a hateful expression, I will end you."

The jolt sizzled between us, and my heart doubled in size. Mom had always been in my corner, but not even she could match his devotion. I wasn't sure what I'd done to deserve such a sexy and amazing person, but I wouldn't complain. With Thorn, I was happier than I'd ever been, even when dealing with constant threats.

Jaw twitching, Peter closed his eyes as his Adam's apple bobbed. "I got it."

Saphira snorted. "Are you sure? Because you said that earlier and got knocked out again. I don't even know why." She pouted and glanced at Thorn. "What did he do?"

Turning to the side, Thorn lifted his shirt to reveal where Peter had cut him. The cut was just a scab thanks to shifter healing. That healing speed was the only reason I'd survived the fall in the woods when I'd cracked my skull. If Thorn hadn't accidentally changed me, I would've died.

Seeing his injury had my blood boiling. "If he does anything to Thorn again, I'll kick his ass."

A huge smile crossed Cassidy's face. "I'm so glad Thorn found you."

"I'm not," Peter grumbled so low he had to think we couldn't hear him. "If he hadn't gotten involved, Everly would be with Drake, and none of this would've happened. Once again, it's all *her* fault."

A snarl rattled Thorn's chest, but I tugged him back and wrapped my arms around him—well, as far as they would go. Though Peter was a jerk, he hadn't meant for us to hear him. When my arms touched Thorn, some of his anger eased as our connection thrummed at full speed.

"Just so you know," Tyson said as he sat on the couch close to the back door. "Every one of us heard you. Dragons have excellent hearing. Everly is the only reason you didn't get knocked out again."

Face blanching, Peter suddenly found the floor very interesting.

"I'm going out for some fresh air." Eva walked across the den.

Before she could reach the back door, Cassidy shook her head. "I'm sorry, but we all need to stay inside. A dragon could fly overhead, and if the wedding was broadcast, they'll know your face. I'll order us pizza, but we are stuck inside."

"Then it's a good thing we have this to keep us entertained." Brenton strolled to the pool table and grabbed a stick. "Come on, Errol. I bet I can still kick your ass."

Elliott and Eva sat on the couch next to Tyson, and Elliott pulled out the Switch and gave one of the controllers to Eva. Tyson settled in to watch them play, while Cassidy removed her phone from her pocket and headed to a door on the left that led to the kitchen.

"I've been sitting enough," Peter grumbled as he moved to the corner of the room farthest from everyone. "I'll just stay here."

"Fine with me." Saphira sat on the couch closest to us and patted the middle seat. "Come watch something with me, Everly."

Not wanting to stand around, I led Thorn over and sat down, and Saphira searched for something on TV. I snuggled up with Thorn, relieved to be with him and not in danger. For this moment, the two of us could just be.

The next morning, my body thrummed, and my eyes fluttered open. My body felt rested despite barely having any room on the full-size bed. Thorn took up almost all the space due to his size, but that meant I'd been wrapped in his arms all night.

Last night had been rough. Thorn and I had wound up in the room upstairs with Peter and Elliott, with Cassidy and Vlad in the master bedroom close by. Saphira and Eva had taken the master bedroom downstairs, and Tyson, Brenton, and Errol had stayed in the other room downstairs with a bunk bed and a twin.

After spending some time with his parents, making things right with his dad, Vlad had arrived in better spirits.

A large, warm hand slipped under my shirt and rested on my stomach. My body warmed, and I bit my inner lip, trying to keep my head on straight. Peter and Elliott were right across from us in the bunk bed.

But that didn't stop the desire from knotting in my stomach. Thorn's lips were on my neck, and I'd begun to forget why this was a bad idea when there was a loud knock on the front door.

Thorn's arm tensed around me. Then he released me and jumped to his feet.

Peter and Elliott were still snoring loudly across the room, but even that couldn't block the noise from downstairs.

After a second, another series of loud knocks pounded on the door, and my lungs seized.

Thorn threw open our door just as Vlad and Cassidy ran past, heading down the stairs. By the time I made it out of the room, Vlad was opening the front door with Cassidy beside him and Thorn halfway down the stairs.

"Mom?" Vlad asked breathlessly. "What's wrong? I thought Dad was supposed to come."

My heart pounded as I reached the bottom step and stopped next to Thorn.

Alina stood in the doorway, eyes wide and cheeks pink. She glanced around, as if expecting someone to show up, then put a piece of paper in Vlad's hand. "Go there. Now. The warriors are at our thunder."

CHAPTER TWENTY-ONE

"WHAT?" Vlad stiffened. "How did you get out of there?"

"I'd already left the house this morning to help set up the booth at the local farmer's market with some of the thunder women." Alina rubbed her hands together, her head haloed by faint pink and dark purple clouds that indicated the sun was about to rise. "Luckily, we usually do go to the market together, so it wasn't out of the ordinary. Aiden linked, telling me they were on their way and to come here and let you know." She hugged her son as she rasped, "I've got to get back. They're demanding everyone return. Go there." She pointed at the paper. "The leader of the thunder can be trusted, but he's not happy about getting involved. He's doing it for your father. Make sure the human man behaves."

I froze. Everything kept getting worse instead of better.

Thorn wrapped an arm around my waist, and I leaned into his side, both of us experiencing the sadness of watching Vlad and his mom say goodbye again. They'd already lost twenty-one years together because of the king, and now they would lose even more time.

Alina pulled away and glanced at Cassidy. Alina placed her hands on the younger woman's shoulders and gave her a heartbreaking smile. "One day, I hope I get to know you. From everything Vlad told us about you, I know you're an amazing woman, and you already feel like the daughter we always wanted. Keep him safe."

Cassidy's eyes glistened. "I promise. I'll do anything in my power to protect him."

"I know." Alina turned to Thorn, and her lips mashed into a line. "I'm sorry for the hell you've gone through. We need you to prove to the world that our king and prince are wrong in how they lead. It's your destiny."

My dragon inched forward, brushing against my mind. She agreed with everything Alina had said, and my human side did too. The king had allowed fear to govern his decisions, and Drake was an asshole. Thorn was a good man who understood the struggles of living like no other royal could.

"Screw destiny." Thorn's eyes glinted. "I'm not interested in helping the very people who turned their backs on me without a moment's hesitation. There are only three people I'm concerned with keeping safe—Everly, Cassidy, and Vlad. They've never betrayed me, not even when the opportunity presented itself."

His fingers tensed, digging into my skin. The jolt shot through me, giving me a feeling of peace only he could provide, but part of me ached for him. Though I agreed with Alina, I understood where he was coming from. Even Saphira hadn't wanted to believe or help him at first, and she would've turned her back on him if not for me.

Alina winced and opened her mouth, but her eyes glowed, and she exhaled. "I've got to go, and you all need to get out of here. They're already spreading out to search the area, so it won't be long until they come here." A tear trickled down her face as she scanned the four of us again before turning around. She darted to her vehicle before she paused and glanced over her shoulder. "Like I told Vlad growing up, fear forces people to do stupid things, and sometimes, you've got to be the bigger person to prove to everyone they're wrong."

Her words washed over me. If what the king had said about Thorn's grandfather was true, there was a reason people feared Thorn's magic. Though they were wrong, they had no way of knowing they were associating one person's horrible actions with Thorn.

Vlad cleared his throat. "Just...please, you and Dad be careful, and if you need help, you have my cell phone number."

"I love all of you. Be safe." She got into the car and drove away.

We stood in silence until her headlights blended in with the trees. I hadn't been up for ten minutes, and already we'd found ourselves in yet another threatening situation.

Thorn's anger wafted through our bond, and I wrapped my arms around his waist to calm him, before the stress of fleeing again added more strain to the tension running thick within him.

He kissed my forehead, the jolt zinging to my core. He connected, *I'm fine. I promise.*

My head tilted back. *Are you sure? And how did you know I was worried?*

The corners of his mouth tipped upward. *With you here beside me, I can get through anything. And I can feel your worry.* His anger faded into warmth and the same emotion he usually emanated toward me—love.

I hated to ruin the moment, but we had no time to waste. "Let's get packed."

We split up to inform the others that we had to leave, and I headed to the bedroom on the main level where Eva and Saphira were rooming together.

Within five minutes, we were loaded up in the vehicles and heading toward the main road. Like last time, Vlad drove one vehicle and Cassidy the other. If something were to happen, the two of them could use their fated mate link to communicate without a phone.

This time, Eva rode in the front passenger seat next to Cassidy, with Thorn and me in the middle row, and Peter and Elliott in the back. At first, Eva had complained about not sitting with Elliott so they could play a game, but Peter wanted to sit in the back, so she'd jumped into the front seat willingly.

She'd grown up a lot during the past week, and the fact was bittersweet. She'd needed a little bit of grounding. Eva and Elliott usually retreated into video games and each other, instead of dealing with their problems, but I *hated* that her wake-up call had come through Drake. The man could have stripped her innocence away at a time of his choosing, a thought that had my blood run cold. I had to hold on to the fact that she hadn't actually experienced that.

The address Alina had given us was over an hour and a half away, near the small town of Abingdon, Virginia. Elliott grumbled and groaned in the backseat, while Peter breathed loudly as he sat behind me on the passenger side.

Thorn had fetched Elliott and Peter, and when my stepdad had come downstairs to join us, he'd been pale and visibly shaking. Obviously, Thorn had said something to get him to cooperate, but I hadn't asked Thorn what. As long as Peter behaved, I didn't give a damn. Peter deserved whatever he got, and I knew Thorn wouldn't actually kill him because of me and my love for my siblings.

When the GPS alerted us that we were twenty minutes away, Eva fidgeted in her seat. "What are the people helping us like?"

Cassidy stared straight ahead as we drove through a charming downtown. Brick buildings stood to our right, and to our left was a small community park with a water fountain in the middle. She answered, "I have no idea, and neither does Vlad."

A hateful snort came from Peter. "Figures. You kidnap me and Elliott and take us to people you don't even know. How do we know we aren't walking into a trap?"

My dragon snarled as my breathing quickened. He always had to be negative and patronizing, and I couldn't let it roll off me like I had so many times before.

"Technically, I'm here willingly." Elliott lowered his Switch. "Which means it's not kidnapping."

Turning around in my seat, I narrowed my eyes. "You'd rather have stayed home so Drake could use you to force Eva to return to be his human breeder? Is that what you're saying?"

"If you—" he started.

Thorn's growl was so loud that my ears rang. He rasped, "If the next words out of your mouth insult my wife in any way, I will *end* you. I'm sick and tired of the way you treat her."

My dragon purred. The Everly from a month ago would've been appalled and considered his threat a red flag, but not this version. I wanted to rub my body all over him to show my appreciation for how much he loved me.

Peter huffed and leaned back in his seat, and I faced forward. Thorn's pupils turned to slits as he scanned me.

My body warmed, needing him in a way that was very inappropriate while in a car, surrounded by other people and headed into unknown territory.

The bond between us sizzled.

I bit my bottom lip, trying to force some sanity back into myself. *I love you,* I connected with him. Those were the three best words I could come up with to start expressing the extent of my feelings for him.

You own me, he replied, the spicy scent of his arousal surging between us.

Those words had a desperate need building within, stronger than before. Every cell burned, and I had the overwhelming urge to unbuckle and straddle him.

"We're fifteen minutes out," Cassidy said a little too loudly, and my face burned.

She must have smelled my desire, which would have been awkward enough without her being my mother-in-law.

My heart pattered. Thorn was my mate and husband. I couldn't get over that. Though the wedding had been forced and I would've preferred something Thorn and I had planned together, I'd already known he'd be my husband someday. I wished it had been about the two of us and not Drake and me.

We turned onto a road that took us deeper into a thickly wooded area, away from downtown, which I would've loved to visit if Drake hadn't been hunting us.

Thorn chuckled, the sound warm and sexy. *Don't be embarrassed. We're fated mates. New ones at that. Our reaction to each other is expected and normal.*

Maybe. I suspected my emotions for him would never change, and that was both terrifying and thrilling. *But she's your mom.*

Remember, you'll smell her and Vlad for the same reason. He winked.

My body felt light and carefree. He made me so damn happy, and I couldn't figure out how I'd lasted twenty-two years without him.

The remainder of the ride passed quickly as the two of us enjoyed each other's company. When we hadn't passed anyone for several miles, Cassidy turned onto a dirt road that we would've likely missed if the GPS hadn't given us a hundred-foot warning.

The road curved as the white and chestnut oaks and loblolly pines thickened. The area seemed more remote than Thorn's cabin and Vlad's parents' thunder. We continued along the curving dirt road with nothing but woods thickening around us.

"Y'all, I hate to agree with Dad, but am I the only one who has ever watched a horror movie?" Elliott grumbled. "I mean, come on. I say we turn the fuck around."

"El, chill." Eva turned toward us and rolled her eyes. "You know I've watched them. I was sitting right next to you every damn time, holding your hand so you wouldn't cry."

"Gah, don't *lie*," he scoffed. "I told you, I had something in my eye."

She tilted her head. "Every time someone jumped out with an ax or machete?"

"I admit, the timing wasn't the best, but my eyelashes clearly have a mind of their own," he retorted. "Yes, it sounds suspicious, but dammit, you'll just have to trust me."

Does he really cry during horror movies? Thorn connected as he smirked, stealing my breath away.

Just one little move, and he turned me into complete

mush. *I don't know. They didn't include me in all things twinning.*

His brows bunched together. *Twinning?*

That's what they call their one-on-one time—or when they say things at the same time. I realized they hadn't used the phrase in the past day or two, probably because Eva still wasn't quite herself. This moment right here was the closest she'd been to the Eva I was used to.

"Will you two stop it?" Peter snapped. "I don't know what's worse. Hearing you babble back and forth or being stuck around—"

Thorn's head jerked toward Peter, and my stepdad blanched.

"Woods," Peter finally said. "There's no telling what kind of wild creatures are out here."

Laughter bubbled in my chest, and I bit the corner of my mouth to prevent it from spilling out. My humor died, though, when we rolled over a hill and the woods opened to reveal a modern white barn. A red truck with an extended cab was parked next to it, and a sizable man around Vlad's father's age leaned against the wall by the large wooden door.

As we descended, the side of the barn came into view. This place was the size of a large house. There were two windows in the front and two on the visible side, and they were covered by some sort of barrier, likely wood, which prevented me from seeing inside.

When we all got out of the vehicles, Thorn marched over to stand between Peter and me and took my hand. He cut his gaze to Peter, who stiffened.

Good.

The older man's gray hair was styled back, and his muscles bulged from under his polo shirt. His warm tanned skin gave his six-and-a-half-foot frame a healthy glow.

His rich brown eyes narrowed as he lifted his chin and settled his gaze on Thorn. "I'd hoped that Aiden was wrong, but the resurrected dragon prince who steals other shifters' dragons is, in fact, part of the group he asked me to hide."

"My father wouldn't lie." Vlad stepped forward, blocking Thorn partially from the man's view. "And here I thought you were his oldest friend, Theron."

Theron snarled and arched a brow. "I am, but that doesn't mean I couldn't hope he was mistaken."

Uncomfortable heat emanated through my connection with Thorn. His hand tightened on mine as he rasped, "If you didn't want to chance me being here, you should've said no."

"You're right. I wasn't thinking clearly, especially since you've come here seeking shelter and are speaking that way to the very person who's risking so much by taking you in." Theron sneered. "Your presence here puts my entire thunder at risk, especially my son."

Especially his son? That was an odd thing to add.

"If you don't want us here—" Cassidy started.

Theron lifted a hand. "I *don't* want you here. Alerting the warriors to your presence would be the smart thing to do."

Thorn tensed, and my heart stopped.

"But Aiden has never asked me for a favor, so I'm doing this for *him*. Make no mistake—if anything goes awry, you *will* leave without putting up a fight. If you can't promise that, I won't give you access to the hiding spot." The man's face was lined with worry, and his voice grew thick with emotion. "Sol is already on Drake's radar, and I can't make him more of a target. He's already lost too much."

His heartbreak called to me. His tone was so familiar, reminding me of when I'd had to tell people that my mom had cancer.

The words were rough against my throat, but I asked the one question I'd hoped to ask when I was a doctor. "What's wrong with your son? Why is Drake a danger to him?"

Theron's head jerked back, and he inhaled sharply. "Drake is hunting him, too."

CHAPTER TWENTY-TWO

I WAITED WITH BATED BREATH, but I wasn't sure I wanted to know the answer. That was the thing about knowledge. Once you had it, there were no takebacks. Knowledge was power, but sometimes, it had the power to destroy you.

Theron's face twisted as if he smelled something horrid. "Is this a joke? You're the royals' advisor."

"No, I'm the *king's* advisor." Errol winced. "Or I was. Pretty sure I can't do that when I'm on the run."

"What's the difference?" Theron snapped, his nostrils flaring. "They're one and the same."

Everyone was focusing on the wrong thing. I took a step forward. "Can you humor us?" I waved my free hand between me and the others. "I have no inkling of what you're referring to."

"I'm with her." Saphira placed her hands on her hips and stared him down. "Drake shouldn't be *doing* anything. He's just the prince, not the king."

Theron's brows furrowed as he studied us. Then his jaw slackened. "You really don't know?"

"I just learned about the existence of dragons, so..." Elliott quipped from behind me, where Thorn and I had positioned ourselves to keep the humans from Theron's attention.

Thorn closed his eyes as if he'd already learned there was no stopping my brother.

That was probably true, but I'd at least try. I gave him a stern look over my shoulder.

"Hey, you may be my older sister, but you don't get to *mom* me." Elliott moved so he could see Theron. "There should be no surprise about my lack of knowledge. I just wanted to be upfront and clear."

Eva groaned. "El, for goodness' sake, I'm with Everly on this one."

"I'd rather never have learned about dragons or been forced to come here," Peter complained. He glared at Thorn in challenge, the very thing Thorn had told him not to do.

Hot rage boiled through our bond, and his dragon roared, hurting my ears. But that had been my stepdad's point.

Babe, he wants you to blow up and give this man a reason to call Drake, I connected. I understood how Thorn felt, but Peter was intelligent. He knew exactly what he was doing. *If you want to teach him a lesson later, fine. Just not now.*

The heat cooled marginally, informing me I'd gotten through to him.

"And humans? Really? Harboring the prince and the runaway fiancée wasn't enough?" Theron hung his head, but then his gaze jerked back up to me. "Wait. They're your family?"

He didn't have to say more. I understood the unasked

question. "Yes. Thorn changed me, which is why Drake took Eva, my sister, to become his human breeder and wanted me as his..."

Thorn fisted his hand.

Yeah, I couldn't force myself to say *wife,* so I could only imagine how he felt thinking I might say it.

"He's a prick." Tyson sneered, his body shaking with such rage. "He ruins everything he touches."

"Son," Brenton warned. Then he bit his bottom lip.

"Dad, we aren't back *there.*" Tyson spread out his arms and glanced at the sun, which had risen high in the sky, indicating it was close to noon. "Theron has his own grievances with Prince Drake, which I still want to hear."

"So do I." Errol rubbed the back of his neck. "Do you mind sharing?"

Theron pushed away from the barn and strolled past the edge of the group and onto the dirt driveway. He kicked at the ground, raising a small dust cloud, which the faint, cool breeze blew away from us toward the trees.

"The past few years, Drake has made an unofficial decree." Theron placed his hands behind his back and stared into the trees. "I only learned of it this past year. He's been eradicating the weak, and with every week, he's been searching closer and closer to here."

Eradicating.

The word hovered around us, making the air so heavy I couldn't breathe.

Inhaling sharply, Brenton placed a hand on his son's shoulder and asked, "What do you mean by 'weak' and 'eradicating'?"

"The weak—as in any dragon who isn't at their peak." Theron straightened his shoulders. "The old, the weak, and especially the handful of dragons with some sort of disability...like my son. And you know what 'eradicate' means."

I grew lightheaded, and Thorn's shock ran through our bond, adding to my turbulent emotions.

"Are you saying Drake is *killing* dragons?" Saphira clutched her chest. "His own people?"

Theron nodded, his face flushed. A vein bulged between his eyes. "It's been happening for the past three years, apparently, but we just learned of the trauma when a thunder in Utah alerted us a year ago. Forty dragons were killed, leaving the thunder at a total of fifty."

The numbers didn't make sense. "Wait. I thought you said only the old, weak, and disabled. Forty out of ninety is an awfully large number." That was almost a fifty percent death rate in one attack. That much of the population couldn't be old, and weak, and disabled dragons appeared to be rare. Hell, even though Theron and Aiden had to be in their sixties, they didn't look that old, except for the gray hair. They were just as muscular and strong as Vlad and Thorn, which made sense, given dragons lived for about five hundred years.

"They also killed any thunder member who didn't agree with the man Drake designated as the new leader. A friend of mine who left our thunder to join his mate's thunder gave me a heads-up because he knows about my son. Otherwise, we'd have been clueless until they attacked."

Vlad rubbed a hand down his face. "Drake needs people who won't revolt against him or rat him out to the king."

Theron laughed humorlessly. "You're still sticking with the king not knowing that his son—his heir—is doing these things?"

"He does *not*." Errol's jaw tensed. "I would've over-heard something if he did, and I'm still confused about how it would be possible."

"I believe King Arman is clueless." Tyson's lips curved. "Drake injured me, lied to his dad, and drove us to live on the outskirts of town. He blamed me for it. He's a jackass, and he intends to finish the job of killing me."

Drake was a psychopathic narcissist. The very worst kind in the world.

I turned to Peter and arched a brow. "You still want to go home?"

He scowled but didn't respond.

"That's why it's a huge risk to have you here." Theron scrubbed his hands through his hair. "Because of the potential attack, I bought this land in case Sol and I had to leave fast and go into hiding for a while. We're an hour's flight from my thunder, so the risk is a lot less than having you at our location. As long as you stay put so there's no risk of anyone seeing you, everything should be fine. I stocked the kitchen while you were on your way here."

"We understand." Errol stepped forward, a warm smile on his face. "We appreciate the shelter you're providing."

"Wait." Saphira eyed the barn warily. "We're staying *here*?"

"Won't be much different from how you smell now," Tyson quipped, bumping her arm. "Maybe it'll be an improvement."

"Absolutely not." Peter shook his head. "*This* is where we're expected to stay? Hell no. You all need to take me home. This is the final straw. I'd rather take my chances with Drake."

Thorn snarled. "You won't make it that far because your

death will happen before you make it five feet from me. I will not allow Drake to capture you and use you as leverage against Eva and Everly."

Recoiling, Theron pressed his lips into a line.

He wasn't happy with how Thorn was handling things, and my heart sank.

I was done having the same conversation repeatedly. I lifted my chin and glared at my stepdad. "Peter. There are two ways this can go down. One, you behave and understand that the *only* reason you're here is because you're Eva and Elliott's dad and we're trying to protect you and your children. Or two, we can gag you and tie you to a chair so you can't eat, pee, or get a drink of water without permission. I refuse to let you keep pushing everyone's buttons, and the sound of your voice is getting on my nerves. One more negative thing, and you will have made your choice...permanently."

Peter's eyes darkened and sweat sprouted above his lip.

Apparently, my threat had been more effective than Thorn's, which surprised me, but I'd take it.

Theron squared his shoulders. "I'm serious. *One* more thing to make me regret allowing all of you here, and I will evict you, and you can become someone else's problem. Do I make myself clear?" He glared at each of us. "I've got backup measures in place. If I disappear or show up late, I've instructed several members of my pack to notify Drake. I can use my fated-mate bond to give my wife the barn's location if Drake comes, and if I don't return, she can bring the warriors here."

"Having Drake show up is a risk to your son." Cassidy ran her hands along her stomach. "Surely, you wouldn't contact him."

"First off, my son wouldn't be there when they arrived,

so it's not an issue." Theron crossed his arms. "And second, Drake has made a video stating that anyone with information on Thorn and Everly that results in their capture will be owed a great debt. That would come in handy if he ever does learn about my son."

I wanted to tell him that Drake was lying, but he wouldn't believe me. I could see the determination in his eyes. He believed that, since Drake had said it on the Dragonnet, he couldn't go back on his word. Explaining Drake's treachery would just be another strike against us.

Theron glanced at the sky. "I've got to return home before they get nervous." Then he focused on Vlad and walked over, handing him keys while saying, "I'm trusting this group because of your father. Don't let me down."

"We won't." Vlad took the keys. "I promise. We want to remain hidden until we figure out what to do."

"Don't go into town. We can't risk exposing you and this place." Theron headed toward the tree line. "I'll be back tomorrow to check in and make sure there isn't something you're lacking. There are clothes inside, though I'm not sure they'll fit all of you. What's here is yours, just as long as you take good care of things."

"Thank you." I nodded at him, and some of the weight of the world disappeared from my shoulders. This man seemed like a good guy, and I hoped we'd have a few days to regroup.

He darted into the tree line to shift and go back to his thunder.

The eleven of us remained quiet, and soon we heard the faint noises of limbs cracking, indicating Theron was in his dragon form. In animal form, he'd be able to sense us, even that far away.

My dragon grumbled, and the urge to shift damn near

overtook me. It'd been almost a week since I'd shifted, and she was growing restless. *Do you think the two of us could go flying tonight?*

Thorn grimaced, and guilt squeezed our bond. *Of course. I should've thought of that before now.*

My shoulders sagged. I hadn't meant to make him feel guilty. *It's not your fault. We've been on the run. But yes, my dragon is urging me to shift.*

We'll take care of that, he promised. He placed a hand on the small of my back just as Vlad slid the key into the lock and opened the door.

"Oh, thank gods." Saphira marched inside. "It's not actually a barn."

We entered a large open area that reminded me of Peter's basement back in Asheville where his home office was located. The floor was concrete, and although there wasn't a large desk inside, there were four plastic benches that each seated four. To the left was an island bar that had a few bottles of wine and whiskey, and there was even a black telescope in the corner. A loft overlooked the room, and I wondered where the stairs were to reach it.

On the far side of the room, two white walls divided up more living areas. Each wall had a door midway down.

Saphira hurried to the left side and flung open a door, revealing a hallway. She wandered in as Tyson and Eva hurried over.

Let's check out the other side, Thorn linked as he led me to the right side.

We walked through that door. Inside was a long hallway with the same concrete floor. The first door to the left opened to a bedroom with a queen mattress and cream walls. The mattress lay on the floor, but there were gray sheets and a comforter on top. There was no furniture, paintings, or anything personal, but this was a safe house.

On the far side of the bed, a sliding glass door led out back to a fire pit. On the other side of the room, I spotted sliding closet doors and a bathroom. I wandered over and peered in. The tub was standard size with a marbled shower wall. A toilet sat between the shower and the sink, and the cabinet under the sink was small. The bathroom wasn't tiny, but it wasn't roomy, either.

We headed back out and found a half bath at the end of the hall and, to the right, a den with a big flat-screen TV and an L-shaped, brown couch. Walking through the den, we located a small laundry room to the left and a sizable white kitchen to the right. The stove, refrigerator, and dishwasher were silver, and all the cabinets were white with a gray laminate countertop. On the right side of the room was a round, white, wooden table that seated eight.

Peter, Elliott, Vlad, and Cassidy strolled into the kitchen behind us with Saphira and the others only steps behind.

We fanned out, and Saphira, Eva, Elliott, and Peter sat at the table.

"This place is large enough for us." Cassidy sighed as she brushed past us toward the stove. "I was worried for a second."

"There's only one bedroom over here." Thorn pulled me against the wall beside the dishwasher.

"Yeah, but there're three bedrooms on the other side, as well as three full bathrooms. The one bedroom with a black couch and bunk beds also has the stairway to the loft, which has another bunk bed and a full-size mattress. So technically, there are five bedrooms in total." Saphira ran a hand over the cream wall and wrinkled her nose. "They could have chosen a better color. It's so bright."

That was the least of my worries. "Are there enough beds for all of us?"

"The second bedroom has two double beds, and the last one is a bigger room with a queen, like on this side." Brenton gestured to where we'd come from. "With two fated-mate couples, that works out perfectly."

I didn't know how we'd gotten so lucky, but after all the shit luck we'd had, I was more than willing to take it.

Cassidy opened the refrigerator, and Theron hadn't been lying. The entire fridge was full with no space to spare. He'd made sure we wouldn't need to leave for anything, but with our metabolisms as dragon shifters, I was certain the food wouldn't last long. There were steaks, vegetables, milk, cheeses, hamburger meat, chicken—pretty much anything we could want. We owed this man so much money.

My stomach grumbled. I'd gone way too long without food. We'd run out of the house this morning without eating.

Tyson laughed. "I'm glad that was someone else and not me."

My face burned, and I turned into Thorn's chest. When I tilted my head up, Thorn beamed at me with adoration in his eyes. He kissed my forehead and said, "Let me go make my baby something to eat."

"Nope, I can handle that," Cassidy said, shooing him away. "Besides, Vlad has other plans for the rest of you."

Thorn narrowed his eyes. "Like what?"

"Training." Vlad rubbed his hands together. "Errol, Saphira, Brenton, and Tyson have led sheltered lives. They need to be able to hold their own when the warriors inevitably find us, and Everly is a brand-new dragon."

"It's a waste of time," Thorn said, his hand tensing. "We won't be here for long. We'll leave the country. If we go somewhere remote, we should be able to hide. There's no need to learn how to fight if there's no battle."

"Uh, I have a family business." Peter scowled, but he kept his tone from its usual cruel cadence. "I can't just leave."

His company wasn't our problem, but what Thorn wanted to do was. My heart ached, and I murmured, "You want to run away?"

"Not run away." Thorn faced me, giving me his full attention. "Protect you and everyone we love. Here, we'll be in constant danger."

"Honey, do you really think Drake will stop hunting you?" Cassidy shut the refrigerator door. "You're a threat to him and the throne."

She was right. Drake wouldn't stop looking, especially with Eva and me involved. "And what about your people? We just learned that Drake is hunting and killing some of them." I swallowed hard as I placed a hand on his chest.

"We've gone through this." Thorn brushed his fingers against my face. "As long as you and my family are safe, that's all that matters. The other dragons will figure out their problems on their own."

The jolt penetrated my soul, encouraging me to take a step closer. King Arman had done a number on him, and I could only try to undo the damage. I opened my mouth to speak but couldn't.

"Uh...where do I fit into this picture?" Saphira jutted out a hip. "I'm not your family or Everly's. Are you just going to throw me and *my family* to the warriors and get away?"

Tyson stood, his face twisting in anger. "Figures. You can't take the jackass out of the royal blood."

Thorn's rage slammed into me like a raging inferno. He rasped, "Do not lump me in with them *ever* again."

If I didn't interject, this confrontation would go too far. But with the hurt swirling from Thorn, I feared everyone would know the pain he usually tried to hide.

CHAPTER TWENTY-THREE

MY HEART CLENCHED at the pain and anger roiling through my mate. The resentment he'd built up over the years was so strong it stole my breath. Whatever issues I had with Peter didn't even come close to Thorn's level of devastation. I'd known my mate had deep-rooted issues, but it was worse than I'd realized. He might be stronger because of it, but that didn't mean he wasn't wounded to his very core.

His own parents had tried to have him killed because they feared him.

Thorn took a menacing step toward Tyson, and I jumped in front of him. I placed my hands on his chest and locked eyes with my mate. *Just like you have issues with the royals—I* was careful not to say family—*so does he. Remember what Saphira told us. Drake injured his dragon, leaving him disabled, and now he's learned that Drake is killing people like him. He's got his own baggage, and he's lashing out. Please, be the man I know you are. Understanding, kind, and strong.*

He exhaled, his minty breath hitting my face, and his irises came close to returning to their gorgeous color—just a tad darker. *Only for you. Only because I want to be the man you deserve.*

My heart skipped a beat. Even when he was hurt and angry, his love for me shone through. I couldn't help but fall in love with him more.

As my dragon grumbled, I turned toward the kitchen table. Brenton and Saphira had stood up and flanked Tyson. They were ready to protect their family, and that reinforced my trust in them.

I lifted my hands to diffuse the situation, but I had to stand up for my mate. "Look, that was a low blow. Thorn didn't have anything to do with what Drake did to you or the way the king protected his son. In fact, the king—his own father—tried to kill him. Or did you forget that?"

Tyson closed his eyes.

"I'll be honest. When I met Thorn, I didn't trust him." Saphira remained tense and on alert. "I thought he was full of shit, though I could tell you were taken with him. Now, I understand why—he's your soulmate, and when he turned you, he created his fated mate. Because of that connection, I saw the truth. Drake is much worse than I realized, and Thorn wasn't lying at all. But what Tyson said holds true. Thorn admitted to only caring about protecting the people he loves."

"Yes, that's exactly what I said," Thorn added.

If anyone were to hurt Thorn, I'd defend him, but the urge to smack the shit out of him surged through me. I was trying to calm the tension, and he'd reinforced the words that had brewed up the tension in the first place. I knew he was smart, but he wasn't showing any common sense, allowing his emotions to get the best of him.

"Then why the hell are we here?" Peter spat, his body rigid.

For once, I couldn't blame my stepdad, but I knew Thorn. He had to be talking out of his ass, or I'd make sure to beat some sense into him...maybe while pleasuring him sexually.

Whoa. Where had that thought come from?

"Because if any of you are captured, the people I love will be at risk." Thorn pulled at the roots of his hair. "That's why I tried not to forge connections—because the more people you let in, the more people are at risk." Thorn gestured to Peter. "I can't stand you, but your kids love you. If Drake threatened you, Eva or Elliott would be desperate to save you, which then puts Everly at risk. The same thing goes for Saphira. So yeah, maybe you aren't the ones I'm most concerned with, but that doesn't matter. I care about your safety because that's how I protect Everly."

I winced. That sounded somewhat better, but it still wasn't the most reassuring thing he could've said.

I was surprised when Brenton relaxed.

Straightening, Brenton nodded. "When it comes to someone taking care of their fated mate, we have nothing to worry about. You'll protect us just as valiantly as her."

Saphira lifted a finger. "I allowed myself to get captured to save you, and I don't even make it into the somewhat-loved category?" She tilted her head back. "I'm offended." But humor glimmered in her eyes.

"Well, I like you now if that's any consolation." Thorn chuckled as he placed his hands on my shoulders and tugged me close, so that my back was pressed against his chest. "And Everly loves you, so there's that."

That was true, even though I hadn't gotten around to telling her that.

"Uh…" Elliott raised a hand. "May I ask a question?"

"Technically, you just did." Eva stuck out her tongue.

Peter rolled his eyes, giving me pause. I'd always thought he did that only to me, but my suspicions about his indifference to the twins seemed more and more like a certainty. He didn't treat them as poorly as he treated me, but I could see why they relied more on each other than their dad.

"What is it, dear?" Cassidy asked with a smile. "And you never need to ask permission. There are no silly questions."

Rubbing her hands together, Saphira waggled her brows.

I didn't want to know where she was heading, so I added, "No silly ones, but there are some that could be deemed inappropriate and won't get an answer."

She frowned, closed her mouth, and pouted.

That was what I'd been afraid of.

"What's a fated mate?" Elliott pursed his lips as he looked at me and Thorn. "Because these two moved super quick."

A line of worry creased Elliott's forehead, and my chest expanded. Was he worried about me?

"Fated mates have become rarer among our kind as our numbers dwindle." Errol smiled sadly. "They're an intense version of soulmates. It happens when a soul has been split between two people. When two human soulmates meet, their urgent connection can be confused for lust. The emotions and attraction are immediate, and when it happens between two supernaturals, their magic calls to them and intensifies the connection. Fate intervenes to ensure the two halves find each other. They are destined to be together, and if one dies, it's like a part of the other is lost for eternity."

He spoke as if he understood the loss. "Was Saphira's mother your fated?"

He pressed a hand to his stomach. "She was. Brenton's and my fated mates were leaving to shift, but they weren't careful, and hunters accidentally shot them before they could change into their dragons. It happened sixteen years ago." His voice cracked and died away, the emotions too much.

So both Saphira and Tyson had been young when they'd lost their mothers. No wonder Saphira hadn't mentioned hers during our time together.

"It was an accident. They didn't wear bright clothes, and they blended in with the landscape. The hunters called the police and waited at the edge of the dragon lands, a spot that had become inundated by humans." Brenton picked up the story. "They were let off the hook because we didn't want more attention drawn to our lands, and they hadn't killed them on purpose. If it hadn't been for Tyson, Saphira, and the king, I'm pretty sure both Errol and I would've done something stupid that we would've regretted."

Now it made sense why Saphira had been so opposed to viewing the king poorly. He'd helped her dad and her uncle during a painful time. That was why Brenton held so much resentment toward Drake but not the king—he felt he owed the king a debt.

"Wow." Elliott's jaw dropped. "Having a fated mate sounds intense."

"It is," Vlad added, standing beside Cassidy. "Which is why we *all* need training, including Everly."

A panicked sensation surged through our bond as

Thorn's hands trembled on my shoulders. He rasped, "No. We need to think of a way out of the country and not distract ourselves with something she won't ever need."

Saphira bobbed her head. "So, you're fine with her getting another faceful of someone else's penis? Good to know."

A guttural growl emanated from Thorn's chest, and my dragon purred. I didn't know why, but him almost losing control over that comment had me wanting to claim him all over again. His possessiveness turned me on.

Yes, I'd become that girl...and I wouldn't change it for the world.

But I had to stay levelheaded until he and I were alone. "I'm not asking for permission. I *will* train with Vlad. This is something I have to do. Hell, it's something we all need to do, including Eva, Elliott, and Peter."

"Dude, I can totally buy *Spyro*." Elliott removed his Nintendo Switch from his pocket. "I don't even know why I haven't yet, but that ends now."

Vlad blinked. "Does he really think a video game will teach him how to hold his own against dragons?"

"He's human." Thorn's forehead creased. "It's not like going outside and practicing hand-to-hand combat will make a difference when the time comes to fight. That's why we need to focus on finding a way out of the country, instead of wasting time training them."

I wouldn't say this out loud, at least not yet, but I connected with Thorn, *What if you change them like you changed me? If they agree to it.* I wanted it to be clear that I didn't want them forced into it.

His hands went still. *Maybe. Not Peter—he's a fucking prick—but your siblings, I wouldn't be opposed to. That might make things easier. But even if they agreed to it, I'm not sure I can.*

You took away several dragons back at the chateau. He had done it with ease, so I wasn't sure why that would change now.

I didn't mean to. My dragon and I were fighting to save you. Thorn lowered his hands and stared at them. *I wasn't in control. The magic took over.*

The same had happened when he'd changed me into a dragon shifter. I'd been dying, and he'd reacted. He hadn't meant to do it, but I was so thankful he had. *Okay. That's fine. It was just a suggestion.*

He turned me to face him as if we were the only two in the room. *Talk to them alone, not with Peter around. If they want me to try, we can, but tell them no promises.*

I pushed my love for him through our connection. I wanted him to know how much I appreciated and adored him.

"Uh..." Elliott cleared his throat. "What happened here? He was arguing, and now the two of them are looking at each other in a way that's making me very uncomfortable."

"It's call eye-fucking." Saphira blew out a breath. "And they've been doing that since day one, when I thought she'd lost her mind for looking at our kidnapper that way. I'm glad it's because they're fated and he turned out to be a good guy, or there would be hell to pay."

"Good guy?" Peter scoffed. "That's what you call it?"

"He is to her," Eva said softly. "That's all that matters to me."

That was one way to ruin our moment, but we were with nine other people, so we probably shouldn't be looking at each other this way. Now that I had Thorn's attention and he wasn't being obstinate, I figured now was a good time to try again. "The dragons won't expect humans to be trained. That could buy us more time to reach them if they need help, and I need to know how to fight now that I have a dragon."

"We could train them with guns and arrows." Vlad steepled his fingers. "Even if we wind up leaving the country, we can't right now. Every dragon shifter is on high alert and so scared that they won't think twice about reporting us. It won't hurt to train everyone, and that way, we'll keep up our strength. Dragons live around the world, so there will always be a risk."

Thorn huffed, and I placed a hand on his chest and gave him a small smile. *I want to train, and my dragon is restless with all the running and sitting around we've been doing. What's the harm in me learning how to defend myself?*

"Fine. You're right. It wouldn't hurt for all of us to be more prepared and for me not to become rusty." He mashed his lips together. *I can never say no to you.*

My pulse quickened, and the jolt of the electricity between us only added to the sensation.

"Then go." Cassidy shooed us out. "Let me cook while you all train. Lunch will be ready in a few hours. The protein bars you ate earlier won't sustain you for much longer."

Our group stood, and even Peter begrudgingly obeyed.

THE REST of the day passed in a blur, including our all-too-brief lunch break when we devoured the delicious meal Cassidy had prepared.

Saphira and I teamed up as sparring partners, and

though she wasn't formally trained to fight, she still had more experience than me, and she kicked my ass over and over.

Tyson and Eva partnered up, leaving Peter with Elliott, and Brenton with Errol. Thorn had wanted to work with Saphira and me, but Vlad had intercepted. I was glad because, if Thorn had trained us, any time I got hurt, he'd have been tempted to end the training.

After lunch, Vlad took Errol, Brenton, Saphira, and me deeper into the woods and away from Thorn's watchful eye. We practiced fighting in our human forms, and I caught way too many blows. My ribs and sides throbbed from how many times Saphira had hit me.

"This is our last round before we call it a day," Vlad informed us from beside a white oak at the edge of the small clearing we'd found.

Sweat glistened all over my body. Though I ached all over, muscles burning from my efforts, it felt amazing to be sore.

Saphira lifted her hands and smirked. "Ready for another beating?"

She was as competitive as I was, and unfortunately, she was also way better at this.

I was determined that, before long, I'd beat her.

Raising my hands caused my ribs to protest, but I pushed the discomfort from my mind. I didn't need Thorn homing in on it—he'd already shown up twice to get me to stop.

"Go!" Vlad shouted.

Bouncing on her feet, Saphira watched me, ready for me to strike. I'd been playing offense the whole time, and it hadn't worked, so this time, I'd make her move first.

She snickered. "That won't change the outcome." She

stepped forward and shifted her weight to her left side.

Vlad kept reminding us to watch for our opponent's tells, and this was the first time I'd picked up on a clue. I spun to my left just as she kicked. She hit air, and momentum kept her moving.

I spun back around and punched her in the stomach, bringing her to her knees. My dragon surged forward, urging me to kick Saphira in the face, but I aimed for her side. She caught my foot, lifting it upward.

The leg holding me up wobbled. I pushed off it before I lost my balance and made contact with her side.

She stumbled, releasing my foot, but I couldn't right myself, so I landed on my back, pain surging through my body.

Everly, Thorn connected, his worry swirling through.

I didn't have time to respond. He knew we were sparring. I jumped up just as Saphira caught her balance, her cocky smirk gone.

"I see someone finally learned something," she spat. "It's about time."

She was trying to mess with my mind, but I wouldn't let her. Instead, I lifted my hands, ready for her to attack.

Rushing toward me, she leaned to her left side again, but she didn't put all her weight on that foot like last time. Instead, her right fist surged toward me. I ducked, then punched her in the stomach again.

As she stumbled back, I righted myself and pretended I was going to kick her in the stomach again. She lifted her hands to catch my foot, but I aimed for her ribs, like she'd done to me so many times. She didn't have time to correct as I nailed her in the midsection, and she crumpled to the ground. She hissed as she stood and shook herself, ready to continue the fight, but electricity pulsed through the air.

"That's it," Thorn said, stepping from between two red cedars. His jaw was clenched, and his attention was locked on me. "Cassidy wants us back for dinner." Our bond filled with rage.

"Fine." Saphira sighed but winced. "I could use a break."

I puffed out my chest. This was the first time I'd seen Saphira winded.

"Yeah, yeah." She rolled her eyes but smiled. "You're a quick study, but don't get too arrogant. I'll be kicking your ass again tomorrow."

Vlad came over and patted my arm. "Everly did fantastic today. You progressed a lot faster than I expected. You're a natural fighter, as if you were meant to be one of us."

I beamed. Other than Mom, I'd never received praise from a family member, and that was what Vlad was quickly becoming.

Brenton and Errol both had black eyes, but they had smiles on their faces. Apparently, dragon shifters enjoyed a good brawl.

As the five of us started back toward the barn, Thorn gently caught my arm, holding me in place. He connected, *We aren't going back. I can't. Not right now. Not after what I saw.*

I lifted my chin, refusing to cower. *We agreed I would train. There's no reason for you to be angry.*

"We'll be back shortly," he informed the others. At Vlad's nod, he took my hand and led me deeper into the woods.

The connection between us sizzled as we picked up our pace. Luckily, my body was already healing, a nice side effect of being a shifter, and I didn't struggle to keep up.

As the sounds of the others vanished, Thorn kept moving forward. After a few miles, he stopped and turned to me, his pupils slitting. He stepped toward me, gently pushing me against a tree trunk.

He growled, "I need to inspect you for injuries."

CHAPTER TWENTY-FOUR

THE BARK CUT into the back of my arms, and a knot of desire twisted in my stomach. First, we needed to address the tension hanging between us. "Why are you mad at me?"

"I'm not mad," Thorn murmured as he leaned closer to me. *I was concerned when I felt your pain, but then I saw the end of your fight with Saphira. My dragon and I approve.*

He placed his hands on the trunk, trapping me, and focused on my lips. The sweet scent of his desire mixed with his usual minty amber, hiding the hint of sulfur. My breathing quickened as I stared at his strong jawline and full lips.

I became hyperaware that I was covered in sweat and reeked of body odor. I placed my hands on his chest, holding him back, the jolt of our connection pulling at my soul. I connected, *I need a shower. I stink.*

Smirking, he lowered his head. *It's fucking hot, and in a second, you'll be sweating even more.*

But the food... I tried to be sensible, but my dragon inched forward, and my body thrummed, needing the relief only he could bring. Still, if we didn't show up, everyone would know why.

Food can wait, he interjected and kissed me.

His lips were soft and urgent, and he threaded his fingers into my hair.

The sweet pressure and gentle tug had me coming unglued. I opened my mouth, and his tongue swooped inside. His minty taste consumed me, and I responded to each stroke with eagerness. I slipped my hands inside his shirt, tracing the curves of his muscles. He shuddered and cupped my neck, drawing us closer together.

Each line of his abs was part of a masterpiece. I would have to do a nude painting of him as soon as I had some place to hide it for my eyes only.

He groaned, and my cells sizzled as his hand swooped down and moved under my shirt, then my bra. He caressed my nipple, and I leaned my head back against the trunk as warmth spread through me.

Trailing a hand lower, I unfastened his jeans and pushed them and his boxers down so I could touch his hardness. I stroked him, and he hissed between his teeth.

He whispered, "Gods, you feel so good." Then he unfastened my bra, lifted my shirt, and bent down, replacing his fingers with his mouth.

I gasped and closed my eyes, reveling in the sensations building inside me. His hips swiveled, keeping pace with my hand, as his tongue worked his magic over me.

You're better than mint chocolate chip, he connected, unbuttoning my pants, then moved his fingers underneath my panties and between my legs. He circled and pressed in perfect rhythm, causing me to move faster.

With my eyes closed, the sensations took over, and the sounds of the breeze rustling through the branches and animals in the underbrush emphasized we were alone out here, desperate for each other.

The friction built, pushing me close to the edge, but I needed him inside me. I wanted him to find his pleasure at the same time I did.

I let go of him and opened my eyes. Watching him had my body going into overdrive. Ecstasy slammed through me, and he slightly increased the pressure. The pleasure intensified as his tongue lapped my breast.

I couldn't wait any longer. I grabbed his wrist and threaded my fingers in his hair, pulling him away from my chest. I spun him around, so he was against the tree trunk, then pushed his jeans and boxers to his ankles.

I kicked off my tennis shoes, and he bent and helped remove my pants and panties. We peeled off our shirts, and as I climbed his body, I tossed away my bra and enjoyed the way our skin crackled everywhere we touched.

His sky-blue irises glowed brightly, and his pupils slitted as I guided him inside me. Our dragons roared through our connection as he slid in, filling me whole.

You are so damn sexy, he connected as he slowly thrust into me.

He grabbed my thighs as I wrapped my legs around him. We moved together, and when I rode him faster, he quickly matched my pace.

I opened our bond, pushing all my love toward him. He responded in kind, and my heart expanded close to bursting. This joyful pain was so damn scary because, if I lost him, I wasn't sure I would survive, but I was lucky to have this magical connection.

His pleasure built, enhancing mine. This was what I'd been so desperate to have. A connection we could achieve only when we were linked together as one.

He moved faster, nearing his release.

As he orgasmed, his euphoria flowed into me, and my body followed suit. Our highs merged, and our bodies convulsed together as our bond swallowed us whole. I was lost in him.

All too soon, the world came back into focus around us. The sky was twilight purple, the moon was rising, and the stars twinkled above us. We'd been out here for over an hour, making love, and I'd enjoyed every minute of it.

As I slowly slid down his body, Thorn's chest rumbled, and my breath caught. It was the first time I'd heard him purr.

When my feet touched the ground, he kissed me and wrapped his arms around me, the cat-like noise growing louder.

As he pulled away, he cocked his head and arched a brow. "What happened? You just got happier, and you have this breathtaking smile on your face."

"You're purring." Never in my life had I imagined I'd be comfortable standing in front of a man, in the middle of the woods, butt naked, listening to him purr, yet here I was. How times had changed.

"I'm happy." He chuckled, then pushed a stray hair behind my ear. "You purr all the time."

"Yes, *I* do," I said and placed a hand on his chest, needing to touch him again. "This is the first time *you've* ever done it. I was thinking..." My smile faltered, and a lump formed in my chest.

"Oh, baby." He leaned forward and cupped my face with both hands. "That's not it at all. I'd be purring nonstop if Drake and the king would just leave us alone. I am happy, but this is the freest I've felt since Cassidy and Vlad were taken. We're alone in the woods, and I don't sense any danger."

Even at the cabin, a threat had loomed over us. At least here, at this moment, it was just the two of us in the woods. Besides, I didn't want to make him feel guilty. When he made that noise, I wanted it to be genuine and not forced... like now. "It's fine. I'm just a little emotional."

He smiled, and my pulse quickened. He pressed his forehead to mine and murmured, "When we get out of the country and we're safe, I'll purr *all* the damn time. You'll get tired of hearing me."

"Oh, whatever." I snickered, lost in his gaze. He was so handsome and easily the most attractive man I'd ever seen, and not just because I was biased. Even better, he was *all* mine. "Just forget I said anything. Please."

"Absolutely not." He placed a finger under my chin, gently forcing my head up so he could lock eyes with me. "I don't want you to ever feel like you can't talk to me about anything. Your well-being, both emotionally and physically, is my top concern. And I *am* happy. Happier than I ever thought I'd be, and I'm sorry I made you doubt that even for a minute."

His sincerity washed through me and settled comfortingly in my chest. There was no reason to hide anything from him. He accepted me for who I was, flaws and all.

"You know what?" he whispered against my earlobe, sending goose bumps all over my body. "I know what we should do."

I warmed for round two. If I had to choose between sex and food, sex with him would win every time. As long as I died while orgasming, I'd count it as a win. I bit my lower lip and whispered, "I haven't got a clue. Why don't you tell me?"

He grinned wickedly. "Well, we're both naked..." He winced and glanced down at his pants and boxers pooled around his ankles. "For the most part."

I laughed as my body tingled. I'd never imagined I could be this happy. "Sorry about that. I kinda got desperate, and that helped me get what I wanted faster."

He winked. "I approve of the strategy."

I trailed a finger down his chest, enjoying how his pecs quivered under my touch. "So...what is this idea of yours?"

"You, my love, have a one-track mind," he growled as he peppered kisses over my cheek. "But I was thinking we should shift and go for a flight."

My heart clenched while I also shuffled my feet. Two conflicting emotions mingled: disappointment that he wasn't speaking of sex and eagerness to take to the sky.

Gods, I love you. He beamed. *You look like a pouting puppy dog that has a treat dangling in front of her.*

I shrugged. *I was hoping for more sex but flying sounds nice, too.*

Then you shall have both. He booped me on the nose and kicked off his shoes. *But your dragon is restless, and it'll cause problems if you don't shift. Let's fly, then have another round of sex before heading back to the barn.*

I leaned against the trunk and watched my sexy mate peel the rest of the clothes from his body. His muscles flexed, and my stomach somersaulted all over the place.

He took a few steps back, so we'd have room to shift. Faint purple splotches appeared on his tanned skin as he transitioned into his dragon. With each second, his scales became more pronounced and darkened to his gorgeous silvery-plum color.

My dragon brushed against my mind, eager to follow suit. I thought to her, *Let's do this,* and she didn't hesitate.

She surged forward, melding with my mind. Our thoughts had already begun to merge, but when we were in dragon form, we were truly one.

The ground got farther away as my bones altered me into my dragon form. Within seconds, my feet and hands became silver-scaled limbs ending in talons, completing my transition.

I turned my head toward Thorn, who had been watching me. His sky-blue irises shimmered in the darkness, and he flapped his wings, lifting off the ground.

Allowing my dragon to take over, I followed Thorn, and we rushed into the sky. The wind blew past my scales, giving me a sense of freedom, and I enjoyed watching my mate in his strong dragon form. We were close to four times our human size, which meant my mate was over thirty feet of pure muscle.

With my dragon-heightened senses, I noticed a group of foxes running underneath us and several owls flying about two miles away. Most importantly, nothing out here could harm us.

The sky was clear, and we were high enough that no humans could see us. I stared into the true night sky, which I was finally able to see with my dragon eyes. The dark blue was peppered throughout the atmosphere with green and yellow splotches and spots of cobalt and pink swirls from the center of the Milky Way. It was second on my list to paint once I finished my masterpiece of Thorn.

Settling into a rhythm next to my mate, I reveled in the sense of peace swirling through me, and the two of us enjoyed our time together.

A WEEK PASSED, and Theron came back every few days to check in, update us with news, and take a grocery order.

Thorn had hoped that the hunt for us would die down, but Drake had increased the number of warriors searching for us. In a way, I was thankful. Thorn was determined our group should leave the country, and I'd been trying to talk him out of it.

Training had been going well. Saphira and I were now on equal footing, and Vlad had promised that tomorrow we would switch partners so I could spar with Errol. He said fighting different people would strengthen our strategy.

My skin buzzed from holding hands with Thorn. We'd finished our nightly routine of sex, flying, and more sex. Since Vlad and Cassidy had taken the isolated master bedroom, I didn't want Saphira, Tyson, Errol, and Brenton to hear Thorn and me in ours. Besides, I liked having sex outside. Being a dragon had changed me so much, and I was beginning to like myself.

We broke through the tree line behind the barn and found Eva and Elliott by the unlit firepit, sitting in two of the Adirondack chairs.

Neither of them noticed us as we strolled closer.

"I wish there was internet out here." Elliott gazed at the stars. "I miss my gamer friends, especially since you've become a stick in the mud, and Tyson is in the house, pouting."

Eva scowled. "First off, I'm not a stick in the mud. I just don't want to be in a position where I can't defend myself again. As for Tyson, he wants to train with the dragons, but he's too weak and stuck with us humans. He isn't pouting. He's depressed. He reminds me of Mom those first months after she was diagnosed with cancer."

My feet stilled as the memory sprang into my mind.

She'd been so upset that she'd become suicidal and would've tried to end her life if we hadn't intervened and gotten her some help.

What's wrong? Thorn connected and scanned the area for a threat.

Tyson. I turned toward him, my vision blurring. *I didn't realize he was struggling that badly.*

Thorn winced. *Yeah, I didn't want to worry you, but I get it. When your dragon is injured and you can barely fly, it makes things difficult.*

That was why Saphira, Tyson, Brenton, and Errol shifted together at different times from us. Vlad and Cassidy would go out later, after Thorn and I got back, but those four always flew at midday while we were eating lunch, and they weren't usually gone for long. It had to be because Tyson couldn't handle a longer flight.

I strode forward, wanting to be part of the conversation. "Do you think he might harm himself?" If there was a chance, we needed to watch him more closely.

Eva yelped, and Elliott's head snapped around.

His eyes bulged as he pointed. "What the *hell?* How did you sneak up on us?"

"We didn't." Thorn lifted a brow. "Remember, listening at all times is something we're supposed to be working on."

"This is why I'm a *stick in the mud.*" Eva lifted a hand. "Because dragon shifters are strong, fast, and quiet."

"There's one easy solution." Elliott waggled his brows and smiled so wide it was creepy. "Our brother-in-law can *change* us."

My mouth went dry. Thorn and I had talked about offering to change my siblings, but we hadn't gotten around to it yet. We'd been focused on so many other things, and

Thorn hadn't seemed eager to treat my siblings as guinea pigs.

When neither Thorn nor I responded, Elliott's jaw damn near touched the ground. "Wait." My brother jumped to his feet. "Is that an option?"

You can offer it to them, Thorn said as he squeezed my hand comfortingly. *If they want to, I can try. It would make things easier if they were strong as dragons.*

We stopped across the firepit from them, and I inhaled, searching for the right words. "Thorn has offered to *try* to change you...*if* you want. He can't guarantee it, and it's not a requirement."

"Fuck yeah." Elliott lifted a fist.

Eva's brows furrowed as if she were perplexed.

"Really?" Thorn's head tilted back. "When you first came to the cabin, you asked if I would change you as if you didn't want it."

I'd forgotten about that, and Elliott's quick yes now made me uneasy.

Elliott bobbed his head. "Well, yeah. At first, I was like, uh...no. But now that I've had time to acclimate...I've decided it'd be badass. So, fuck yeah, I'm down. Where the hell do I sign?"

I wasn't expecting that level of enthusiasm, Thorn connected, apprehension swirling through our connection.

Same. He hadn't taken the time to think it through. He was just gung ho. "What about you, Eva?" I wanted to see how she reacted.

"The thought has merit, but it's a huge change." She rubbed her arms. "Even though you're growing more comfortable with yourself, that only happened recently. I... I need to think about it."

Now *that* was rational. "How about you both think it

through? It's not like the offer is now or never. It doesn't expire. Besides, Thorn isn't even sure he can do it. This would be a whole life change. You'd have another being inside you that was never there before, and you'd see and hear things that don't make sense. It's not an easy transition, so at least, take a night to decide."

Elliott pouted and rolled his eyes. "Fine. I'll take the night, but my answer will still be yes tomorrow."

He reminded me so much of a young child.

"I'll try, then." Thorn mashed his lips together, trying not to smile.

"Wait." Eva's face lit up, and her attention landed on my mate. "Is that something you can do for Tyson to fix his dragon?"

"No. He's already a dragon..." Thorn spoke slowly, speaking to her delicately. "I can't give him another one."

My stomach swooped alarmingly. She'd made me think of something I hadn't before.

Something that might prevent everything Drake was killing for.

CHAPTER TWENTY-FIVE

IF I HADN'T KNOWN any better, I would have thought I was floating as my breath stuck in my chest. "You said you took Arman's dragon and gave it back, right?"

Thorn faced me with furrowed brows and nodded.

I didn't want to jump right to the end, needing to think everything through before I got ahead of myself. "And you mentioned you can use your magic to pull the energy of past dragons from the air to create a new dragon shifter, like you did for me, right?"

He scratched his head. "Yes. I don't know how, but when that magic pulses from me, I can feel the essence of dragons who've passed and the energy of the dragon inside the person as well. They feel the same, just...one is inside a living person."

That information enthralled me, but that was a discussion for a later time. "Hypothetically, what if you took Tyson's dragon and gave it back? Maybe whatever injured his dragon could be replenished from the surrounding essences. Maybe you could heal his dragon's injury."

Eva smiled, her irises lightening with hope. "Do you think that could work?"

"I... I don't know." Thorn rubbed his hands together, his face lined with worry. "My magic is a curse. I don't see how it could do something good like that."

My heart panged. I didn't believe that, but Thorn did. Why wouldn't he, after his own father tried to kill him for having this ability? If healing Tyson worked, it could convince other dragon shifters that Thorn wasn't a threat, and he would see the good he could do for his people. "If Tyson is willing, what's the worst that could happen?"

"I'll go get him." Elliott jumped to his feet and jogged to the house. "I'm sick and tired of seeing him mope around."

I frowned. He sounded similar to Peter with his lack of empathy, but I had to remember he was young, and he'd been raised by his father for the past six years with me visiting only intermittently.

When Elliott went into the barn, Thorn kicked at the grass. *I'm not sure this is a good idea. What if I mess him up further?* His trepidation weighed on our connection.

Moving closer to him, I placed my hand on his arm and looked into his eyes. I pushed all my love toward him and connected, *We'll be honest with him about the risks, and if he says yes, it won't be your fault. We warned him. Babe, you changed me, and you've taken the king's dragon and given it back. I don't think there's much at risk here, since you'll be learning to connect with your magic, and potentially relieving a dragon shifter of something that is impacting him.*

His sky-blue irises locked on me, and I reveled in them, memorizing each diamond fleck. The next words flowed out before I could even think about them. *I believe in you.*

His eyes widened, and his breath hitched. Something nebulous crossed his face before strong emotions swirled between us. The sensation was both heartbreaking and joyful.

He wrapped his arms around me, pulled me close, and kissed me.

You don't know how much that means to me, he connected as his tongue brushed against my lips.

"Uh..." Eva cleared her throat. "I know I'm not usually the mouthy one, but no one else is here to say anything, so it's on me. I'm pretty sure I just got pregnant watching you two."

I laughed and took a step back, enjoying the moment. This was what normal felt like: being in love with an amazing man and having my little sister there to rag on me about it. I could only hope there were many more moments like these in our future.

The back door opened, and Saphira, Brenton, Tyson, Cassidy, and Elliott came out. Saphira had an eyebrow arched, while Tyson's eyes were downcast. Brenton had a curious gaze, and Cassidy scanned the surroundings as if looking for answers. Elliott's body language was the most unique. He had a bounce in his step and a grin on his face.

When they reached the firepit, Saphira stood behind the chair across from me and crossed her arms. "What exactly do you want to talk to Tyson about?"

At least, Elliott hadn't run his mouth. There was no telling what would've come out. I'd imagined something like, *You want a new fucking dragon?* or an equally blunt question.

"Well, I—" Thorn bit his lip, our bond cooling as his insecurities filled it.

"I wanted to run something by Tyson." I'd take the blame so if it didn't work out, everyone would be mad at me and not Thorn. I refused to let Thorn carry a mistake on his shoulders, when it would be my fault for suggesting we heal Tyson in the first place.

Tyson pursed his lips. "Let me guess. You want me to hide if there's a fight since I'll only cause more problems." The agony on his face broke my heart.

They hadn't exaggerated the pain he was enduring.

"No, not at all." I stepped forward, wanting to be seen as the leader. "I was wondering if you'd be open to Thorn attempting to remove your dragon and give it back to you. It might reverse the injury Drake gave you that day in the clearing when you stood up for Saphira against him."

"Wait." Brenton lifted his hands. "Thorn can fix him?"

Tyson flinched.

"Not that you're broken." Brenton huffed and pinched the bridge of his nose. "I didn't mean it like that."

"How else could you mean it?" Tyson glared at his father, his eyes glistening.

Drake had caused so much strife in people's lives. He'd hurt Tyson, forcing him to feel inadequate.

"Sometimes, people phrase things ignorantly or make mistakes." Eva rubbed her arms and glanced at me. "They might say the wrong thing or say nothing at all—which could be worse—and act distant because that's all they've known since someone important passed away."

My breath caught. Was that her way of addressing what our relationship had been like during the last six years since Mom passed?

"What are the risks?" Cassidy asked, changing the direction of the conversation.

That was probably the safest bet.

"The biggest one is that I don't know what I'm doing." Thorn's shoulders were hunched slightly. "I changed Everly from human to dragon shifter, and when I was six, I took

King Arman's dragon and gave it back to him immediately. Other than those two instances, I've only recently taken dragons, and that was mainly fueled by my need to save Everly. After making her a dragon shifter by accident, I tried to take her dragon away, and it didn't work. The risk is that I might not be able to take your dragon if I'm not being fueled by emotion, or I might take it away and not be able to give it back, making you human permanently."

"Do it," Tyson said without hesitation. "I'm good with you trying whatever."

"Hell yeah." Elliott pumped his fist. "That's what I'm talking about."

Saphira scowled and growled, "Let's not encourage him to act irrationally."

"I'm with Saphira," Brenton said as he placed a hand on Tyson's shoulder. "We need time to think it through."

"No, *we* don't need time." Tyson glanced from Brenton to Saphira. "Maybe you two do, but that doesn't matter. I'm a legal adult now, and I want Thorn to try. I'd rather try and become a human forever than be scared and never have a way to truly fly like I should be able to. At least, if I'm human, there'll be a reason I'm not like the two of you, and I won't have a dragon going stir-crazy. I want to try, and that's my choice."

Saphira rubbed her chest as Brenton rubbed his temples.

Cassidy exhaled. "I'm not trying to push my opinion, but I've had to come to grips with Thorn and his magic. One of the hardest things about caring for someone is knowing when to let go and when to push back. This is a choice between Tyson and his dragon, just as it's up to Thorn whether he tries to use his magic."

My vision blurred. I hadn't considered that Thorn using

his magic might impact Cassidy. Maybe this was something he and I should've discussed with her. She had given up everything to protect him. "I'm so sorry. I didn't think about what I was suggesting."

"No reason to apologize, dear," Cassidy assured me with a sad smile. "You didn't do anything wrong. If Thorn can use his powers for good, that would be beyond amazing."

That was the point. I believed that if Thorn got over his fear of using his magic, it could be a blessing and something that could help dragons if they wanted it.

"She's right." Brenton clasped his hands. "If Thorn and Tyson want to try this, knowing all the facts, who am I to try to stop them?"

"His dad." Saphira lifted her hands. "Even if Tyson becomes human, Drake will still hunt him. It's not like that's his get-out-of-jail-free card."

"Why does that sound familiar?" Elliott tapped his chin. "What video game did you take that from?" He snapped his fingers. "It's from *A Way Out*, isn't it?"

"No, dumbass." Eva shook her head. "It's from *Monopoly*. We used to play it with Mom and Everly on board game night."

His mouth dropped open. "Oh, yeah. Back when we were heathens and didn't own electronics." He shivered. "Those were hard times."

"Seriously?" Saphira lifted a brow. "You're derailing a serious conversation."

"Saphy, you know I love you." Tyson gave her puppy-dog eyes. "But if Dad can get behind this, why can't you? Either way, Thorn is going to try. I'm asking for your blessing, but it's not required."

She scoffed, then took a deep breath. "Fine, but only

because I love you and you got injured protecting me. I guess it's the least I can do."

The dread and fear rolling off Thorn increased, and our connection became heavy and cold.

"When do we try?" Tyson lifted his chin and focused on my mate.

"Whenever you want?" Thorn swallowed, his Adam's apple bobbing. "Now, tomorrow, a week from today."

"Now." Tyson took an eager step forward. "If you *can* heal me, I want time to train with Vlad and the others. I need to be as strong and healthy as possible to hold my own if something happens."

Thorn stiffened but nodded. "Remember, you might turn human."

"It's a risk worth taking." Tyson surveyed the area. "Where do you want me?"

"Wait." Elliott bounced on his feet. "Do we need candles or to chant something to help with the magic?"

"What?" Thorn stared at him as if he had two heads.

Sometimes, I wondered about my brother. "He's not hosting a seance. He's tapping into the magic he has naturally. There's no need for blood or sacrifices." Wait. I didn't actually know that for sure. When he'd changed me, I'd been bleeding, and when he took the warriors' dragons, the people had been left human. *Or do we need a sacrifice?*

Thorn sighed. *Technically, pulling the essence from the air means a sacrifice has already been made—the human part of the shifter has already died for it to be released. Even though I'm not a witch, all magic comes at a cost.*

Good to know, I replied as I looped my arm through his. As expected, some of his anxiety ebbed at my touch, making me feel treasured.

Thorn chuckled dryly. "Though I don't need a witchy

setup, I would prefer it if everyone but Everly and Tyson would go inside."

"No candles and chants, and now I can't even watch." Elliott hung his head. "This is sorely disappointing."

"Elliott, sometimes, it's not about you." Eva rolled her eyes. She took her brother's arm and tugged him toward the barn. "Let's go kill some people."

"Okay. Those five words are my most favorite to hear, and they make this sting a lot less." He picked up his pace. "I'm going to kick your ass."

"Your brother." Cassidy snickered and shook her head. "That's what I thought raising a teen boy would be like, but Thorn wasn't like that, so I thought I'd been misguided. Now I'm learning Thorn was the exception and not the norm."

My brother didn't have the same background as Thorn, but I didn't want to mention that. No one needed that reminder. "Thorn is the exception to every rule." I glanced at my mate, the warmth of his love spreading through my body, even reaching my toes.

"I was about to argue about staying out here, but I'm afraid if I do, I might vomit." Saphira gagged, her face scrunching. "I thought those two were bad before. Oh boy, I was wrong."

That was the second comment like that in the past hour. I should have been offended, but I was more than pleased.

Cassidy winked at Thorn and me before nodding to the barn. "Let's get you inside before you throw up your dinner."

Brenton wrung his hands. "I'll stay close to the door. Just shout if you need me."

That was what a good parent did for their child —worried.

"Of course," I breathed.

Saphira, Cassidy, and Brenton went inside. Once the back door closed, Thorn took a deep breath and said, "Maybe you should sit down."

Hurrying to the chair in front of Thorn, Tyson sat, facing the firepit. "I'm ready."

I wish I were, Thorn replied as he rubbed his fingers.

My chest tightened. *If you don't want to try this, don't. I wasn't trying to push.*

I'm willing to try. This way, I'll know if I can actually change your siblings. Thorn placed his hands on Tyson's shoulders. *I need you next to me, but not touching me. I don't want to mess with your dragon by mistake.*

That I could do. *I'll always be at your side.*

He smiled. *I know. There's no doubt in my mind.* He closed his eyes, and his jaw clenched.

A few minutes passed, but neither he nor Tyson reacted or made a noise beyond breathing.

I can't do this, Thorn connected. *I don't feel anything.* Frustration wafted from him.

Remember what it was like when you felt the magic at the chateau and when you changed me? That was all that I could think of to help. *Remember the emotion and hold on to it.*

Okay, he replied as he closed his eyes tighter.

A strangling emotion surged through me, reminding me of when he'd been desperate to reach me. His hands glowed as his magic swirled inside him. My eyes widened.

Tyson gasped as the connection between Thorn and me grew hot and vibrant. Something swirled between us, a sensation that I'd felt once before, as if I could feel the brush of Thorn's magic.

The intensity increased, and Tyson whimpered, "It's gone."

"Give me a second," Thorn rasped as his eyes opened and focused on me.

The air around us buzzed. Not quite like the connection of our fated-mate bond but more like a warm hug brushing over my skin.

Pupils slitting, Thorn stared into me, and something inside me tugged as if he could see my soul—which wasn't far-fetched, given he was my other half. Air sawed through my lungs as my body thrummed and warmed in ways that had never happened simultaneously.

That night, when I saw you fall down the incline and hit your head, I was devastated and crazed, he connected, and a shiver ran down my spine. *Now I understand why. My dragon recognized you despite you being human. He refused to allow you to die and, by doing so, created our fated mate. When I made you a dragon shifter, there was so much blood I feared I couldn't save you. But you are strong—the strongest person I've ever known—and I'm so damn glad you decided not to reject me as your mate. I doubt I could've survived that hurt.*

I could never reject you. I inched closer, needing to be next to him. *Even when I was human, I didn't want anything bad to happen to you. Hell, even the night I first saw you in your car outside Drake's bar, your eyes captivated me.*

When you marched into that bar, I almost raced after you, wanting to protect you from him, he confessed. His hands dimmed, and the strange buzzing in our connection lessened.

For a minute, Thorn and I couldn't peel our eyes off each other.

Finally, my mind cleared. *What was that for?*

You said to recreate what I felt the night I changed you, so that's what I did. He smiled shyly. *And I think it worked.* Pride swirled through our bond, and my chest puffed out for him.

I gulped as my body tingled. Now we'd find out if Thorn could heal dragons that were impeded. "Tyson, how do you feel?"

He jumped to his feet and faced Thorn and me.

I expected him to show joy and relief, but his face was a shade paler than normal. He whispered, "Something's not right."

CHAPTER TWENTY-SIX

MY HEART THUDDED against my rib cage, and Thorn frowned. Our connection became frenetic as concern replaced the pride he'd felt.

"What do you mean something's not right?" I asked, touching Thorn's arm. This time, my touch didn't have as much of a calming effect. He barely relaxed.

I winced. I was the reason for this, but I couldn't take it back. *Before we panic, we have to hear the facts.*

It's been the same since I was a child—I'm cursed. No good can come from my magic, he replied as our bond heated with his anger. *This was a mistake. I shouldn't have tried. I should've known better.*

The urge to hang my head and close my eyes surged through me. Instead, I forced myself to stand tall. If I crumbled, I suspected Thorn would only struggle more.

Tyson stared at his hands as if they would reveal the answer. With each second that ticked by without an answer, Thorn's emotions became more turbulent.

"Please, Tyson," I said softly and leaned toward him.

"Your explanation doesn't have to be perfect. Just tell us how you feel."

"Different." He dropped his hands, and his forehead wrinkled. "It's like it's *my* dragon, but not."

I tilted my head. "Does it feel different or react differently to you?" At least, he had a dragon that was somewhat familiar.

"It's *mostly* the same, but I don't recognize it completely. It feels weird." Tyson rubbed his hands together. "Like when you get bandaged or something."

"Gods, Tyson." Thorn's voice broke, and his shoulders sagged. "I'm so sorry. I should've known better." Heartache penetrated our bond, and I damn near collapsed to my knees.

Thorn was letting his emotions get the best of him, and I refused to allow it. "Before we assume the worst, maybe you should shift and see what's different."

If he can shift, Thorn connected but thankfully had enough clarity not to say it out loud. *I might have made his situation worse. Maybe the king was right, and I shouldn't be around other dragons. All I do is harm them.*

I clenched my free hand, allowing my fingernails to bite into my palms. I would not let the king ruin this amazing man. He was spiraling, and it was my fault. I hadn't realized he'd take it this hard if it didn't pan out, especially when we'd warned Tyson that we didn't know whether it would work, and the young man had agreed to try anyway. *Thorn, none of this is your fault. Let's see what happens.*

"Yeah, I can do that." Tyson rolled his shoulders and inhaled. He called toward the house, "Dad, wanna go on a flight with me?"

Part of me wanted to go with him, but I bit my tongue. He hadn't been comfortable before when he'd known his dragon had issues. The last thing he probably wanted was Thorn and me hovering around, inspecting his dragon. Some insecurities were hard to get over.

The back door opened, and Brenton hurried toward us. His face was tight, and his eyes narrowed as he inspected his son. "Of course. Are you all right?"

"I'm not sure." Tyson nodded toward the tree line. "But I guess we're about to find out."

Brenton nodded. "Let's go."

"We'll be back soon." Tyson exhaled. "I won't leave you two hanging."

The two of them headed off, leaving Thorn and me alone. My mate paced the open grassy area between the barn and the firepit. He ran his hands through his shaggy hair and kept his gaze cast downward.

I'd never seen him like this. "I'm sorry, Thorn." I took a step toward him and stopped. He might not want me close after what I'd encouraged him to do. Maybe that was why my touch hadn't calmed him as much as normal. "I understand why you're upset with me."

He stopped and turned to me. His face twisted. "I'm not upset with *you*. I have no reason to be. You wanted to do something good for someone. That's one of the reasons I love you—you truly care about others." He lifted his arms. "And I want to be able to do that *for you*, but almost every time I use my magic, bad things happen." He hurried a few steps closer to me. "I'm afraid of what might happen when you realize that, and I'm afraid something bad might happen to you because of me."

My breath caught, and I didn't hesitate. I closed the distance between us and touched his cheek, enjoying the jolt that thrummed under my hand. "Was changing me a bad thing?"

He flinched. "Of course not, but at first, you weren't happy about it."

"I was caught off guard, and there was all the crap with Drake and Eva." I caressed his skin. "But I wouldn't change it for the world. I'm happy now, all because of you. You need to see that. You need to see that nothing bad has happened because of *you*. Drake was already targeting my family, and I was already *promised* to him. The only detail that changed was that I would be his wife, instead of his breeder, which wasn't that much of a difference."

A low growl emanated from his chest. *I hate hearing about that, and one day, we will get the hell out of here so he can't breathe down our necks.*

If we leave and don't fight, he'll always be hunting us. I understood he wanted to believe there was somewhere safe we all could go, but a place like that didn't exist. Not with someone like Drake, a powerful royal whose ego was more important to him than anything else. We'd embarrassed him in front of his people; he wouldn't let that go. If anything, every day that hate and resentment festered inside him made the danger worse.

But there were more pressing matters, so I pivoted. *You said your magic is a curse, but you made me into a dragon.* We stared at each other. *I don't feel cursed. I, for once in my life, feel complete and like I belong.*

He leaned down and pressed his forehead against mine. *Of course, I don't feel like changing you into a dragon was a curse, but I did it without your permission. It's like, whenever I want to do something the right way, I mess up. Remember, you wanted me to take your dragon away, and I couldn't.*

I had forgotten about that. I couldn't imagine being human again and giving up the amazing connection I had with him. There was nothing in the world more important, not even my promise to Mom. *Maybe you couldn't because we're fated mates. You took Tyson's from him, and you gave it back. Maybe your magic changed me because, as you said, your dragon recognized what I was.*

Brows furrowing, he straightened. *I hadn't thought of it like that. It would go against everything within me to turn you back to human, but still, you asked, and I couldn't deliver.*

And I'm so damn thankful for it. I tugged at our connection, pushing the magnitude of my feelings toward him. *Then we wouldn't have this, and I will never give it up.*

His irises lightened, and some of his turmoil lifted from our bond. Though the feelings were still there, they weren't as strong.

The back door opened, and Saphira, Vlad, and Cassidy joined us in the backyard.

Saphira chewed on her lip and scanned the trees behind us. "Is Tyson okay? I heard Brenton come out but was trying to give them a few minutes before I barged in to check on him."

I lifted a brow. "I didn't realize you were capable of such self-restraint." I tried schooling my expression because I was teasing her. If she didn't have self-restraint, she would've ratted Thorn out to the cops who had come by the cabin before we'd learned everything.

She scrunched her nose. "I have my moments, and I know how Tyson is struggling. I didn't want to make things worse for him." Her lips tipped downward.

Thorn placed an arm around my waist. "We aren't sure. I took his dragon away and gave it back, but he said something didn't feel right. He and Brenton went for a flight to see what happened."

Wings flapped overhead, and our group glanced skyward. Two dragons came into view, flying over the treetops, barreling toward us. They were similar in size, but the one on the left was cream-colored and the other was maroon. Both were flying without issue.

Thorn's arm tensed around me.

"Is that them?" Vlad's cornflower-blue eyes reflected the rising moonlight, now that darkness surrounded us.

"Yes, but Tyson's reddish color is lighter than it was." Saphira's eyes narrowed. "Like a shade lighter. And he isn't flying wobbly like before."

The two dragons descended and landed in the open area beside us.

Tyson flapped his wings and threw his head back, roaring faintly before taking to the sky again.

"You did it, Thorn." Cassidy beamed, her attention locked on Tyson. "I'm so proud of you."

I'd expected the pride to return to Thorn, but the bond constricted in a way that stunned me.

He said he felt different, and his color has changed. Thorn's breathing turned ragged. *I don't know what that means.*

You had to use some of the ancestors' essence to make his dragon whole. Maybe that's the result. I burrowed into his side, placing my head on his shoulder. *It makes sense that it would no longer be exactly the same magic, and he did say it felt mostly the same, just a little odd. Maybe that's why. To heal him, you had to change him a little. But the point is, you did heal him, Thorn.* I needed him to focus on the miracle. *No one but you could've done that. Now he won't be in danger, like before.*

A happy lightness filled our bond, and when he smiled,

my heart skipped a beat. The anger disappeared as he watched Tyson fly high into the sky.

This was what he'd needed. A true win. Maybe...just maybe...he'd stop seeing the magic as a curse and understand the possibilities it could open for his people—the safety he could provide.

THE NEXT FEW days were rewarding. I was competent enough to hold my own, and Tyson joined the dragons' training. His enthusiasm was better than anything else to make the atmosphere feel less threatening. He'd acclimated to his dragon, which he found to be more similar to his original dragon than he'd feared. All he'd needed to do was shift and fly with it for them to settle in with each other.

Eva still hadn't decided whether she wanted to become a dragon, and I was thankful she wasn't rushing into anything. It wasn't a decision to take lightly. Thorn had agreed to turn Elliott, but only after Eva had made her final decision, regardless of what she landed on.

Saphira and I were in the middle of a fight. She stood in front of me, waiting for me to make a move. Despite the chill of the late May breeze, our bodies were slick with sweat.

Not wanting to disappoint, I glanced at her stomach to make her think I was going to kick. When she shifted her weight to protect that area, I lifted my leg to continue the ruse and tapped her jaw. We'd agreed on no hard hits to the face.

She frowned and gritted her teeth. "Dammit! That's the second time I've fallen for that!" She settled back into a fighter's pose.

"That's good," Vlad called from his corner where he was sparring with Tyson. "You're learning your weak spots. Keep it up."

He was an excellent teacher. Tough when needed but also encouraging when someone felt discouraged.

I prepared myself. The one thing I'd learned about Saphira was that, when she was emotional, she tended to be rash.

Ev, Theron is here, Thorn connected with me from his spot with Eva, Elliott, and Peter in front of the barn. *I thought you might want to know.*

Hearing his voice, I was slow to notice Saphira's kick and pain exploded in my stomach, and I doubled over, falling to the ground.

"Whoa!" Saphira squealed. "Everly, I'm so sorry. I thought you'd block it."

Eyes burning and blurring, I hissed through my teeth. I had let Thorn distract me, and now I was paying the price.

Everly, what happened? Thorn's voice popped into my head. *I'm on my way.*

My thoughts were scrambled, but I knew he needed to stay there with Peter. There was no telling what he'd say or do around Theron if one of us wasn't with them. *I'm fine. Stay with Peter and Theron. I'll be there soon. Saphira kicked my ass. That's all.*

His dragon roared.

It was my fault, not hers. Unable to see the world around me through my unshed tears, I watched a blurry form hurry over to me and place a hand on my shoulder. A musky cinnamon scent wafted around me.

Vlad.

"Hey, you okay?" he asked, concern thick in each word.

My skin prickled, indicating that everyone was

watching me. I hadn't gotten hurt like this before, meaning I'd royally screwed up. I gritted, "Yeah. Thorn connected with me and said Theron is here."

"Ah, you were distracted," he said and patted my arm. "Though it's a hard lesson to learn, it was one best served here. Even when your fated mate talks to you, you have to pay attention to your surroundings and not get lost in your bond."

"Believe me." I gasped, but the pain began to recede. "I learned."

"I'm so—" Saphira started.

I lifted my hand. "We were sparring. You didn't do it on purpose."

"I wouldn't be so sure about that." Tyson snorted.

"Hey! No one was talking to you," Saphira snapped.

I blinked, a few tears trailing down my cheeks.

Brenton and Errol shook their heads at each other, and Errol said, "And I thought these two were done acting like siblings."

"Come on. I'll help you up." Vlad held out his hand.

I took it, my sides screaming as I straightened. It was a damn good thing I was a dragon shifter. I'd bet this would have taken days to heal if I'd been human.

"Cassidy said lunch will be ready in thirty. Let's take a break and head in." Vlad waved toward the barn but stayed next to me.

Tyson, Errol, and Brenton led the way, trying to get Tyson away from Saphira before he riled her up more. Saphira had a deep scowl on her face, feeling guilty for what she'd done.

"I promise. I'm fine." I smiled. "Like Vlad said, it was better for me to learn this now instead of in battle. This way,

I have time to lick my wounds before getting even with you later."

Her mocha irises twinkled. "Oh, you think you're going to get even? Please. Next time, I'll kick your ass and not feel bad about it."

Now *there* was the Saphira I knew and loved.

"Let's see what updates Theron has." I headed for the barn, knowing the two of them would follow me.

Within minutes, we stepped into the clearing and found solemn faces...except Peter's. He smiled as if he'd won the lottery.

"What's going on?" I asked, picking up the pace.

"The warriors." Theron placed a hand on his stomach. "Aiden alerted us that they're at his location, which means my thunder is next. You need to leave, so I can bring my son here."

"But he can stay here with us," Thorn rasped as his neck corded. "I don't understand why we need to leave."

Theron bared his teeth. "If my son finds out about you, that will put him in more danger. I'd hoped the warriors would bypass us, but they're getting closer, and I have to protect my son. I'm sorry, but you all need to leave."

Theron and Thorn were reacting emotionally and not thinking clearly.

"If your son isn't there when they arrive, they'll ask questions." Vlad lifted his hands. "I get the need to protect your son, but if the warriors realize something is amiss, you'll only reveal to them that you have something to hide. I'm not saying I don't sympathize, but that alone could place a target on his back."

"There's something that could protect both groups," I said and glanced at Thorn. He'd healed Tyson's dragon—maybe he could do the same for Theron's son.

Theron laughed harshly. "Like what? It's like you think I haven't tried to find a solution."

Everly, no, Thorn connected. *I did that for Tyson to help us.*

You're going to let a dragon shifter get marked for murder when there's something you can do to save him? I asked, lifting a brow. *Thorn, you can't mean that.*

Thorn flinched, my words hitting their mark.

Before he and I could finish our conversation, Tyson stood tall. "I had an injured wing, and Thorn healed me. I no longer have that issue."

Mouth dropping open, Theron glanced from Tyson to Thorn. Then his face went red as he growled, "Oh, *hell* no. He's not touching my son. I saw what he did to those warriors. Your group needs to leave."

Thorn's hurt slammed into me, and I marched forward. No one made my mate feel that way.

I'd bring Theron to his knees.

CHAPTER TWENTY-SEVEN

HURT AND ANGER rolled from Thorn, adding to my rage. Even when Thorn proved his magic could be used for good, some scared dickhead made him feel as if that wasn't good enough.

I strode to Theron and pressed my finger into his chest. The older man blinked several times.

"You want to condemn Drake for hurting the weak, but you're as bad as he is." I lifted my chin as my dragon inched forward. "You're letting the opinions of others, and what you *thought* you saw, paint a picture of my *mate*, a man who's a million times better than you, because you're allowing your fear to control you."

Theron's pupils slitted as his dragon peered through. I couldn't blame him; I was being aggressive, so naturally, his dragon would sneak out.

He sneered. "They've replayed the wedding several times, and you can't say he didn't steal those warriors' dragons."

Everly, let it go, Thorn connected, warmth spreading

through our connection. *We need to leave before the warriors get closer.*

If he thought I'd let this asshole say what he had without putting him in his place, Thorn would soon learn better. I continued, "Of course, he did! Because Drake manipulated me into giving myself up, supposedly to save my sister, Saphira, and Thorn's parents. Drake wanted me to be his breeder, but instead, when he realized Thorn and I had completed our fated-mate bond, he decided to make me his wife so Thorn would expose himself to save me. What would *you* do if your mate was taken against her will and forced to be with someone else?"

"I know I'd be going crazy," Vlad interjected from behind me. "And I would've done worse than Thorn. He didn't kill the warriors. He just took the dragon of anyone who attacked him when he was trying to get to his mate."

Something unreadable passed through our connection, but I didn't have time to focus on what Thorn was feeling. I had a threat to put in his place.

Theron looked over my shoulder at the group behind me.

"If it's any help, I didn't trust or like Thorn at first," Saphira said and moved to my side. "But after a short time, I realized he wasn't what the king and Drake had portrayed. I'm the daughter of the king's most trusted advisor, and Drake threw me in a jail cell because I'd sided with Thorn. He promised Everly, in front of me, that if she handed herself over, he'd release the four of us, but when she did, he went back on his word. He said he was above the law. After seeing what a difference Thorn made to my cousin"—she gestured to Tyson—"if I were you, I would let him help your son. That's the only sure way to protect him."

Theron yanked on his hair. "I... How do I know you're telling the truth?"

"The king asked me to help his son, Thorn, to save his fated mate before Drake could force her to marry him." Errol strolled to Saphira's other side. "He trusted me, especially after what Drake did to my daughter. I wouldn't be here if I believed Thorn was the real threat to the kingdom. I willingly left the king's side to protect my daughter and obey the king's command. You have a son. You should understand this completely."

"And you know my dad," Vlad added.

Theron sighed. "Let's say maybe I was overreacting, and I'm open to the possibility of Thorn helping my son." He turned to my mate. "Is that something you're willing to try and can do?"

I swallowed, waiting for the inevitable no from Thorn.

Our bond fluttered, and Thorn replied, "Yes, on both counts."

My chest expanded, and I looked at him and asked, *Really? I thought you didn't want to.*

I don't, but you're right. If I don't help, we're sentencing an innocent dragon shifter to death just because he's different. And after Vlad, Saphira, Tyson, and Errol backed me, I don't really have a choice. Thorn winked as our connection heated. *And you telling him off was hot. Besides, if I help his son, we can stay here longer. Then we'll have more time for lovemaking, which I desperately need.*

I smiled. *I'm always open to sneaking away to spend time alone with you.* As long as he'd decided to help on his own, I was here for it. Obviously, he did care; he was just jaded, and I couldn't blame him for that. I believed that with each positive thing he accomplished with his magic, he would see things differently.

His pupils slitted, and my dragon purred. Thankfully, only internally.

"Okay." Theron exhaled and nodded. His irises glowed. "My wife will find Sol and tell him to meet us at the edge of our thunder's territory. It'll be best if only Thorn comes, so we can remain undetected."

"I need to come too." The thought of Thorn heading to a thunder alone, when the warriors were nearby, didn't sit well with me. Theron's focus would be on protecting Sol, not my mate.

"And me." Vlad tensed. "If the warriors come, we can't leave Thorn there by himself, and he is *my son*."

"Fine, but no more." Theron rubbed a hand down his face. "I'm only agreeing because I understand those bonds, but we need to move. We have a couple more days before the warriors appear, but I'd rather try it now, while it's less risky."

Why don't you stay here? Thorn frowned. *It would be safer.*

If I were heading off somewhere, would you stay behind? I arched a brow. I already knew the answer, but I needed to hear him say it.

He surprised me when he sighed. *Fine, but at the first sign of anything suspicious, you leave, even if I can't yet.*

In other words, if he hadn't finished replacing Sol's dragon. *Fine.* Hopefully, we wouldn't get into that situation.

The front door opened, and Cassidy strolled out. Her face was lined with worry. Vlad had been keeping her apprised of what was going on.

She rubbed her hands down her pants and jerked her chin toward the barn. "Lunch is ready."

My stomach growled, but food would have to wait. We

needed to act, not only due to the threat the warriors posed, but also because Theron could change his mind.

Vlad must have had the same thought. He said, "Will you put aside plates for Thorn, Everly, and me so we can eat once we return?"

"I'd think twice before letting my stepdaughter go with you." Peter scowled, his beady eyes darker than normal. "She causes more problems than she's worth."

When Thorn took a menacing step toward him, realization washed over me. That was the exact response my stepdad wanted. He wanted to make Thorn look bad in front of Theron.

Don't, I connected, my urgency filling our bond. *He's manipulating you.*

Thorn halted just as Eva crossed her arms and said, "Dad, the only person who causes problems is *you.* You embezzled money from the Hales, which is the only reason Everly and I got involved. So go look in the mirror to find the person who's to blame, and stop trying to drive a wedge between Everly, me, and Elliott."

My gut tightened. Was he the reason Elliott and Eva had treated me with so much indifference for so long? Since the Hale situation had arisen, the twins had been treating me differently. They actually felt more like siblings than mere acquaintances, and I'd seen a side of them that had disappeared when Mom died.

Theron's forehead creased, and I wasn't sure if it was from confusion, concern, or both. Either way, leaving before Peter got more riled up was our best option. I should've known he would pull something like this, but he'd been playing along the past few days, so I hadn't thought twice about it.

"We can finish this conversation later," Cassidy said,

glaring at Peter. "Thorn, Everly, and Vlad need to go." She went straight to Vlad and hugged him. Their eyes glowed, and she pulled away and patted Thorn and me on the arm. "Go on. Brenton, Errol, and I have it from here."

"Hey!" Saphira placed her hands on her hips. "Don't play the old-people card on me. I'll help watch Peter and his sniveling ways."

Vlad nodded. "Let's go. I don't want to drag this out."

Theron hesitated, and my stomach sank. Then the older dragon glanced at Tyson, and something firmed in his expression. "Yes, let's go." He spun on his heel and marched toward the tree line, and Thorn, Vlad, and I followed.

Suddenly, I paused. "Wait. We need to pack a bag, so we have clothes to change into."

"It'll be fine," Theron replied, not breaking his stride. "My mate will bring things for you to wear while you're there. You won't be staying long, just enough to do...whatever Thorn does."

That would work. And anyway, the clothes he'd stocked here were slightly too large for my human size, and I'd learned that wearing shorts was my best option. I had to wash my panties and bras each night because none of the extras here fit me.

"Let's shift, and you all can follow me." Theron turned toward us. "Let me be clear. I'm not comfortable taking you this close to the thunder, but Sol can't travel far in his dragon form. If something goes south, I will do anything to protect my thunder."

He didn't need to spell out what he meant—he would tell Drake where we were. Even if we ran, the dragons would know where we'd started.

Aggravation swirled from Thorn, and he growled.

But I understood both men. Theron was helping us as a

favor to a friend but didn't fully trust us. And Thorn didn't like being threatened, especially when I was involved.

"We understand. You've already made that clear. But know that when someone is helping you, they don't want to hear the same threat again." I tried to keep a level tone. We were all highly emotional. *Thorn, remember, he's taking us to his mate and son. How would you feel if someone you didn't trust was about to meet me? Try to see it from his perspective.* That was a trick I'd picked up over the years when dealing with Peter.

"I agree with Everly." Vlad smiled, and there was pride in his eyes.

"All right." Theron marched into the tree line. "Let's take flight."

Within a few minutes, the four of us were flying skyward, higher than we did at night, since the sun was out, and we needed to stay away from human eyes.

Theron's Carolina-blue dragon took the lead. Thorn and Vlad flanked me, Thorn's gorgeous plum dragon on my left and Vlad's olive-green dragon on my right. Among such colorful dragons, my dark silver color didn't seem as vibrant.

Peter better be damn glad that Theron was there, and you stopped me. I could've easily killed him, Thorn connected, his sky-blue eyes locking on me. *He wanted Theron to force us to leave so Drake would have a better chance of finding us.*

Which is why you didn't act impulsively, I reminded him as I brushed the tip of my wing against his. *You need to let that go and enjoy the moment. We can worry about him when we return. You need to focus on your magic.*

I didn't react because you were there as my voice of reason. He focused forward. *But you're right. We'll deal with him on our return.*

For forty-five minutes, Thorn and I enjoyed our flight. We hadn't ventured far from the barn, so traveling faster and farther away was amazing.

All too soon, Theron began a descent into a thick section of trees. We'd reached our destination.

Using my dragon senses, I searched the area. I detected rabbits hopping below, a few elk roaming, and other woodland creatures enjoying the wilderness.

Two human forms waited as well.

That had to be Sol and Theron's mate.

Not sensing anything threatening, our group swooped down. Thorn and Vlad did their own assessment.

Stay close to me, Thorn connected. *Though I think he's trustworthy, we can't be too careful.*

I have no intention of wandering away from you, I assured him. My time of trying to sneak away and act on my own was over. Drake had cured me of that.

We landed where the two people stood waiting. Theron's mate was shorter than six feet tall, with shoulder-length ash-blonde hair and forest-green eyes. She looked to be in her forties, though there was no telling how old she truly was.

A man in his mid-twenties stood next to her. If he had a dragon injury, I never would have guessed. He was close to six and a half feet tall and looked strong, like his father, with dark blond hair, chestnut eyes, and a light brown goatee that was neatly trimmed.

I'd expected Theron's son to be closer to Vlad's age than mine, but Theron's wife was younger than her mate, so maybe that explained it.

"Here are your clothes," Theron's mate said, gesturing to the four outfits laid out in front of us. "Go shift. People in our thunder saw Sol and me head this way alone after searching for Theron all morning."

Great, now there was even more urgency around our plans.

After carefully grabbing the clothes, we dispersed into the trees. Thorn and I stayed together and shifted into our human forms. We dressed quickly and headed back out to join the others.

When they saw Thorn, neither of them flinched. Theron must have warned them.

Theron's mate took an eager step toward Thorn and asked, "Is what you told Theron true? Can you heal Sol?"

My skin itched from the nervousness swirling through my bond with Thorn.

"I'll try," Thorn replied as he took my hand. "I healed someone in a similar situation a few days ago, but there is one thing I have to prepare you for."

"What?" Theron scowled. "You didn't imply there was anything my son had to worry about."

Vlad lifted a hand. "Hear him out, please."

My mouth went dry, but I needed to contribute. "It'll make sense if you do."

"Honey, they're right." Theron's mate touched his arm. "We can always decide not to let him do it."

Theron sighed and leaned into his mate. "You're right, Hydra. I just worry."

"Please, tell me everything." Sol leaned forward, his eyes wide.

Fidgeting, Thorn launched into what we'd learned from Tyson about his dragon changing slightly.

When he was done, Sol nodded. "I'm in."

Unease prickled through our bond, and I squeezed Thorn's hand tighter, silently telling him I was right there. I connected, *You've already done this once, and I'll be right here beside you.*

That's the only reason I can go on, he replied, and my heart missed a beat.

"Are you two okay with it?" Vlad added as he moved to Thorn's other side. "We don't want anyone to get upset over whatever happens."

Hydra smiled sadly. "If it's what our son wants, we won't stop him."

"What do we do?" Sol crossed his arms.

A quick look around confirmed there was no seating like back at the barn. Instead, Thorn stepped in front of Sol. "I need to touch you. Remember, I'll have to take the dragon away first, and you'll feel the loss."

Sol nodded.

Thorn released me and placed his hands on the younger man's shoulders. He inhaled deeply, and the flutter in our bond started.

He was nervous, and having Theron and Hydra watching wasn't helping matters. But I doubted they'd be willing to leave. *You've got this. I believe in you.*

I hope you're right, he replied as he closed his eyes. *Remember not to get too close.*

A long moment passed, and nothing happened.

Theron and Hydra glanced at each other, and Sol shuffled his feet.

Panic swirled through our bond as Thorn struggled with his magic.

Remember what it felt like when the warriors attacked you at the chateau? I almost reached out to him but stopped short. *Take your time.*

Thorn inhaled again, and after another moment, his hands glowed. Hydra's, Theron's, and Vlad's eyes widened.

None of them had seen Thorn use his magic before.

The same strange feeling soared through our bond, the vibrations warm and consuming. As soon as it started, the sensation vanished.

"It's gone." Sol sounded startled.

"I warned you." Thorn closed his eyes tighter. "Now, I'll give it back to you." His face twisted in agony for a moment before his hands sparked and the thrumming filled our connection. His magic tugged at our bond, and his hands glowed brighter.

Hydra gasped.

When Thorn's hands dimmed, Sol gasped as well.

"Did it work?" Theron asked as he rushed to his son.

Sol nodded. "I feel my dragon, and like he said, it feels different."

"All you need to do is fly, and you'll settle into each other." I smiled, seeing the joy light up Sol's face. "That's what helped Tyson."

"Thank you so much." Theron scratched the back of his neck. "I know I was cynical, but this—"

Vlad lifted a hand. "Don't. You've already helped us more than we can ever repay."

A branch snapped several yards away, and the six of us tensed.

Someone was spying on us.

CHAPTER TWENTY-EIGHT

THORN TURNED toward the noise and stepped in front of me, partially blocking me from view.

I wanted to yank him behind me, especially if the threat was a warrior, but I understood he was acting on the same instinct to protect me.

My lungs seized. If it was a warrior, they would've already notified the others that we were here.

Theron hurried toward the noise, racing between a yellow poplar and an oak tree, and disappeared from view.

"Dad," Sol whispered loud enough that Theron could hear.

When there wasn't an immediate response, Sol took a few steps forward, but Hydra clutched his arm and murmured, "You're not acclimated to your dragon yet. You need to stay put. Besides, he found the person watching. It's Wyvern."

My lungs started working better. The name seemed familiar. "Who's that?"

"Theron's righthand man." Hydra dropped her hands to her sides. "Ever since we learned the warriors were near, everyone's been on edge. Wyvern noticed us hurrying away, and he couldn't find Theron. He must have been making sure everything was okay."

The sounds of footsteps drew closer, and both Theron and Wyvern stepped into view.

Vlad and Thorn went rigid. If I hadn't known better, I would've thought a warrior was here, but maybe their wariness had to do with the frown on Theron's face.

Wyvern was shirtless, which didn't help matters for Thorn with me here. The new dragon was muscular, his warm, medium-brown complexion enhancing the curves of his muscles. He placed a cell phone in his back jeans pocket and folded his arms over his broad chest. His dark eyes assessed Thorn and me, and I noticed his eyes had a fold in the upper eyelid in the inside corner.

"Why are *they* here?" Wyvern asked, rubbing a hand across a scruffy goatee. He sneered at me like he thought his look of disgust would impact me.

A laugh bubbled in my chest, but I held it in. Laughing wouldn't help, but seriously, Drake had the menacing look down pat. Compared to him, Wyvern looked as threatening as a kitten.

"The less you know, the better," Theron rasped and pointed behind them. "Why don't you head back to the thunder?"

"Are you serious?" Wyvern jerked his head back. "Why have you allowed them here?" He paused, his cheeks reddening. "Wait. Are they blackmailing you? Is that why you've been disappearing so much lately?"

Thorn shook his head and bared his teeth. *This is why I didn't want to help them. I get accused of horrible stuff, even when I do something good. It's not worth putting us at risk.*

My heart ached. Every time he felt good about something, something else came along to ruin it. My hands clenched. "No, we aren't blackmailing him." I lifted my chin, refusing to cower, and flanked Thorn. "My *mate* just healed Sol so when the warriors do come, he won't be targeted."

Wyvern's brows furrowed. He looked at Thorn. "Why would you do that?"

"Because Thorn is a good person," Vlad interjected as he stepped up beside Thorn.

It was clear we would protect Thorn, no matter the cost.

"How did you..." Wyvern's eyes bulged. He turned back to Theron. "Have you been *helping* them?"

Jaw ticking, Theron glanced at us and said, "You three, go on. I'll handle things from here."

Thorn's nostrils flared. "Gladly."

The three of us spread apart, readying to shift.

Sol hurried to Thorn and touched his arm.

My mate tensed, not meeting his eyes.

"I just wanted to say thank you again." Sol dropped his hand. "You saved my life, and I will *never* forget that."

"The same goes for me." Hydra smiled but stayed several feet away. "Your secret is safe with us."

Wyvern frowned. "We can't let them go. The prince is searching for them, and we all saw on the Dragonnet that this asshole stripped those shifters of their dragons." He scoffed. "I can't believe you allowed him to touch Sol!"

A deep growl emanated from Thorn's throat. Hot anger and cold tendrils of fear swirled through our bond. A hot fudge brownie with ice cream was an amazing combination of the two temperature extremes, but *this* sensation was far from comforting. It was unnerving. If Thorn felt I was under threat, who knew what he'd do?

I grabbed his arm. Some of his turmoil ebbed, but not as much as I'd hoped.

"You will let us go," Thorn rasped. "The only reason those warriors lost their dragons was that they were keeping me from my *mate*." He wrapped an arm around my shoulders and pulled me to his side. "Drake and the warriors tried to force my mate to marry *him*, despite her being mated to *me*. So I did what I had to do to save her." He lowered his arm. "Let me be clear. If you prevent us from leaving or put my mate in harm's way, I won't hesitate to do the same to you."

There was no question Thorn loved me and would do anything for me, and I treasured that. But I wasn't sure if threats were the right route to go with Wyvern.

Wyvern's jaw dropped as he stared at Theron and asked, "Did you hear him? He said he would take my dragon!"

"Because he senses you're putting his mate at risk," Theron growled and gestured at me. "If I had that power, I'd do the same if you talked like that about Hydra, especially if the person hunting her wanted to make her his wife."

"By helping them, you've put the whole thunder at risk." Wyvern shook his head. "What do you think will happen if Drake finds out? Hell, they knocked out the king!"

Vlad touched Thorn and me and murmured, "We need to go."

He was right. Wyvern was distracted, arguing with Theron. If we gave them time to calm down, we could be stuck here, especially if Wyvern had a fated mate, or if he'd texted someone in the thunder to alert them about us.

Taking Thorn's hand, I guided him into the trees as Sol and Hydra moved to stand between us and Wyvern.

"Hey!" Wyvern shouted. "You're not going anywhere!"

Thorn tensed, but I tugged him deeper into the woods after Vlad. There was no doubt the three of us could get out of here with Hydra, Theron, and Sol there to protect us.

"Yes, they are," Theron replied. "I'm the leader of this thunder, and I'm telling you to let them go. He healed Sol. Do you understand? Or do I need to remind you why I'm in charge?"

There was a moment of silence before Wyvern sighed. "Fine."

Thorn relaxed as the three of us continued into the woods at a quick pace.

"Let's shift." Vlad stopped in his tracks and turned toward us. His skin took on a green hue. He'd already called his dragon forward.

Moving far enough away from Thorn and Vlad, I did the same. As my dragon surged forward, my vision sharpened, and my hearing amplified. My body expanded, and I found myself in my dragon form.

When Thorn completed his shift, the three of us took off, soaring back to the barn, but a chill still ran through me.

THE REST of the day passed. We filled everyone in on what had happened back at Theron's thunder, and soon, dinner was ready. The scent of meaty lasagna filled the house, and my stomach grumbled.

Though I wanted only the pasta, Eva, Elliott, and Peter enjoyed a salad with their main course. My appetite for greens had vanished since I'd become a shifter, but I craved meat and carbs all the time. Thorn had explained that needing more calories, carbs, and protein was a side effect of being a dragon.

Thorn, Vlad, Cassidy, Saphira, and I headed outside to the firepit to eat. I sat between Saphira and Thorn. I tilted my head up to stare at the night sky and enjoyed all the new colors and views I hadn't been able to see as a human.

"So... Sol and Wyvern." Saphira twirled a piece of hair around one finger. "Were they attractive? The only dragon males I've met are the ones who live around the chateau or Drake's friends, who, let's be real, are pompous and unappealing."

Putting his fork on his plate, Thorn glared at Saphira.

"What?" Saphira stuck out her tongue. "Just because she's mated doesn't mean she can't find other men attractive. She's taken, not blind."

I smirked. Since I'd met Thorn, all other men had paled in comparison. Someone I would've found attractive a month ago, I wouldn't even glance at today.

Cassidy leaned over the arm of her chair and patted Thorn's leg. "I bet their looks didn't even register on Everly's radar, now that she has you."

"Oh, come on." Saphira rolled her eyes. "There's no doubt Everly is devoted to him." She mouthed to me, *You can tell me later.*

Thorn snarled.

I took his hand as I answered, "I won't have a different answer." We were concluding this conversation now. "Thorn is hands down way more attractive than either one of them. It's like comparing a kid's fingerpainting to *The Starry Night.*"

"Uh..." Saphira glanced up at the sky.

"The painting *The Starry Night* by Vincent van Gogh.

Not the actual sky." Sometimes, I forgot that many people didn't love paintings the way Mom and I did.

Vlad nodded. "That is a gorgeous painting."

Okay, at least *someone* was cultured.

"To put it more bluntly, once you find your fated mate or complete a bond with a chosen mate, you inherently don't notice anyone else in that way." Vlad shrugged and smiled at Cassidy adoringly. "And I wouldn't want it any other way. She is the sun, moon, and stars to me."

Saphira's face twisted in confusion, and she blew out a breath as she stabbed a large bite of her food. "Forget I asked."

"I'm more than happy to do that." Thorn took another bite.

Something dinged. Vlad leaned over in his seat, removing his phone. "Dad texted me. That's odd." After he swiped the phone and read the message, he jumped to his feet, his plate crashing to the ground.

Thorn was a second behind him. "What's wrong?"

I swallowed the bite I'd just taken, the food almost lodging in my throat. I climbed to my feet too, putting my half-eaten plate on the seat.

Vlad answered, "Dad received a text from Theron. Theron wants us to run. The warriors are there, and they're picking up our trail from a few hours ago."

My stomach heaved, and it wasn't because of the food. "They can't do that, right?"

"If they know we were there earlier today, they'll assume we're close." Thorn assessed the area as if he expected Drake or the warriors to pop out at any second. "They'll eventually find us here. We need to flee *now*."

Chest constricting, I shook my head. "What if Theron and Hydra are in trouble? They helped us. We can't turn our backs on them." I understood wanting to get away from danger, but running would mean abandoning our allies.

He turned to me and placed his hands on my shoulders. He lowered his forehead to mine and said, "I helped them, Ev. I healed Sol. We've done our part to give back. All I care about is keeping you safe."

We always came back to the same conversation. "Running won't keep us safe. The only way we become safe is by facing the threat together, which means we can't abandon the people who could be our allies."

"You heard Wyvern." Thorn lifted his head, his determination wafting through me. "He had no interest in giving me a chance, despite Sol, Hydra, and Theron telling him I helped Sol. He was ready to hand us over to Drake. Staying here will only lead to our capture. I can't lose you again. I can't survive that." His fear and agony crashed through me.

My insides knotted, and my dragon whimpered. I'd hurt him so much when I'd handed myself over to Drake. It didn't matter if my intentions had been good; we'd come so close to losing each other.

But if I hadn't tried to do the exchange and someone had died, I would've had to live with that regret my entire life. "These are *your* people. Drake is hunting down the weak and old and slaughtering them. I understand you feel abandoned and betrayed, but Theron didn't turn his back on you...and that was before he knew you could help Sol."

"She's right." Cassidy set her plate on the grass. "Thorn, the dragon shifters never turned their backs on you. Your parents did. And they feared you because they haven't been given a reason not to. We will *never* be safe. Isn't it better to go there and help—which Drake and the warriors won't expect—than let them attack us when they're prepared?"

Thorn cut the air with a hand. "The thunder isn't under attack. The warriors are looking for *us*."

"Oh, please." Saphira crossed her legs and finished chewing her bite. "We *all* know Drake will be with the warriors. He wants to be there when you get captured. He'll hurt some, if not all, of the thunder to make sure no one knows your real location. Theron may have told you to run, but that doesn't mean they're safe. He just feels indebted to you."

Thorn closed his eyes, chest heaving. I could sense how much he wanted to leave, but he was in the minority.

Sometimes, the hardest part of life is doing the right thing when you don't want to, I connected to him and squeezed his hand. *And you're the type of man who knows right from wrong. If we run, you'll regret it. Maybe not today or tomorrow, but eventually, it will catch up to you.*

Something strange passed between us, and his voice popped into my head. *I'm not that guy, Everly. The world could burn to the ground, and I wouldn't care as long as you were safe.* When he opened his eyes, his pupils had slitted.

My traitorous body warmed as my dragon purred. His overwhelming love for me was intoxicating.

I also want to be the man you deserve, which means I'm willing to do this...for you. He brushed his fingers along my cheeks, leaving them flush in their wake. *But at the first sign of something going wrong, we leave. I will not allow Drake to capture you again and force you into something you're unwilling to do. Keeping you away from him matters most to me.*

Of course. The same for you. Though I wanted to help Theron and his thunder, I couldn't watch Thorn be taken. If they caught him, they'd kill him. *But Vlad is right. They won't expect us. This could be our best chance to end this.*

"We'll go." Thorn took my hand and moved to face everyone else. "But if the warriors aren't harming or threatening the thunder, we leave.

Vlad and Cassidy nodded, while Saphira arched a brow.

"We better get going." Saphira took her last bite, chewed, and swallowed. "If Drake is involved, as I suspect, it's probably already bad."

The five of us headed into the barn and found the others in the kitchen and den. We informed them of what was going on, and everyone was on the same page as Vlad, Cassidy, and me. Brenton and Errol were especially determined to help. They couldn't stand idly by while Drake acted the tyrant, and Tyson hated Drake even more after learning that Drake had been targeting people with injuries like his.

We also decided that Eva, Elliott, and Peter needed to stay. It would be too risky to take three humans into battle.

As everyone got ready, Thorn found some rope and tied Peter to a chair in the kitchen. We didn't trust him enough to leave him free to roam.

Everyone headed outside with Thorn and me in the rear. As we left, I heard Elliott mumble, "If he'd changed me, they would've had another dragon on their side."

I smiled. Several days had passed, and he hadn't changed his stance about becoming a dragon, so maybe when we got back, Thorn could change him.

Soon, all eight of us were flying toward the thunder. We were lucky we'd gone there earlier, or we wouldn't have known the way.

Even flying couldn't calm my frazzled nerves.

Keep an eye out, Thorn connected as he flew close to me. Each time we flapped our wings, they brushed together.

Vlad led the way, and Thorn and I stayed at the back so the dragons wouldn't see us first.

As we approached, I became aware of a group of people down where we'd landed earlier. None were in their dragon form, so we weren't at risk yet.

"If you don't tell us who the abomination was meeting with, I'll cut the throat of a thunder member of our choosing. The person who informed us of Thorn's presence here and the leader of the thunder know what's going on." Drake's cold voice echoed up from the spot. "Maybe I should kill someone now so you can see I mean it."

My heart raced, and I flapped my wings harder.

There was a scuffling sound, and Theron cried out, "No, not my son!"

CHAPTER TWENTY-NINE

EVERLY, *Thorn connected as he easily caught up to me.* I remained focused on the area where Drake and the others were below. *We can't rush in. We need to be smart.*

Maybe that was true, but someone important to the man who'd helped us so much was in danger. There were only ten others there, besides Theron, Wyvern, Sol, and Drake. We wouldn't be grossly outnumbered. I suspected Sol and Theron wouldn't attack us, especially if we handled Drake. It wasn't like we were rushing into a fight with fifty warriors.

Vlad flew faster, which was good, seeing as he was in front of the group. If anyone was going to reach them first, it would be him. And Thorn couldn't connect with him like he could with me.

We are being smart. We agreed to come here and help if this thunder was in danger, and there are only ten warriors down there. I kept up my quick pace as our group plunged toward the thunder. *They're under threat. I promise, if I get in harm's way, I'll let you know, and you do the same for me.*

The clearing we'd landed in earlier came into view just

as a warrior grabbed Sol by the neck. The sound of our wings must have finally registered because Drake's beady eyes turned upward and focused on Thorn.

A cruel smirk spread across the ugly prince's face, and I was ashamed I'd ever found him physically attractive. His onyx eyes seemed even darker, and his dark brown hair was still styled perfectly in spikes. "Here they come, proving how stupid the abomination and his disciples are. They willingly enter the dragon's lair."

Please, whatever you do, don't let them capture you, Thorn begged as his trepidation weighed down my wings.

Then it clicked. Thorn was terrified of losing me because he was petrified of the royal family. He wanted only to keep those he loved safe, but not because he didn't care about his people. It was because, since he was six, he'd been hiding from the king. The fear he'd felt as a little boy had grown as he'd gotten older, and he was merely trying to survive.

My heart ripped in two. I hated that I hadn't seen it before.

I pushed the warmth of my love and confidence toward him. *You don't need to fear them. You're a force to be reckoned with. They should cower before your strength and determination. Only you can end Drake's plans. You're the firstborn heir to the throne, and you can take his dragon. Do that. Reverse the roles. Make him quake at the sight of you.*

The warriors raised their weapons, and my heart constricted. They had tranq guns, which meant they planned on capturing us instead of killing us.

Drake wanted to put on a show.

"Shoot!" Falkor commanded from his position next to Drake. "Remember, we don't kill them...yet."

Ladon rushed to flank the ugly prince's other side to

protect him, and the other eight guards fired.

I stopped moving my wings, ending my forward progression, and Vlad, Cassidy, and Thorn did the same.

Saphira, Errol, Brenton, and Tyson didn't. The four of them changed their trajectory, but they weren't in danger, since all eight guards had been aiming for Thorn and Vlad.

Of course, the guards recognized the four of us in dragon form. Not only that, but they knew Thorn was the plum dragon, and six of the darts had been aimed at him.

As they reloaded their weapons, Thorn flew forward. His strength shone through as he sped past everyone and darted downward.

My heart clenched. Okay, I'd wanted to inspire him, but I hadn't meant for him to do *that*. I couldn't take it back now, or I might distract him and cause him harm. But that didn't mean I would leave him alone to take on all the warriors. He was strong, but he needed help.

The seven of us charged forward as Thorn swooped down. The warriors aimed their rifles at him, not focused on the rest of us. They viewed Thorn as the real threat.

I'd never seen anyone fly as fast as Thorn, and as the guards fired at him, each shot missed by mere inches.

Thorn spread out his talons and snatched the tranq rifles from the hands of two guards then barreled into the last four, who had their tranq guns trained on him.

Gunfire exploded as I surged to the head of our group, adrenaline making me faster than ever before.

I had to get to him. If he got tranqed, I'd need to carry him away quickly.

A loud, guttural roar came from deep within as I reached the treetops. Vlad and Cassidy were a few feet behind me, almost as desperate to reach their son as I was.

"Falkor! Ladon!" Drake barked. "Get him *now*!"

That settled my target. Eliminating Drake would also end most of our other problems. King Arman would let Thorn live as long as he didn't make waves.

My blood boiled with rage, and my stomach heated as flames scorched my insides. Drake was a tyrant and weirdly obsessed with getting his way, feeling entitled to whatever he wanted.

Several guards screamed, and Thorn jerked his head up. The sensation of his magic took hold, telling me what he was doing—stripping the warriors of their dragon.

Falkor and Ladon aimed their rifles at Thorn, but Vlad, Cassidy, and I had caught up. Vlad stopped short, shielding Thorn from a shot as he attacked a guard close to him.

Cassidy took Ladon, while I expelled flames on Falkor. Of course, I'd be stuck with him, as if Fate were giving me hell for dropping his drawers. My flames licked his skin as the rest of the group reached Thorn and Vlad to help fight the remaining three warriors, who were readying to aim their tranq rifles at Thorn and Vlad again.

Grimacing, Falkor stood strong as my flames engulfed him. His skin turned pink from the burns, and he didn't move. My flames were having an impact on him, but unfortunately, it wasn't as much as I'd hoped, probably because he was a dragon. Something was better than nothing. I still had so much to learn about dragons.

All too soon, I didn't have any flames left, and my fire thinned as my lungs burned for oxygen.

Falkor narrowed his eyes and swiveled his tranq gun at me.

Too little too late. I chomped on the arm holding the rifle. The metallic taste of blood filled my mouth as he grunted. Vomit inched up my throat. I'd never tasted blood like this before. The idea of having human fluids in my mouth didn't sit well with me. I'd cut up all sorts of things in my premed classes, and I hadn't expected to have *this* much of an issue.

With his other hand, he punched me in the nose. Pain exploded in my snout and shot into my head. Tears burned my eyes, and I jerked back as my jaw went slack, but I'd managed to keep a firm enough grip that my teeth ripped his skin. Despite the damage, he still held on to the rifle.

My dragon roared, loud and angry. She was upset that I'd allowed myself to get distracted by something so silly as the taste of blood. Despite all the training back at the barn, I hadn't been fully prepared for an actual battle in dragon form. But failure wasn't an option.

"Make sure you don't permanently hurt Everly," Drake commanded as he stumbled back, spun on his heels, then raced toward Theron's thunder.

He was a scaredy-cat or whatever the equivalent was for dragons who lacked courage. Maybe he should put *himself* on his list of weak dragons for deserting his men.

Falkor swung at me again, but I was prepared. I caught his arm with my left talon, digging my claws into his wrist. I wanted to injure both his arms so he couldn't use any weapons on us. He was one of the strongest fighters. Putting him out of action would hurt their cause, especially if he was injured enough that he couldn't command the others.

Drake's getting away, I connected with Thorn. The only thing keeping me going was the magic thrumming through our connection. As long as he was using it, he was alive and well enough to function.

We all saw his cowardly ass scurry away, Thorn replied.

A loud snarl sounded behind me, and out of the corner of my eye, I watched as Tyson lifted himself into the air and chased after Drake.

Thank goodness. Someone needed to go after him, and I was glad it was Tyson. It would serve Drake right if Tyson took him down.

Falkor kicked at my back talons, trying to knock them out from underneath me, then swung the arm with the rifle at me, but it didn't get far. I wondered if it was broken.

Even though his kicks hurt, my legs didn't give out. With my right talon, I swiped the rifle away and pushed him backward. He tumbled down and landed on his back, his eyes bulging.

Sol appeared at my side and swiped up the rifle. He straightened and fired it, lodging a tranq right into Falkor's stomach.

Blood oozed from Falkor's arms and dripped into the grass as he snarled, "None of you will get away with this." His eyelids lowered slowly then closed as the dart knocked him out.

Sol pivoted to where Ladon and Cassidy were fighting. I turned toward them in time to see Ladon lodge a dagger into Cassidy's left side. Cassidy drew her head back and snarled just as Sol fired the gun. The tranq hit Ladon in the neck.

The strange magical feeling from Thorn ebbed, and my breath caught. Something might be wrong...but as I focused on the bond, I didn't feel any further discomfort coming through.

As Ladon collapsed, Cassidy grabbed for the dagger with her talons, but blood coated the edge, and her scaly skin slipped off the blade.

"I've got it," Theron said. He rushed past Sol and me to her side, then yanked the dagger out as Vlad reached his mate.

Are you okay? Thorn connected. The ground shook as

he raced toward me.

I took in the area. All eight guards were lying on the ground, out cold. All of our people seemed all right, but Saphira's gaze was fixed on something just beyond me.

I jerked in that direction. Wyvern stood there, equally still. He was focused on Saphira as if nothing else in the world mattered.

Clearly, Saphira had found one answer she'd been so desperate for earlier—whether Wyvern and Sol were handsome. Apparently, she approved of Wyvern, judging by the tangy smell of arousal wafting off her.

Now was *not* the time for this.

Thorn roared, rushing toward Wyvern. Though he was in dragon form, it was clear that Thorn was beyond pissed. Wyvern was obviously the one who'd ratted us out to Drake.

The threat was enough to snap Wyvern out of his daze.

"I'm sorry." Wyvern lifted his hands. "I thought I was protecting the thunder! I didn't know he'd come here and torture us."

Smoke trickled from Thorn's nose.

In fairness, no one understood that the prince is that horrible. I'd hoped that no leader could be that cruel, but Drake was obviously a product of his grandfather, the former marked dragon who'd used his magic to force people to do his will. *At least, they hoped he wouldn't be.* I touched Thorn's arm to send him some calm.

"Look, I know Wyvern messed up, but we have a more pressing issue." Theron rubbed the back of his neck. "There are forty more warriors back with the thunder. Drake left the majority there to ensure no one slipped away. If he makes it back, he'll send them here, and your scent won't have time to dissipate if you leave now."

My pulse thundered. We should've expected more warriors. Of course, Drake would bring a large number with him after what had happened at the wedding.

Worse, we couldn't fly away, not after Sol had nearly died at Drake's hands.

Shit. Tyson, Thorn connected.

I couldn't swallow. Tyson had flown after Drake.

A gunshot rang out. Something horrible was going down.

Brenton took off toward the noise with Saphira and Errol on his tail.

Even though Tyson wasn't blood, he'd become my family. When I flew after them, I expected Thorn to argue, but he and his parents followed as well. We all raced toward the threat.

As we rose higher, I saw twenty dragons winging toward us in the distance with just as many in human form on foot below.

Drake had mobilized his troops.

Thorn, I connected. *You need to go.* This was all about catching and killing him. I couldn't risk that.

There's no way in hell I'm leaving you, Thorn replied, his own stress seeping through. *Even if I run, they'll chase after me. It would be hard to get away with numbers like this.*

I looked at the ground and noted two figures closer to us than the oncoming warriors. Drake and Tyson. Tyson was naked and passed out on the ground. Drake squatted next to him, one hand gripping Tyson's hair to keep his head up. He held a dagger at Tyson's throat, and blood trickled down his neck.

Despite my being airborne, the world shifted around me.

CHAPTER THIRTY

DRAKE LIFTED HIS HEAD, a victorious sneer on his face.

Leaving to save Thorn wasn't an option. Neither was allowing Drake to cut Tyson's throat.

Throwing his head back, Brenton let out a thunderous roar.

"Stay back," Drake spat. "Or I'll slit his throat."

He won't, I connected with Thorn. Unfortunately, he was the only one I could communicate with in dragon form. *He needs Tyson alive to ensure he survives.*

Don't be so sure, Thorn replied as his mistrust thrummed through our connection. *He only cares about control, and the warriors will be here in seconds.*

My stomach hardened. Drake only needed to hold off for another minute and he'd have plenty of backup. *You need to go.*

I'm not going anywhere without you, and he won't allow either of us to get away. He'll kill Tyson as soon as we try to leave. Thorn's fear chilled our connection.

And this is why we had to come here. Sol would be dead

if not for us. If we turned our backs on people we could help, we'd be no better than Drake. I needed Thorn to realize that.

"*All* of you are going to shift back into human form now." Drake tightened his grip on Tyson's hair, pulling at the scalp.

Even unconscious, Tyson moaned in agony.

All of us paused. Since we'd come in dragon form, we hadn't brought any weapons. If we changed into our human forms, we'd be defenseless against the warriors, who were armed with guns.

The seven of us glanced at one another as if we were all thinking the same thing.

Drake's face reddened. "Now! Or I'll slit his throat this instant!"

The first of the warriors came through, and I recognized two of them—Jessie and Uther. Uther's face was scrunched with discomfort, while Jessie's eyes homed in on Thorn and me.

The rest of the warriors filed in behind Drake. There was no way we were getting out of this.

Errol, Brenton, and Saphira landed first and shifted back into human form. A few of the warriors watched them, but most were focused on Thorn, Vlad, Cassidy, and me.

They thought we were the biggest threat, perhaps because they knew Thorn cared about the three of us, but they thought he might not see Tyson as family, and there-fore, might not care about his death as much.

They were wrong.

The four of us landed behind Errol, Saphira, and Brenton and pulled our dragons back. I hated being trapped like this. Before long, I'd be exposed to Drake and his men in ways I'd never wanted to be. My mouth filled with saliva.

My body shrank as my dragon begrudgingly separated from my mind.

"Let him go," Saphira cried. "We've all landed and shifted as you demanded."

Drake pouted. "I'd hoped that Thorn and Everly would need more convincing." He chuckled and removed the dagger from Tyson's neck, replacing it in the sheath at his side. "But the abomination is a coward. He's all big and bad when he catches us off guard, but as soon as my warriors and I are prepared, he cowers. And *this* was the son my father feared."

I took a hurried step forward and pointed my finger at the dickhead. "He's not *afraid*. He cares about Tyson. One would think you'd feel the same way, seeing as he used to live next door to you."

"Ah...Everly." Drake scanned me, making my blood turn cold. "With a body like yours, maybe I won't need a breeder after all. You are quite delicious, in both dragon and human form."

A menacing rumble shook the ground as a strong arm wrapped around my body. My skin caught fire.

Thorn.

He tugged me behind him, chest heaving with each breath. "Do *not* look at her. She is my mate and wife, and I will *kill* you for everything you've done to her."

I wanted to step around Thorn and tell Drake exactly where he could go, but Thorn's hatred and anger flooded our connection. He didn't want anyone ever seeing me this way, especially not *him*.

I couldn't blame him. If someone had been trying to force Thorn to be her husband and lover, I didn't think I'd have been keeping it together as well as Thorn was.

Drake laughed, the noise like sandpaper to my ears. I

winced but refused to cover them, not wanting to show a hint that he had influence over me.

"You really think you're going to make it out alive?" Drake glanced over his shoulder at the warriors. "He's delusional. Though he may be the firstborn, I'm the true heir. Everyone sees him as an abomination."

My patience snapped. I poked my head from behind Thorn's back and said, "Just because you keep throwing that word around doesn't make it true. Thorn is the one trying to save dragons you're determined to kill. That's why he attacked the chateau—you were forcing me to marry you against my will."

"Don't forget, *love*." Drake tilted his head as he released his hold on Tyson. The unconscious man dropped to the ground. "You're the one who hunted me down in the bar that night. You *asked* me to choose you. Don't make this into something it isn't."

I flinched. I *hated* that he had me there. "You were planning to take my little sister, who'd just turned eighteen."

"None of this matters." Vlad lifted his chin. "Like Thorn said, you won't be taking Everly or hurting my son. Give Tyson back, and we'll leave. No one needs to get injured."

Jessie snorted. Her black helmet had pushed her bleach-blonde bangs into her cinnamon eyes. "There are forty of us to your seven. You're in human form with no weapons. Do you really think that's how this is going down?" She aimed her rifle at Vlad.

Sol, Theron, and Wyvern weren't here. I wondered briefly why they hadn't shifted into dragon form.

"What would King Arman say about this?" Errol hung his head. "Your father is a good man. He didn't raise you to threaten your people and kill your brother."

The sound of more people approaching made me freeze. Theron had said there were forty warriors. Who were these newcomers? Maybe it was Theron's thunder, but that wouldn't make things better. They would follow their prince to protect their thunder from harm.

"My father is *weak*," Drake snarled and bared his teeth. He spun around to the warriors. "Surround them and take them back to the thunder."

"Wait." Uther frowned. "We aren't going to kill Thorn here?"

"No," Drake's snarled, "We need to get it on video so all dragons can see. After what he did at my wedding, they need to know I won't tolerate actions like that."

We can't go with them, Thorn connected. *We need to grab Tyson and get the hell out of here. Everly, if the warriors detain us, our chances of escaping will be low. I won't lose you. I'll make them all pay for the hell they've caused.*

My vision blurred as the warriors closest to us removed handcuffs from their belts. The dark shiny metal was distinctive—Wolfram Dwinn. If they put those on us, we wouldn't be able to shift back into dragons, and Thorn wouldn't be able to access his magic.

"Jessie," Cassidy said in a broken voice. "We were friends. You don't have to do this."

I started. As a former royal nanny, Cassidy would know many of the warriors.

"We *were* friends, but when you took off with the prince and protected him, everything changed." Jessie kept her gun trained on Thorn. "You won't get any help or sympathy from me."

That was the thing. Drake owned his warriors. *Even the ones who don't agree with him, like Uther, will follow because he's threatened their families.*

Thorn hissed, his pupils slitting. *That's exactly what my grandfather did when he was king.*

More warriors raced out of the trees and surrounded us. Thirty of them kept their guns trained on us, while ten moved closer, ready to handcuff us.

I spun and pressed my back to Thorn's.

When I tell you to run, go, Thorn's voice popped into my head. *As soon as the warriors with the handcuffs get close enough, I'll steal their dragons.*

That would cause chaos, if only for a moment.

I tried to breathe slowly, needing a clear head. If shit hit the fan—er...the flames hit the scales—I didn't want to be caught with my pants down, like Falkor. Granted, I was already buck naked. But still.

The ten guards split up. Four headed toward Thorn. Their hands shook as they got closer, as if they knew he planned on using his magic.

A woman warrior was in front, her jaw trembling harder with each step. "Now, don't do anything stupid. There are thirty guards with weapons aimed at all of you." Her voice quivered.

"If you're going to handcuff me, just do it," Saphira gritted out, her irises glowing as her dragon showed through. "Don't be timid...unless the only warriors Drake could get on his side were those too weak to go against him."

"Get them *now*," Drake bellowed. "And knock them out, if that's the only way to get them to stop talking."

I couldn't see him, but I pictured him stomping like a toddler.

Uther appeared in front of me, his face twisted with regret. He opened the handcuffs and lifted both hands so I could see what he was holding. His gaze remained on my face and didn't travel down my naked body.

Drake had forced him into this.

When the woman reached Thorn, a white light glowed around them, brighter than the midday sun.

Thorn was channeling his magic.

"Merigold!" the male warrior behind her shouted.

The warning came too late. Thorn touched the woman, and magic thrummed through our bond.

"Grab a warrior!" Vlad exclaimed, and thanks to our training, none of us hesitated.

I jumped toward Uther as he pivoted to catch me. His intention was clear, but at the last second, I switched direction and grabbed his arms.

Gunfire erupted, and my dragon jerked forward, tapping partially into my mind, which she'd never done before. I sensed a tranq barreling toward me. I dropped to my knees, and the dart passed over my head by mere millimeters and lodged in Uther's chest.

"Shit," he rasped, but the damage was done.

Another warrior aimed his rifle at me, and I gripped Uther's arms, forcing him to turn toward the warrior as the tranq flew toward us. The tranq hit Uther, just an inch away from where my hand held him.

The warriors were taking into account what I was doing.

A thud sounded to the left, and Saphira yelped, "Uncle Brenton!"

He must have gotten hit.

Screams came from near Thorn, and I saw four warriors positioned deeper in the trees to my right, training their rifles on him. I had to do something.

Uther's body grew heavy as the drugs took effect. I wished I'd been dragon born so I'd be stronger. I released him, and he dropped like a brick as I moved toward my mate.

They're shooting— I started as Theron, Sol, and Wyvern appeared from behind a tree and jumped on three of the warriors. One fired a shot.

"No!" Cassidy shouted as she lunged in front of Thorn, taking the dart to protect her son.

Theron knocked out the fourth warrior, and the three of them ran back into the shadows of the woods. They were helping us while staying out of sight. Drake and his warriors remained focused on Thorn.

The rest of the warriors raced toward us, rifles ready.

We couldn't escape. There was no way.

A loud, familiar voice broke through the chaos. "Stop this. *Now!*"

Everyone froze. The warriors lowered their weapons, and I spun around to find King Arman and ten more guards stepping through a thick section of trees.

"Father," Drake gasped. "What are you doing here?"

"I heard Thorn might have been found." King Arman's neck corded. "I told you I wanted to go with you when he was located. Why did you not alert me?"

Oh, I knew that answer, but I figured I didn't need to say anything. From the expression on King Arman's face, he already knew as well.

"I want to prove what I'm capable of, Father." Drake's warmer persona slipped on like the slimy skin of an actor on stage. "Isn't that why you put me in charge of the family business, so I could prove I'm fit to lead?"

Saphira laughed, not bothering to cover it up. "You're not fit to breathe the same air as us."

Drake's eyes flashed, and the monster within snuck out for a second. "Say that again, and I'll—"

"You'll *what?*" King Arman snapped. "Threaten her like you have the thunder here when they called and informed you that they'd seen Thorn? And now you have an entire group, including my *royal advisor*, standing here naked in their human forms without weapons, while warriors attack them?"

"Oh, please." Drake rolled his eyes, unable to maintain his fake persona. "They're all traitors, and every one of them will die...except my darling Everly."

Thorn snarled and took a menacing step toward Drake.

Jessie aimed her rifle at my mate again.

"Remember not to kill him." Drake rocked back on his heels. "That's what he'll get when we arrive home, along with everyone here...including Errol."

"No." King Arman marched to his son. "You will let these people go. For the past twenty-one years, Thorn has stayed hidden, causing no problems or harm. He's no threat to us."

Drake straightened and glared at the king. "Yeah, I learned that when I found his address in your desk a few years ago. You allowed him to live, risking *my* claim to the throne. When I asked Falkor what he knew about Thorn, he told me everything, and we made a plan to eliminate him."

That was why Falkor had told the king he needed to protect Drake all that time ago.

"You're just as bad as my father," King Arman spat. "Thorn posed no harm, and now you've hurt others in our thunder because you're fixated on him and Everly."

Drake pounded his chest. "I'm doing what's needed to ensure the dragons survive. That's what a king does. You're content to let us die off."

"He's killing injured dragons, sire," Errol murmured and gestured at Tyson, who was passed out on the ground.

"That's what we learned here. But Thorn healed Tyson. He can fly and fully connect with his dragon again."

King Arman's attention swung to Thorn. "You healed an injured dragon?"

"Not just one," I interjected. "Two. He mended them both, and he changed me. His magic has far more potential than just stealing someone's dragon or forcing people to change for his own selfish gain."

The king strolled across the clearing to Thorn. He placed his hand on his son's shoulders and stared into his eyes. He whispered, "You're not like my father after all. I'm so sorry that it's taken me so long to see that."

Our bond filled with uncertainty. Maybe we'd survive this. The king was finally supporting his son.

"Father, he's an abomination," Drake spat. "He took four dragons here, and eight more not too far from here. Maybe even Falkor's and Ladon's since they're not here."

The king's eyes flashed with anger, and he kept a hand on Thorn's arm as he turned to address his other son. "No, *you're* the abomination. You forced him into doing that to protect the people he loves. I see it now. You, Drake Hale, are *not* fit to lead." He dropped his hand and stepped toward Drake. "I denounce you as the official heir to the throne."

"Thank gods," Saphira rasped.

"You can't do that," Drake snarled. "He wasn't even raised royal. No one will follow him, not after what they've seen him do."

"In time, everyone will see what he is like, just as I see who you've become." The king turned back to Thorn, his shoulders slumped. "Son, I'm so sorry. If you'll give me a chance—"

Before he could finish, Drake removed the dagger from its sheath.

I charged forward, pushing past Thorn. "King Arm—"

Before I could reach him or warn him, Drake had stabbed King Arman in the back.

His words were cut off, and his eyes widened. He turned slowly and blinked at his son. "What...have...you...done?"

The positioning of the dagger was so precise, and I knew from my time at university exactly where Drake had hit the king. His heart. My hope that we would soon be free lessened with each strangled breath King Arman took.

No matter who you were, even if you were royalty, doing the right thing could result in someone closest to you stabbing you in the back.

The world tilted as the king stumbled, his lavender shirt turning crimson. His heartbeat stuttered. Even as my mate's warmth pressed into my back with that comforting buzz, I knew.

Drake had won.

ABOUT THE AUTHOR

Jen L. Grey is a *USA Today* Bestselling Author who writes Paranormal Romance, Urban Fantasy, and Fantasy genres.

Jen lives in Tennessee with her husband, two daughters, and two miniature Australian Shepherds. Before she began writing, she was an avid reader and enjoyed being involved in the indie community. Her love for books eventually led her to writing. For more information, please visit her website and sign up for her newsletter.

Check out her future projects and book signing events at her website.
www.jenlgrey.com

The Marked Dragon Prince Trilogy

Ruthless Mate

Marked Dragon

Hidden Fate

Shadow City: Silver Wolf Trilogy

Broken Mate

Rising Darkness

Silver Moon

Shadow City: Royal Vampire Trilogy

Cursed Mate

Shadow Bitten

Demon Blood

Shadow City: Demon Wolf Trilogy

Ruined Mate

Shattered Curse

Fated Souls

Shadow City: Dark Angel Trilogy

Fallen Mate

Demon Marked

Dark Prince

Fatal Secrets

Shadow City: Silver Mate

Shattered Wolf

Fated Hearts

Ruthless Moon

The Wolf Born Trilogy

Hidden Mate

Blood Secrets

Awakened Magic

The Hidden King Trilogy

Dragon Mate

Dragon Heir

Dragon Queen

The Marked Wolf Trilogy

Moon Kissed

Chosen Wolf

Broken Curse

Wolf Moon Academy Trilogy

Shadow Mate

Blood Legacy

Rising Fate

The Royal Heir Trilogy

Wolves' Queen

Wolf Unleashed

Wolf's Claim

Bloodshed Academy Trilogy

Year One

Year Two

Year Three

The Half-Breed Prison Duology (Same World As Bloodshed Academy)

Hunted

Cursed

The Artifact Reaper Series

Reaper: The Beginning

Reaper of Earth

Reaper of Wings

Reaper of Flames

Reaper of Water

Stones of Amaria (Shared World)

Kingdom of Storms

Kingdom of Shadows

Kingdom of Ruins

Kingdom of Fire

The Pearson Prophecy

Dawning Ascent

Enlightened Ascent

Reigning Ascent

Stand Alones

Death's Angel

Rising Alpha